Guban

Guban

A NOVEL *by*

ABDI LATIF EGA

TO MY SON OMER MUKHTAR
& THE MANY FIERCE WOMEN WHO BELIEVED!

CALIBAN MUST GO WHERE CEASAR
HAS NEVER BEEN.

C.L.R.JAMES

Guban

 ONE

The Water Bearer

. . . .

THE JOURNEY TO THE WELL WAS LONG AND SCARY WHEN Tusmo was younger. She would start before the shadows cast, and would usually reach the well when there was a significant shadow in the day. It was scary because the land was an endless darkness. Her camel, a ten foot beast, would not avail her any form of protection from the many dangers lurking out there – the wild animals in search of a succulent morsel before they returned to their dens.

Tusmo, at this tender age, felt she was being thrown to the hyenas in the darkness, shrouded ominously before the break of dawn. Whenever she felt she could not possibly go through with it, the voice of her mother in her head would sternly urge her on, resoundingly stating how it was her duty to the clan, family, and a further duty to her own homestead of the future.

In the light of the day, brought on by an unrelenting sun, the land assumed an indistinguishable form. Every thorn looked like the others, every ant hill looked identical, there were thousands of well-trodden footpaths all around. The small footpaths in the sandy earth, marked by spaces of grass in the ground resembled a translucent head of thinning hair. The trees were mainly thorn trees – all emaciated and small in stature from a sparse diet of nothing but very little rain-fall. The trees had this in common with every living thing in this desolate abode of collective harshness.

It was a most barren part of the world. Everything that grew here had to put up a great fight to merely exist. Plants were as fierce as the rest of the environment; they abounded with thorns to ensure life. The lay of the land was unforgiving, cruel as if still despondent from its volcanic eruptions of long ago. Sand lodged in places where seasonal rivers once flowed. Barren volcanic mountain ranges in the background presided over everything, stoically, aloof to the daily proceedings, as they unfolded. A flat enormity of semi–arid land was dashed here and there by thorn trees too short to hide or give shade to anything. Mingled with thorny shrubbery, that translucent head of hair grass resembled hay growing out from the earth, what perhaps used to be long luscious grass when this was a savanna.

The ten foot camel followed obediently through a nose lead. This animal with all its clumsy glory reigned supreme to the fierce pastoralist. This animal was the end and beginning of all things. There was conflict as to which was more important: water or the camel. Disputes were always over water rights for the camels, goats, sheep – in that order - which invariably involved bloodshed. Only the camel sufficed as payment for the disputes, often heralding the end to hostilities, although there were those rare individuals who chose a life for a life instead.

The currency of the camel was used in all manner of occasions. It was used for bride price. Since marriage was one of the most important events in a Somal's life and procreation, the object of the nomad's very existence, the fierceness of life without the camel demanded large congeries of sons to protect the wealth and general well-being of the family from other such families and from treacherous often barren lone operators, barren precisely as a result of the lack of this clumsy currency in abundance.

Wealth in this part of the world is truly in the eyes of the beholder. The camel is the most rugged and austere of the domesticated animals, reflexively so are the wealthy in these parts. If you see a rather gaunt, lanky red and dusty man, he could be rich in camels and sons, or he could just as well be impoverished.

Tusmo would often hear her Awowo describe many such men of many sons and camels. She cut a picture of one in the throws of death induced by sustained hunger brought on by their own miserliness.

After a long solo journey, Tusmo would arrive at the well, as did many of the girls, having walked a quite lengthy distance, exhausted. They would then wait for the men, usually their kin, to draw the water for them. The wells were very deep in the earth and, as the men worked, there was a chance for a slight reprieve for the girls before the arduous journey back home, leading a camel now laden with fifty liters of water on each side. The water was rusty in color approximating apple juice, a color which permeated everything. It seeped into the clothes, fingernails, and was red, being the color of the loose sand of this region.

After the journey, there were other chores awaiting her return. She would tend to the needs of Awowo, filling his abolition water container full before the night prayer, bringing him milk - and most of all - the tea before he would retire for the night.

By this time, Tusmo had kraaled the livestock for the night, surrounding the encampment with thorn tree branches as an impenetrable defense against would-be wildlife intruders.

 TWO

The Arrest

. . . .

YUSUF WAS ASTOUNDED BY THE CITY ITSELF. HE WAS EXAS-
perated with the desire to break the monotony of the perpetual
moving, grazing and general animal husbandry of it all. It was here
in these desolate places of nature's barren garden that he would first
hear of the larger world outside. This eventually kindled his desire to
see beyond the confines of the limited world of the harsh plains, a
world of constant movement in search of pasture and water. A world
existed beyond this utter desolation, he had heard, and it had cities
that abounded with people who never moved. Incredibly, they stayed
put for years.

Yusuf was determined to become part of the city and identified
as such, but he had to shed his much ingrained camel ways. For this,
he looked to Commander Ali for questions. In Ali Deray, his commander, he saw one who wielded the respect and fear of his fellow city dwellers. Yusuf sought to understand the intricate ways of
what made him, at barely a few years his senior, so prominent. Yusuf
had met many officers outside and inside the military whose rank
equaled that of Ali Deray, but who, despite their rank and file, were
just plainly ignored.

Yusuf rationalized that whatever he knew in his previous life did
not apply to the ways of the city, and by extension, the ways of government. So, when he was ordered to complete the arrest of a man

named Hoagsaday, there were many layers of adherence in his undertaking of the orders.

On the morning he was ordered to do so, he summoned the other soldiers and commenced toward Hoagsaday's house. He knew of the man. He was one of many who had left the country in search of better economical prospects and had returned after a long sojourn with much more. The soldiers arrived at Hoagsaday's in early afternoon and knocked with the usual arrogance most coercive forces are known for. Everyone was indoors, refugees from the midday's naked sun. Such was the custom of Mogadishu that from around one o'clock to at least five – longer for others – those who could ate a hearty lunch - quite excessive, particularly if guests were being entertained – and, afterwards, an afternoon siesta was agreed upon by all who lived in this city.

This time proved quite opportune for Yusuf to present the full regalia of coercive bravado and intimidation. It was an added effect of humiliation for a prominent member of the community, as Hoagsaday was, to be rounded up at their home by the government and in such an manner and at such an ubiquitous time and place of privacy. The intended audience was the public, who would know of the incident before long. It was a nation populated by news chronicles and worthy disseminators, the news would spread like a tsunami, instilling fear in the almost fearless nomads turned citizens of a modern city state.

Hoagsaday heard the knock which at first drove him quickly into a fit of anger, commonly induced by afternoon sleep – it was probably a mannerless person, particularly rude, probably an impatient person having some business with him who thought nothing of invading his privacy, rather than wait for him at the store during the normal hours.

He called to the servant to answer with a firm admonition to the knocker, then again, he quickly changed his mind, brushing past the servant in a haste of fury to answer the door himself. "Who is it, don't you have any sense at all? I just can't understand how a mature person can be so inconsiderate."

As he opened the door with a forceful jerk with one hand, he was confronted by the khaki brown color of a soldier's uniform.

Hoagsaday simultaneously heard, "Are you the rich guy from over-seas, we have orders from my commander, to arrest you, Hoagsaday. Come with us now," almost barking, "Get in the truck."

Hoagsaday saw a military truck behind his vehicle in the driveway full of non-descript beige berets, hunched in the back. In a flash of second, Hoagsaday went through a montage in his mind in search of anything that might shed some light on why the military wanted him. The thought of this event at his home at this hour when most people were resting in the privacy of their homes was surreal. Since nothing was amiss, Hoagsaday grew more and more agitated with these lower ranking enforcers that dared to show up like this. Momentarily regain-ing his stature as a prominent businessman from one of the larger clans, he stood barreling his chest, now returning the bark, "What in the name of God makes you think you can come to my home, at this time, and under such pretentious allegations, and barge into my compound and ask to take me, Hoagsaday, an upstanding member of this city, to the station just like a common and habitual criminal?"

By this time, his children, wife, and a number of his relatives both visiting and staying with him were all shocked out of sleep. They were all heading outside towards the fracas on the veranda, alongside the official intruders.

"Hear this big mouth? Come along quietly before we drag you by the scruff of your neck in front of your wife, children, and your entire family."

Hoagsaday had by now gone from disbelief to belief in the reality that these goons meant business. There was no doubt in his mind now: this madness was real. It was futile at this point to plead with rocks, and he made a split second decision to acquiesce which was heavily influ-enced by the gradual milling on the veranda of more and more male family members as they woke up to what was going on.

Abukar, a male cousin just arrived from the hinterland, started an abrasive verbal assault on the soldiers, "What kind of animals are you? Has the government stopped recruiting humans into the military? How dare you come here with this nonsense? What great balls are these you come with? Do guns have brains? This is not a govern-ment matter. When you come here like this, you don't come here as a government, but as a clan. Everyone has a clan too, and you will reckon with Hoagsaday's. We see you behind the clan camouflage of your uniform."

With that, Abukar was descended upon by two soldiers who had come for Hoagsaday. The berets were now quickly unloading from the truck, all heading to the veranda to help subdue Abukar who was by now pinned to the ground with two soldiers on top of him, engaging in the scuffle as best he could from beneath the two soldiers. He continued to harangue the soldiers with open threats, as other males decided to join in on the now potential melee.

One of the soldiers shouted a command, while the loud cocking of several machine guns was simultaneously heard, launching the all too well known severity in the air, a severity that garnered instant access to obedience. Precisely at this moment, Hoagsaday stated loudly, mainly for the benefit of his family and to calm the soldiers, that he would obey though he requested to go back into the house and change out of his ma'wiss, a long sarong worn by males used both privately in the city and regularly in the hinterland. In a brave posture, he reassured his family and went outside onto the back of the truck, where Abukar was already lying prone on the floor, bloody at the soldiers' boots.

The truck drove fast speeding through the empty roads of siesta time, making its way to a non-descript and heavily guarded isolated building. Both men were manhandled off the truck, barely making the distance between the flatbed of the truck and the ground on their feet because the soldiers were all busy thumping them with their boots and rifle butts. Abukar was given extra rations of hurt for his earlier infraction and continued defiant disposition.

They were separated at the entrance of what looked like a front greeting area office, taken down steps leading to a dark underground, and then lead into a holding cell that had no bars but a thick metal door that was promptly shut behind when Hoagsaday was inside. He sat down in a grand stupor, sitting on the floor of this small rectangle enclosure with nothing - no furniture or even a mat to help you brace the concrete floor. It was a concrete slab of drab nothingness. Hoagsaday was on the floor wondering if what had just transpired

. . . .

was real. If so, who was involved? How does one go from a routine day to some underground holding concrete pit? He started to get out of the haziness of blurred thoughts, slowly thinking about Abukar, Tusmo, his young wife whom he had just left hysterically crying, along with his children, during the fiasco.

He was not so certain anymore whether he could get the ear of someone, anyone. What had just transpired had all the makings of quite a serious problem. There was nothing he knew. He knew absolutely nothing, not even a mere inkling of what he was up against. He now tried in his mind to go back to that earlier montage of events in recent memory to somehow put some feet on why the government had interrupted his life today.

Hoagsaday was not in the government. He was a private business man not engaged in anything even remotely breaching any law of the land. He paid his taxes regularly, never borrowed from the government, nor was he engaged in any way with those who were part of the government, in any partnerships, neither did he solicit any official of the government for powerful whispers on behalf of his company even though this was quite common. Hoagsaday was simply a man who had worked hard for several years to acquire what minimal capital he could as seed money, to start a business and buy a home in the city.

He was slightly reassured by the thought that someone from his clan was probably already inquiring on his whereabouts in the hope of finding his location, and on who needed to be talked to in order to gain his release. As things were in Somal, there would be a hodgepodge of government in the western sense, the traditional pastoral ways of adjudication, and with a large dose of clannishness.

In the meantime, his eyes wandered around this hot dungeon of sorts, the cracked concrete wall full of graffiti, left by those who had had the dubious privilege of passing through this bare and dirty place. This was quite a change from the normal day for Hoagsaday, who had until this point worked himself into the psyche of the city dwellers, known as an ambitious and innovative hard-working man. He had within no time established an operational business that quickly blossomed into many other ones. With prominence came the multitudes of the envious, of course in varying degrees. Some said he dug in toilets, others said he had done a lot of common street begging when he was abroad in the Middle East.

Still others said he beat a hasty retreat after a long career as a thief in the Middle East when his gang made a final career ending score. The rest of his gang were reputed to be non-Somals and prominent in their countries as he was here.

This adventurous mystique was created around the person of Hoagsaday, sort of like a modern day version of the famous Ali Baba fable. But one did not need to look far to find the origin of these rumors. They were generated by rival businessmen and the collective of idle naysayer who had witnessed Hoagsaday's quick ascendancy to the parapets of business circles in the city and who had been astonished at his conscientious efficiency. There was that, and then there were the others who wielded power in the government and used their high positions as a means to public and private coffers.

Hoagsaday, having spent a significant amount of time overseas, had indeed dwelled in nostalgia. Ideas heavily flavored by a hybrid existence in the Middle East at the confluence of many cultures. He cultivated some ideas from the West, the Middle East, as though he was somewhat delusional about the reality of life where he had left. For reasons unknown he somehow did not configure in his hybrid ideas about the very spot he came from. The things he had left were now worse! In this way, one could say he was quite delusional. Hoagsaday was hunched in a cell passing away the time in deep reflection, or what others would rightfully deem as anxiety about a looming uncertainness over his life, his property.

Tusmo, the wife of Hoagsaday, right after the incident involving the military took place, felt a more ominous feeling in relation to the occurrence of her husband's unusual arrest. She therefore summoned the driver and was off to a relative to get things done, as that was how things of such magnitude were broached.

 THREE

The Bloodlines

. . . .

THERE WAS AN UNWRITTEN LAW THAT WAS INCORPORATED
into fabric of life – a hold over from the people and their culture
of pastoralism – which was the hierarchy of clan bloodlines. This
clan hierarchy was entrenched in religion, government, and in general, with all of the Somali. So whatever one was, he was above all a
member by blood of a clan. Blood affiliations ran deep in the society,
forming the trajectory for all the modern occurrences such as a the
modern state, the officials within it, and consequently the society at
large. Every philosophy, Western or otherwise, was grounded in this
concept of the bloodlines. And it followed that distant clan rivalries
were a pretext for altercations in the now.

In this spirit, Tusmo went immediately to a prominent member of
weight in the affairs of the clan in the dislocation of the city. Somal's
clan system was based on patrilineal blood relationships, comple-
mented differently by matrilineal blood relations. The male blood
line, however, and thus the male, dominated clan affairs. Though
Tusmo was particularly aggrieved in the case of her husband's
sudden arrest, Hoagsaday's clan could never be represented by her.

The car arrived at the bungalow of her husband's relative, an
elderly businessman like Hoagsaday and long-time resident of the
city of Mogadishu. The gate was open. The car drove into the driveway. Tusmo quickly got out of the car and knocked at the door

purposefully in abandon. A worker came to the door and recognized her. As she brushed past him, straight to where the women of the household were sleeping, she quickly explained the situation, waiting anxiously for an audience with the elder.

He came into the main living room, his face a little puffy from sleep. He had the thin chiseled features typical of the Somal. His features were accentuated by the wild saffron of his beard and uncovered head, normally covered by an Islamic skull cap called koofiyad.

"Hayeh Tusmo, Hafadi Kawaran."

"Our house has been confronted by a disaster. Soldiers came to the house during our usual siesta, and took Hoagsaday along with Abukar for no apparent reason. Initially they asked for Hoagsaday but when Abukar came out to the veranda and saw what was going on he could not remain watching. He openly protested, calling the soldiers animals, after which two soldiers descended on him with many more coming out of the truck to help restrain him. They were ruthless, cocking there machine guns at us, including the women and children. This action was completely unprovoked based on the way these men came with such force and their lack of respect for anyone at the home. I am frightened by what might be the fate of Hoagsaday and Abukar. I plead that you act quickly, considering the nature of their arrest."

"How long ago did this happen?" "Three hours at the most."

The elder received the news with the dignity typical of an elder, with a degree of solemnity, urgency. But he was very careful not to portray the inner convulsions of alarm which he concealed in front of women.

He then cleared his throat and said, "Tusmo, go back to the children and the house and open the business. Wait for my word as regards Hoagsaday's whereabouts and whose wrath he has incurred. We will immediately try to get to the bottom of this. How dare they! Do they think we are dead? Or we are not men? Go back home now. Leave the matter to us."

The elder sat for a while, forlorn after the departure of Tusmo. He was alone sitting in the same spot lost in the potential of all the overwhelming possibilities. Some were quite dire, some were not quite so dire, but all converged into the absence of the realm of the unknown.

An abyss was created by the fact that he was well aware of Hoagsaday's disposition as a man. He was humble and not one who was interested in political office, nor was he arrogant to people in general, particularly government functionaries. He went through the beginnings of Hoagsaday's life to the point of his abduction by the military. He could not see where the two tussled in any way possible. He had come to the conclusion that it was way beyond the routine problems officialdom had with their citizens.

Most of all, he was preoccupied with the way forward. The elder quickly came out of his thoughts. He ventured towards his sleeping quarters to prepare himself to leave in search of the members of his clan to consult with in relation to this sudden occurrence.

The elder decided to go to a prominent member of the clan-who happened to also be a high ranking military officer-to alert him first of the disappearance and to see if he could first locate what exactly was the reason, if any, that Hoagsaday was taken into the military's custody.

In the view of city dwellers, nomadic life was a life of endless nothingness and, for what they concluded, the mere sustenance of camel milk! Or, the distant promise of some meat, unless, that is, a camel lingered in illness, or the perchance of a goat offering when there was the rare guest visiting the encampment.

The city dwellers had become spoilt in the pseudo-modern ways of the city. A largely sedentary existence, they had an expanded diet of processed food, regular meals at certain times of the day, an abundance of water and more things to buy from overseas markets. The harsh, semi-arid-plains, the natural habitat of this irrepressibly rugged duo of camel and the Somal nomad-was deliberately moved to the back recesses of the city dweller's mind, in the hope the mind might forget the indelible mark ingrained through the centuries by generations of this mode of life. They could not, try as they might, get rid of the nomadic idiosyncrasies that had a habit of showing up at the most inopportune times, even in the most seasoned of the city dwellers.

The city dwellers fancied themselves as far removed from what they saw in a nutshell as their primordial past, certainly an existence far from the white limestone facades of Mogadishu. Unfortunately for them, this past was not even a generation away, even the for the educated in the western sense. Their parents knew no other ways, and they themselves had spent some significant part of their lives in between school recesses as nomads tending to the camels. They engaged on a relentlessly arduous journey in search of the pregnant rain cloud which would bring forth a vibrantly replenished landscape from emaciated dry brown off-red to a stunningly opulent green of deferring shades, contrasting the off-beige of the camel with the silver-grey of the newborn's coat.

The nomad transplants, in their new habitat of the city, felt and acted far removed from the ways of the pastoral hinterland. The essence of a Somal was irrevocably harnessed to the ways of the camel, the gathering of them. The near worship poetic odes to the beauty of this animal, the particular disposition accumulated from the wellspring of a very harsh reality, of a not-so-giving earth, seem to produce a heightened sense of love for the earth. Every prickly plant or even miserly waterhole would be reshaped through the poetic form, or a descriptive narrative into something gushing with a softness of natural fertility. The misery waterhole would become, through poetic license, something bountiful and rich with minerals that nourish man and camel alike.

 **FOUR**

The Saffron Council

. . . .

THE ELDER ARRIVED AT THE SPRAWLING RESIDENCE OF HIS clanmate, the military official. The house had a lot of uniformed soldiers milling about the place. They saluted the elder as he passed them in the compound, knowing him as a frequent visitor and relative to their commanding officer. The elder was ushered into a small waiting area reserved for those seeking the audience of this important person. He was served tea while he waited. Soon he was joined by Abdi, casually dressed in a Somal sarong, the elder then greeted him. "War iskawarran," to which Abdi replied, "I am ok."

"Everyone by the grace of Allah is fine at my home, but the house of Hoagsaday your cousin the businessman has endured a sudden loss. Hoagsaday's wife Tusmo came to my residence an hour ago to inform me that Hoagsaday and Abukar, our cousins, were both taken away from Hoagsaday's home this afternoon by soldiers and piled into a military truck. The destination and why or what the problem is what has brought me to see you right after she left."

The officer could not contain his shock, it showed openly. It was as if he had been hit or slapped from an unknown place.

He managed a, "Hm," momentarily leaving in his mind the scene of the elder.

He then got up from his chair and said to the elder, "Wait, I'm going to get to the bottom of this."

He went into another room and started calling, "This is Commander Beheyeah. Put me through to the resident senior officer in charge.

"Yes" came the response on the other end. He heard a few rings of the senior officer's extension, and a prompt, "This is Junior Commander. The senior is not at the post now."

"Yes, Commander, I would like to know who it is who arrested a businessman this afternoon, what for, and where they took him. Who is it that authorized the arrest? I want a report within the hour at my residence, Junior Commander, I am waiting."

"Yes sir, right away."

He then returned to the elder, who was sipping his tea, clearly perturbed by the incident that was relayed to him.

He sat down and started a conversation with the elder who interjected with, "What is happening?" After regaining some of his composure, he briefed the old man as to what had just transpired.

"I am expecting some answers within the hour. I am as surprised as you are. I don't know what this is. The military does not do the work of the police."

"Well that's exactly what happened this afternoon. What really baffles me is why Mohamed, of all people? I have heard of people in politics who were openly against this regime arrested and shot, but a law abiding businessman we all knew to be humble and pious?"

"I have no answers to give at the moment, but let's wait a little. I am sure there is some rationale to this."

"What do we do?"

"Nothing until we know the situation exactly."

"There is an ominous sign in my inner being when I saw the fear in the eyes of his wife earlier today. I could not see it as a run of the mill thing between some disgruntled or even stupid officer, but rather something bigger than that, simply because he was a prominent businessman in the city, he was known to all - the low and the high. A man like that can not just simply be arrested at the whim of some lowly officer, or a high one, for that matter, simply because Somals are much aware of the stature of a man like Hoagsaday.

And the extended value attached to such a man to any clan. We know that whoever did this was well aware of the consequences from his relatives who invariably were higher ups. Furthermore, his circles were quite prominent and well-to-do. These are the reasons of my forlorn and wonder".

"I am quite aware of what you are saying myself, but I do not want to jump to conclusions. I would be lying if I said I was not shocked by this peculiar news, and yes I do take it personally that my cousin was snatched right under my nose. I further agree that whomever it was took me into account. However, let's wait to see what actually transpired."

With that, a servant came in and summoned him to the phone. "Hello, Commander Beheyeah."

"Yes, it is Commander Beheyeah."

"Commander, the arrest of the civilian Mohamed Haji Hashe was ordere by commander Ali Deray of army intelligence." "That will be all."

He returned with the news to the elder that he had located where the orders had come from. But that was all he had at the moment.

"I am right now on my way to find this Ali Deray, to get the bottom of this nonsense. Meanwhile, go ahead back to your house. I will send someone to fetch you and the other elders, if necessary. We have to have a long counsel tonight."

With that, he dispatched one vehicle to the take the elder and then summoned a captain, his aid de camp, and went upstairs to put on his full military regalia. He put on a crisp uniform with the gleaming star and red collar, displaying for all to see his rank of general, and his conspicuous side arm badge. When he came back down, stepping out to the veranda, all the soldiers inside his compound dropped all and froze at attention. The guards in front of the veranda made a loud sound with their weapons as they froze to attention, and the ADC, standing slightly ahead, opened the back door for the general, who promptly sank into the back seat. The Captain then sat in the front seat. The driver removed the cover from the general's flag, which was red and emblazoned with one star in the middle, and to took the cover off the back metal plates, also red with a star, as was the military protocol, indicating that there was a general on board the vehicle.

On his way to the High Command Headquarters, the General planned his move based on what he knew to be a sudden turn of events. He had shown his worth in revolutionary mettle as one of the young officers, ideologues, committed to a socialism which was closer to the structure of the egalitarian pastoralist. But though the situation was increasingly running counter to the ideals of equality and more toward a hegemony of one group trumping state, rank, and law onto themselves, he did not confide the worry of recent internal movements, promotions, of individuals outside the military's standard order upwards from middle-rank captains, majors, and colonels to generals. There was also the replacement of career military officers, from majors to colonels, who were abruptly assigned to diplomatic missions, and others at very mature ages who were being enrolled in military academies in the Soviet Union.

As such there was then an influx of new officers minimally trained at the local academy moving up rapidly in the ranks in a matter of a few years attaining senior ranks, then replacing these officers without any qualification other than being a member of the clan of the Head of State. The General was aware of this change, subtly at first, and regarded it as something minor and not of consequence to the progress of Somali as a whole. After all, one could not expect a semi-literate driver of camels to comprehend das capital in an African setting, without expecting some digressions back to his camel ways.

The group of ideologues were even happy to bite the bullet for such transgressions, partly lulled by the assumed sincerity of the old, big-mouth father. And likewise the General was just a harmless police general who had worked his way up from the time of the Italian Protectorate, and then was installed by the ideologues hastily as a compromise figurehead to give the revolution a wider public appeal through the use of an elder officer in a country that valued age at the head of the table of reckoning.

As a group, the drawback of the ideologues was youth. In hindsight, their collective youth did have an adverse affect on their choice of this man. Altruism was largely a youthful enterprise and was perhaps what broke the wall of rational wisdom and made them overlook a crucial obstacle. General wisdom, however ill-informed, had a bad habit of trumping youthful ideals.

The General was at a loss. When he stopped to look, there was an encirclement of tribal loyalists, ill-equipped to command much less run a country. Now even some of the middle of the revolutionary cadres had been swallowed by the upsurge of this new system that was based on the old affirmed loyalties of bloodlines. Mechanized units and weapons galore all at the hands of one clan greatly upset the old balance of power in which other clans could adjudicate some reprieve from an over-belligerent clan.

As it had worked, the elders of the more numerous clans had reasons to abate wanton destruction, particularly when a larger clan was involved in victimizing a much smaller clan who could not match them. In the lore of the nomad, it was an eye for eye. Elders of the larger clans interceded to stop the wanton violence by pressuring the aggressor with both veiled threats of violent retaliation by the collective and eloquent entreaties to resolve the problem amicably. But first, the underhanded violence had to stop. In this way, the more aggressive larger groups were held at bay from the arrogance of might released unbridled upon women and children caught in the fury of irreconcilable pride. Such pride was unreasonably fraught with violent destruction of the ordered, natural calm and for it men folk would willingly incur heavy losses rather than compromise the name and pride of their bloodlines, bequeathed from their father's father's fathers. This name was theirs at all costs, in victory or in mayhem, till the last man stands, if that only be an infant. The bloodline consumes all in the name of itself, but the quicksand could be abated with deterrence from outside, in the form of larger numbers, and with a promise of more violence from a larger collective on the side of the vanquished weaker group.

This promise quickly brought about reason to the unreasonable. Or rather, it was not based on rationality but on a firm promise of the other to deliver the same havoc unless there was a definite cessation to this brute madness.

And so, there would be calm again: good enjoined between the two; brides exchanged to ameliorate the loss of fathers and sons; camels thrown in as a further measure to ensure the calm. Indeed, the promise of collective violent punishment brought the clans to the table for peace. Light weapons, machine guns, spears, more sons, more horses: this was the equilibrium of might in the society of Somal.

As the General arrived at the National Defense Headquarters, an unnervingly loud call to attention was sounded by the one of the sentries. There was also a simultaneous cocking of machine guns, now all pointed at the approaching vehicle of the General. The driver then slowed to a halt, after which a sentry approached the vehicle, saluted, and made a little pretentious attempt at asking the driver for particulars.

He shouted to the sentry manning the barrier, "All clear, open!" and shouted the General's rank and name at the top of his voice, freezing in salute as did the rest of the sentries. The vehicle went further on through the military complex, each barrier opening as the sentries relayed the call to attention and froze in salute as the machine guns echoed the salute noise from the soldiers clutching salute. The vehicle was well known and the sentries were just going through the motions of formality. No one could pass without the sentry stopping and identifying the vehicle.

The General went into the large building, made appointments with his fellow ideologues - those he could trust - and went about waiting for the officer who gave the order of Hoagsaday, the officer whom he has summoned to come to his office pronto.

The Aid de Camp handed him some of the routine work, but the General was curt, unusual for one who was usually gracious in spite of his high position to his underlings.

He asked instead to be briefed in the background of Ali Deray. "What have you gathered so far on the officer I ordered here?"

"General, so far what is streaming in has been scant. At the moment, we know that he is a junior colonel, is from the Mid-South, and that he has risen remarkably quickly through the ranks, replacing your former colleague, who, as you know, is now the military attaché in Bulgaria."

"I see. Do we have a time?"

"He should be here anytime now. Will that be all, General?" He saluted the General. "Captain, I want the report given to me now, before he comes here. This matter is for my eyes only." "Yes, sir."

As the General started looking through some of the more mundane routine work, the phone rang. It was his ADC at the other end of the buzzer.

"General, the Colonel is here and ready to be seen by you." "Send him up."

The door was opened and a tall, lanky young man entered the door and stood at attention. The General motioned to him to sit down. He did on one of the plush, leather upholstered chairs, taking in everything with a roving look about the office. He saw a red and black telephone and flags, both with the country's and the military's insignia. Apart from all this, behind the huge oak table, sat the General. The General looked to him to be in his late forties. With a salt and pepper head, and glasses, seemingly engaged in a ponderous stare right past him, the General was acutely observing this young man.

"Colonel, what is the military doing going into private residences to arrest civilians?" "We were acting according to intelligence reports. As you well know, we have intelligence that the business man concerned was an intermediary in a very large arms deal and is a member of a group of dissidents who are bent on the overthrow of this revolution. General, sir, I will be forwarding a full report to the high command in a few hours, but the preliminary full report will be forwarded to your office in a matter of an hour. In essence, the reason the military is openly involved in this case with civilians is a matter of national security."

"Who is the commanding officer in this matter?" "It is General Global Change to Waybee."

With this, the General dismissed the junior officer. It was protocol for him now to follow further with the aforementioned general. Ali briefly stood at attention then proceeded to leave the General's office. He was passed at the door by the General's ADC, carrying the report.

The ADC came in with the report in hand, having scanning it, as was his duty, and placed it in front of the General. The General

looked through the report. It listed Hoagsaday as a co-conspira-
tor with another prominent business man, also from the same area
as Hoagsaday, and reported them both as the bankrollers of a
cadre of malcontents. The report even suggested the involvement of
a neighboring country which for Hoagsaday would mean an indict-
ment of high treason, punishable by death by a military tribunal.

The General winced from the deluge of incredible information gathered with such great detail. The Hoagsaday he saw in the
report was an entirely different person from the one he had known
for a lifetime. At the outset, there seemed to be quite irrefutable
evidence of Hoagsaday's complicity in committing crimes against
the revolution. The general asked his ADC what he had thought of
the report.

"The report is intricate and requires a thorough evaluation,
but from the little I have discerned there seems to be a great deal of
incontrovertible evidence against the group of individuals, however
unlikely the main players seem to be. Collectively, they are probably
the most unlikely band of conspirators I have ever encountered, but,
then again, a perfect deception for the untrained eye."

"Get General Kumanay's office."

Soon after the ADC had left the office, the phone rang.

"General Kumanay speaking. This is General Beheyeah. How is
the family?"

"Very good, Kumanay. What is this report? And why has the military brought up all these unlikely players for charges of espionage?"

"Yes, Beheyeah. It seems rather odd at first, but there is quite a solid
case against all these individuals, notwithstanding all their previous
run of the mill collective histories. Espionage, my friend, has, as you
can see, has assumed unlikely avenues, quite different from what we
know in the more traditional sense of the word. I would like us to
meet so that I may go over some of the overwhelming evidence we
have on this group of individuals. I know Hoagsaday is a close member of your family and that you know him as an upstanding member
of the country. I will be on my way to my house and I was hoping
to discuss this issue with you there. Please read the brief now, and
I will wait for you at the house."

. . . .

"Alright, I am wrapping up over here. See you in around an hour."

With that, the General scanned the briefing from Ali Deray again and summoned his ADC.

"I want you to investigate this brief tonight. I would like comments on my desk in the morning. I am aware the full report is not due yet. Make the comments on what you have. The Colonel said there is irrefutable evidence that suggests foreign meddling and so forth. Also, prepare my escort for a trip to General Kumanay's home."

The General arrived at Kumanay's house with the usual freezing salutes. He was ushered in to a large living room area, detached from the main house but connected by a shade corridor of sorts. He was now charged with General Kumanay's ADC who rushed ahead slightly. He opened the door, announcing, "General Beheyeah, sir."

Beheyeah observed that Kumanay was at the large window, standing behind a large ornate wooden table and a plush sofa. Kumanay turned towards the door as the General came in and broke into smiles, showing with his whole body his excitement to see his fellow general.

Kumanay's gregarious personality, booming voice, tall stature, with a dark, shiny complexion struck the General as Kumanay greeted him.

"Welcome, welcome, Beheyeah! How are you my dear friend? It seems like ages since we last spent more then a few minutes in between some official function or other."

"I am fine everything is good. I wish we had more time to discuss recent events and things as we used to when we were at the academy overseas."

"I feel the same way. Most of these young chaps are so inclined to their own ways rather than the ways of revolutionary progress, it seems we have to teach both the young and old what should ideally be in their own interest."

"Yes, yes. There is a lot of the old we have to deal with. It is in most cases a huge stumbling block."

"I know. How does one explain the working of the state? The position of the national rather than the position of the clan as the main point of cohesion for the state?"

"I have thought on many occasions of the same subject. So far, I am still pondering." "The usual to drink?"

"Yes."

Kumanay went to the tray that was on an ornate table in the corner and mixed a drink of vodka with sprite and handed the drink to Beheyeah while he poured himself another drink of rum. They both then sat down on the plush sofas. The large room was decorated in a very spare but tasteful way. They began to reminisce about their old military college days.

They had both gone to the Royal Sandhurst Academe, one older than the other, almost two years apart. Beheyeah had been in his last year when Kumanay was in his first year and so Beheyeah had been on his own for two years, with no other student there from the home country. When he came, Kumanay struck Beheyeah as an affable young man, in fact, it was Kumanay who had come looking for him then.

The two got along famously within the cadre of other such students who had come from distant, soon to be independent nations. They bonded, found they had a lot in common, and developed lifelong relationships with each other, meeting together with the very powerful few when they returned to their respective home countries. They were assigned to read the standard European war stories, leaving out, in most cases, how the rest of the world was ill-equipped to play the war games. Plunder was replaced with civilization, religion, and the many benign things. Foreign students were force fed, all the while thinking themselves quite elevated from their brethren. But for this fortuitous knowledge they were now privy to would still be languishing in the desolate past of the rest of the uncivilized world.

Before Kumanay's arrival, Beheyeah had been secretly aware of a cadre of older Africans in London who led liberation-focused meetings in London, both by Labor and, underneath the surface, Communist party ideals. He had been particularly friendly with a West Indian student of philosophy who lived and breathed the destruction of Western domination on all the people of the South. And though the man's demeanor had been unassuming, one only had to step back once he started to speak to feel the turmoil, as powerful as sea currents, lurking just beneath the surface of his deceptively soft spoken exterior. He thought of the world and all that was in it. He kept talking about the Western canon – Hegel, Marx and all the others.

It was these friendships that had kept the General up at night reading variously outside of the military curriculum. And this is where he thought of the world, his country with himself in it; this was where the world opened itself to his endless examination. So when Kumanay came, Beheyeah became his tutor in terms of both his military education and the global education he was getting from the Africans from the rest of the world.

The air was one of change, movement, general revolution. Whereas Beheyeah had arrived thinking in the sense of a very small place, he ended up with an entire world to relate to. Of the two, Beheyeah returned to Somal first. He came back to a country that had made quite a bold move through the unification of the British and Italian colonies of Somal. But that's where it had stopped.

The rhetoric of pan-Africanism had taken hold in the elites who had managed to steer the country in the forward direction. But what had proven undoable was the synthesis of the old and the new, making for a very potent mix of clan entitlement and progressive African-centered ideas: a wide birth for the world inside a very tiny frame of the clan bloodlines. This was the Somal that the generals, then junior officers, went forth in earnest to change for the better. Day and night, Beheyeah wanted a Socialist Republic of Somal.

To Beheyeah, still, the reason for this arrest was unclear. All he saw was a man who has done some hard work enterprising with other such individuals. Surely, he thought, was it the government's position to consider all foreign contacts espionage.

With that, he bid goodbye to the General who had reaffirmed his commitment to the goals of progress.

FIVE

Revolutionary Cadre

. . . .

THE NEXT DAY, THE GENERAL SENT WORD TO THE ELDER to come and see him. He then dispatched his ADC to his cousins household to inform Tusmo where Hoagsaday was to be transferred – to a local police station to remain until further notice.

The saffron-haired elder sent one of his sons around to the houses of the other clan members to tell mostly elder and younger men of the bloodlines to meet at his house after the day's siesta.

The General was to also attend this gathering.

The elders came streaming in one by one. They were all ushered into the large seating area designated for such occasions or gatherings. Their hard stuffed pillows, some for leaning, the flat ones for sitting on, were all placed in rectangle formation against the wall with carpets covering the remainder of the room. The men sat in conversation of the day's events, waiting for a quorum, in particular the General, who they all expected to brief them on the details. However top secret the operation was, he was privy, and, as his fellow clan members, so were they. It was funny, they respected him to a large extent because of his position in the government, a position outside the clan. He was their man inside.

The General came in wearing his civilian attire. All stood up to greet him heartily, after he was seated.

The elder started first by giving praise to Allah, and, in his name, the meeting started. "We have gathered in order to see our brother

Hoagsaday out of this problem. We are here to understand why and what is happening to him. So far, we all know that they have moved him from the military's possession to the police, and we will hear more on that from the General, who is here with us. As usual, after the general speaks, all may render their thoughts on the matter as they see fit."

The floor was opened to Beheyeah.

"Brothers, we have all been through several stages of this event. As all of you know, we are going through a crucial time in our history where we are trying to change to a new system. Our old system is wonderful in its traditional ways, but when it confronts modernity, it has to be mediated. The ways of the Somal are just, but the previous government's crooked politicians used the system of the bloodlines to the detriment of the both the old system and the new independent republic with its high ideals. Their use overlooked the larger differences in the hope of establishing a much stronger facade in the face of the more dominant powers of the world. Initially, we had the purity to forgo the regressive outlook of those who later chose to waylay the idealism of an entire continent. But the new republic decided to use its new position not for the sake of that ideal, but as a tool to enrich themselves at the expense of the people of Somal.

"The new dream, as Africans put it, if you will, placed large obstacles in the way of the great foundation for Somal and for Africa, robbing the generations to come of the opportunity to stand as men. The corrupt were able to sideline the noble goals of the Somali vanguard, indeed Africa's vanguard, on behalf of the former colonial masters, so as to continue the malaise of domination at the peril of our nation, continent, and its human resources. This is the hope of those who are to come after us, and this is why I became a member of those who brought back some vision through a forced revolution, in order to put Somal back on the course of those who had the vision, but could not find the temerity from others to see this vision off the ground.

"We have now tried to get that moving. But the revolutionary council is struggling to implement this vision. We are fighting the internal agents of imperialism at the same time we are instituting a system that is first and foremost concerned with the whole nation, and not just a few. We are confronted with those who want to destroy us using the method of the bloodlines, knowing full well the grasp it has on Somal at large. The revolution understands the bloodlines in its traditional, egalitarian way, how it does not discriminate amongst equals, but when messed up with the new state, it becomes the harbinger of nepotism which is bent on sending brother against brother in the final analysis to extermination, all at the behest of the colonial masters, who were until recently replaced by those they put in their stead. They were all from the bloodlines, but not of them.

After all, we are gathered here for some answers concerning the arrest of Hoagsaday. What I want all of you to understand very clearly is that though there have been a lot of misgivings, the core of that vision is still alive and well, albeit with many diversions. For reasons of bloodlines, we must not completely derail to a position of collective self-actualization, nor to the actualization of a very few."

The floor was now open to the gathering of elders. There was the customary responsive affirmations in between the pauses of the speaker's accomplishments, lavish praises sprinkled with the extolling of the virtues of his bloodline. And the affirmations were particularly profound in the tapestry of eloquence.

The next person to speak was a visitor from the Hinterland known for his oratory skills. His family nickname was "one who enters the lyre of the lions," connoting his wild irreverence.

"I have not been so fortunate to have been with the General, nor have I been to school, even in the Somal, much less there in far off lands. Our brother, the great General, has done both, and is wily in their ways which are slowly but surely replacing our ways.

A simple man like me does not understand the aspirations of a greater and larger group with more power than the bloodlines, one that is based on an expansive ideal, that transcends the exclusionary ideal of one or the other bloodlines. Yes, it is true that had we kept forth without compromise to achieve the unity of the Somal from corner to corner, we might have indeed reached a period of great wealth and advance for ourselves, Africa, and the rest of the world.

Unfortunately, my possibilities are tempered firmly with the reality of my time and place as a Somal. However disheartening, the reality of myself and the others in this room is we are animals of our time. We cannot transcend the bloodlines. I would venture that this is not the exception but disgracefully the truth. But I would like to qualify the last statement with a reservation: what has transpired with our cousin Hoagsaday is not political. If I lean on my long understanding of Somals, it is apparent there is a very naked victimization of him because and only because of his clan. Simply because he is not the spy they say he is. The humiliating manner in which he was arrested in front of his children and wife. We know Hoagsaday, we know his father, and we are his immediate blood cousins, the ones who are charged with protecting him, from the infraction of other clans. But today, although it is clear this a clan affair, we can't confront the forest of Government for the tree of clan.

We need your presence with us, General, to see this for what it is – as purely a clan thing – in the hope that you might also utilize the Government's apparatus at the behest of your clan just as we have been shown by those in positions similar to yours. After all, was it not that our cousin was actually picked up by some of your underlings, using the full might of the state? Men are often called to see their time and place clearly so as to better fashion and equip the rest of their fellow human travelers with better choices in this journey called life.

If indeed Allah has blessed you with the erudition of Knowledge, this knowledge should also lead one to clear understanding of the essence of their time – who they are, what are their ideal possibilities, and to what their reality in the form of human capacity is, especially in the example of our times, when our ideals as a nation have been hijacked in the name of clan chauvinism. So, Beheyeah, lead us in the right way and overcome your ideals. Look at the naked truth. Otherwise, you will be party to many more individuals who will somehow become conspirators against the revolution at the cost of so many innocent lives both from our clan and others in a similar position. And all of it for an ideal long since broken by your fellow cadres, *taken your blindness for granted in the interim and final confrontation for certain.*"

 SIX

The Moment

· ·

TUSMO WAS MUCH YOUNGER THAN HOAGSADAY WHEN SHE was formally proposed to by the elder members of her husband's bloodlines. She had been raised mostly in the traditional hinterland ways of the Somal, and even now she went about the chores of the day as if her husband had not been hijacked by the military. She dreaded the messenger the elder would send bearing the unknown news of her husband. She got the children ready for school taking care not to let her state of bewilderment flow over to her young children, although one of them seemed to already understand the atmosphere of the home had changed to a thick air of sullen melancholy. The child was able to discern her mother was not quite there, that she seemed to be walking around absent and somewhere else, unlike her usual engaging demeanor and interested eyes.

Tusmo, was indeed forlorn and mainly reticent and she wished she was back in the hinterland where things were clearer and out in the open for all to see. She thought of the stoicism of her mother, imparting the ways of the women of Somal, the beautiful work of embroidery, a part of many things that sustained the Somal throughout the many seasons of hardship, and the constant moving, she remembered how her mother would impart her tradition, sometimes in poetry, sometimes in certain expected ways, ways that were frowned upon by the men folk. Tusmo also recalled the beginnings of Hoagsaday's entry into the life of her family. She knew there was something in the air although she was barely sixteen when Hoagsaday's clan came seeking her, as their wife.

When married to the clan of your husband, the woman was placed as a transient member in the husband's clan, but always retained her own bloodline. The proverb exemplifying the character of this relation of marriage from the perspective of the woman's clan states, "In the event of a quarrel between your brother in law and your sister, don't burn bridges with your brother in law, because you are never sure of your sister's allegiances."

She had spent her life being prepared for the moment of marriage. She was schooled in all the formal and informal etiquette of marriage, relations and inter-bloodlines, and in particular in the feminine aspects of it. This being the a well defined role that encompassed many roles significant through a bloodline analysis.

The women were acquired for the role of procreation. They were the ones who principally brought the sons into the world. The vehicles, if you will, for the power in numbers, over other clans, were sons and more sons.

Her wedding was done in the ways of the Somal. There were plenty of people, a lot of singing and dancing, a lot of back and forth.

Tusmo could remember well the day, though it had been a many years since and two children after. Hoagsaday's clan had come to the encampment, some of them journeying from the city, and you could tell from the general fatigue they exuded that they had traveled long hours of the journey there on foot. Although nomadic encampments could be reached by sturdy four by fours, hardly anyone did so. In most cases, to reach an encampment one walked. For the nomad, walking long distances was the same as a city dweller taking a bath. The nomad was used to walking great distances at a brisk pace, and in turn he thought the city dweller's attempts at walking, after having modernized their habits in the city, feeble. Long walks left the city dwellers lagging behind, while the nomad briskly made the pace seem easy, as they engaged in quite involved conversations, consciously maintaining a break-neck pace. The city dweller, having accumulated a rather soft all around constitution were quite a spectacle to behold in the eyes of the nomad. A touché in the folly of ridicule, this time the giver was the joke.

Apart from the city dwellers, others came from nearby encampments. The encampment assumed an unusual buzz. As it was the custom for nomads to slaughter a goat without notice upon the arrival of guests, whether the guests had no business, were stopping briefly on their way somewhere, or were relations seeking a family encampment, it was considered terrible to send a guest on his way without the customary meat before they retired for the night and resumed their journey early the next day.

Tusmo reflected, "My mother, or one of sisters, did the slaughtering on the chilab bush, a natural cutting table which looked unassumingly frail and short but was sturdy and held the slaughtered goat suspended in a almost magical form – legs dangling in place – while it was skinned, disemboweled, and cut into manageable pieces."

"My mother was constantly reminding us of our composure – to mind our womanly disposition - and she was urgent, incessant with her corrections, as though we were under imminent danger, always reprimanding us while she leaned down into the work, as if she was taking to the dead goat. But we knew who she was addressing. In the heightened urgency, we performed our duties – gathered wood, started the fire, all on top of the normal duty of the encampment – the kraaling of the goats and sheep inside the cut thorn tree branches that served as an impenetrable wall for common predators like the hyenas, and sometimes the larger cats.

"It was around dusk," she remembered, "when the men arrived, coinciding with the prayer of Maghrib. The men were handed small metal water containers for washing, not unlike the ones used for the tea, and it was quite incredible to behold how a palm of water could wash an entire arm to the elbow, for ablution before prayer. They all prayed in a jam'a (group) and then after prayer, everyone proceeded to the Ardah, a ceremonial Somal dwelling. The walls of it were created by hanging colorful mattes of weave and dark tanned leather ones, and the floor was decorated with a distinctive one, handmade from a variety of assorted scraps of cloth turned into rope and woven.

These rugs were thrown on the floor, capturing the beauty in the color schemes brought about by the different pieces of cloth, and mixed with the tan of the encampment utensils, made of the dark wood and embroidered. The Ardah was a showpiece seating area for important occasions, such as the bride wedding ceremony and the other similar procedures, and, as such, the men were here to ask Tusmo's father on behalf of their clan, for Tusmo's hand.

Then Suleiman, the visible leader of the group because of his advanced age, started off with a eulogy to Adhan, extolling the virtues of how he has raised exceptional girls who were part of a long list of women who had born such men of outstanding character for his clan in the past.

He began, "Today is a day for the clans to remember the long and good relations we've possessed and that we should further solidify this relationship through the proposed marriage of Hoagsaday, an outstanding man of their clan who has distinguished himself from the rest of the clan. Hoagsaday has from a very early age accumulated a lot of wealth from very humble beginnings. We all know his father was not a man known for any very particular thing. He was neither a man of wealth, outstanding bravery, nor of great hikma. But despite this, Hoagsaday has become one of our clan's ambassadors in the capital."

SEVEN

Raw Ambition

HAROLD BRAITHWAITE HAD PONDERED A CAREER AS A STATE department official, and, as such, he was not very enthused by his accidental appointment as an American ambassador in Somal. He had come in from Rome, and the usual process of assignment had been cut short when the previous Ambassador's sudden demise after a heart attack, led to an opening of his job. A quick replacement was made.

Harold's main objective was to rationalize the varied interest of the United States of America, but he had arrived in Mogadishu not very conversant with anything African, much less this most complicated part of it. Needless to say, he had not anticipated such a post, nor did he sign up for this remote and rather ineffectual place in the scheme of the things of the world. He was getting quickly acquainted with this holdover, it seemed to him, from centuries past. Nothing here seemed of the times as compared to the posts he was used to. But with it came certain finalities. There was, after all, his position of Ambassador, which he would not have not gotten if this was a choice capital like Rome. He had to bite the bullet for this position which was usually rendered as a political payback for a more than staunch supporter of the president.

He settled in by going through copies of the previous ambassador's correspondence to Washington. The literature, politics and history of the country he had already gone through before assuming the post. The correspondence gave him an eye into the individuals, the people from the surrounding countries, of Ethiopia, Kenya, and the French Somal, were concerned with in terms of what seemed to be expansionist objectives. All correspondence was copied to all the U.S. embassies in the neighboring countries, with further correspondence between the western powers of France, Britain and Italy, all colonizers of this area. Harold, also backed up his informal education of the position with meetings with both the local and American staff, to help formulate a better view of his posting.

He was under instructions to be ameliorating to Somal officialdom, in this case in particular, the self styled Socialist republic. Before the October Revolution, there was an amicable presence of the U. S. in Somal, although the Somal leadership felt marginalized by the United States overtures to the emperor of Imperial Ethiopia Haile Selassie, the favored alley in this part of the Hemisphere.

The previous government, although in their own estimates fond of the Western system, particularly the Italian and British models, saw no future in an Ethiopian-dictated U. S. foreign policy, particularly when there was also the added centuries of accrued animosity through bloody wars, over the Somal territories annexed by the Former Emperor Menelik as part of his domain when he partitioned it during the scramble for Africa, a reality rarely discussed, because this colonizer did not fit the usual binary of Europe versus Africa. The irony of this Black imperialist is that he also is the symbol of ancient to modern black independence, to all the Africans at home and abroad.

After a brief liaison with the U.S. the Somal leadership were looking elsewhere for assistance in all matters related to the modern state from all who would listen, which was a small group of two in the world in the form of U.S.S.R. and China. Harold was made aware of the previous good relations gone sour with Somal, but nothing was written in stone with the previous government. The new military regime was clearly made of communist ideologues, some already trained by the Soviets as result of the previous misgivings of the previous government's said problems.

Harold thought the post was of no particular significance, but it was dully pressing on him, everyday a little more, that his government had actually bungled this one in many ways. All this in a country opposite the world's largest resources under the sphere and power of his country. In the main, Somal occupied a place quite strategic to the ebb and flow of these valued resources, the world, and in particular the Super Powers, which needed to continue to run their vast spheres of influence. It was pressed upon this new diplomat to do all within his means to beat back the now open Russian influence on this strategic nation sprawled between the Red Sea and the Indian Ocean.

Harold, was determined to win the Cold War battle in this remote part of the world by first acquainting himself with the land and those who ran it. He was in a particular hurry to meet the military diplomatic liaison, having already delivered his papers to the Chairman of the Supreme Revolutionary Counsel, the Head of State at an official function a couple of days ago.

He now called his assistant with a senior member of the local embassy staff. The previous ambassador had written highly about this Somal staff member, extolling his great understanding of his country and personalities. And it was in particular his counsel on personalities that had always made engagement with important Somals that much more beneficial to U.S. interests.

His staff member arrived at the Ambassador's and was immediately shown in. The discussion, directed by Harold, focused on what was going on in Somal and who was most likely to see things his way, as did some of the previous government. The American staff member said that, in the main, he thought it was close to impossible, as long as the new officers who were all idealistic communist ideologues were in charge. "Not much can be done in the form of the regular inducements. This not to say that we will stop trying, but as my local colleague has informed me, whatever it is we do, there must be a focused effort of those who have designs of leadership at all costs rather than ideology. Here we will have a break through. The usual is in place in terms of informants at many levels both inside the circles of power, and without, but unfortunately they are all still very junior in the scheme of things. Information-wise we are close to the heartbeat of everything in this country that matters."

With that he summoned the Sectary to make a appointment for the day after for both the gentlemen. I would also like you to call the Foreign Affairs and invite who you can. I want to see the Somal elites up close, in a more relaxed environment.

Harold, was invited that evening to the British Embassy. He as usual considered U. S. diplomacy what they would call a "bumbling affair" owing to their rather patronizing view of this unfavored young son, who was preposterously naive, particularly in the Native Affairs.

"Ambassador Braithwaite, welcome to this gathering first of all, and may you find solace in the outpost of Western civilization, in this godforsaken torrid land of the Somal."

"Welcome, cheers!" said the group of exclusively European diplomats. Black-tie and all dinners were very formal, the mansions of her Royal Highness's Government was resplendent in all its grandeur, immaculate and well put together in the conservatively repressed way of British upper-class decorum. There was plenty of buzz and plenty of well-placed mutes present who blended well with the ambience, making only quick little movements before fading back into oblivion. They were all Somal, regal, and stoic men, and they looked more aristocratic then the employers.

"Harold, I am the Dean of Diplomats. Not to say no one else has the wisdom of experience to impart to you, but I have been around the Somal 's more than most of you have had a career. These guys we have here are a little different from our usual nomad, in that he has had the great benefit of our civilization through formal Western schooling, some attending our prestigious colleges in the West. What has happened to this often loyal, but easily excitable character, essentially war-like and completely lacking the fundamentals of discipline that has been the corner stone of Western progress. You will find those you work with eager to please you in their quest to be acknowledged as a real friend, always on the lookout for your interests. So, as you see, there is a fierce native, a bag of many tricks. I have wondered how our partitioning the Somal's into five different entities, now in three different independent where there are large tracks of land, but population wise the Somal's are heavily out numbered to have much of a say in any of this groups."

The Italian ambassador, begin his overture , another one who through genetics have considered the particularly no the Somal having colonized this entity for years.

I think we still have strong connections, for example the elder cadres, are mostly from the ranks of our schools, and former administration. Most of the European settler are of Italian extract, they are the ones who run and own those large plantations in the lower Juba. We understand we are most to lose in terms of former and current interests in this former colony. My opinion lies in a consolidated, effort in the interest of our governments, to do all with our means to break the Soviet influence of this corner of this world.

The Dean of the Western Diplomats raised a glass to this, seconding this ideal. Harold was intrigued by the whole setting. This European style mansion with Black Tie guests in the middle of this hot burgeoning coastal town. He was also quite aware of the European snobbery towards him, because of the recent change in Super Power alignments, the British, having been the first subjects of the world, had to concede their accustomed position to the Americans, and the Russians. This was the reality of Global Hierarchy, but the Europeans in general, and the British in particular, continued to act just as arrogantly in their day to day interactions as if nothing had changed the status quo.

Harold was very much acquainted with their condensation, but he was a survivor and knew that indeed these colleagues had more experience, and he was not going to let their delusions affect his judgment when it came to seeking cooperation. After all, they were all in the same line of defense against the Reds.

Harold Braithwaite came into work from his mansion escorted by a Somal military and civilian detail for the National Security Service of Somal and U.S. Marines. He entered his office thinking of the event he was planning later on in the day. He was anxious to help the U.S. regain some prominence in the relations of Somal, as least to make available that counter offer to the Reds, that is, in case things got on the sour side between the reds and the Somal.

He was officially hosting an affair for all the diplomatic missions in Somal. Some friendly and some not so friendly countries all were coming to a dinner reception at the Ambassador's. It was formal, Harold knew there was no such thing as informality in the diplomatic world – one was only informal with countries you were sure needed you for this that and the other, especially if it was coercive power to keep the status quo.

First, though, he checked the correspondence from the State Department in the States. He found a classified document, read it, and noted an urgent instruction. It stated that the aid to Somal would be increased by the Russians through military associations and a ton of advisors, all due in Somal as soon as possible. The State Department also wanted advice on the matter in the form of local reconnaissance. He made a note to consult his subordinates.

 EIGHT

Situations

· ·

THE ELDER, AFTER THE MEETING WITH HIS OTHER CLAN members, went the next day to the business premises of Hoagsaday to go and relay what he could of what they were doing in relation to Hoagsaday's arrest, and partly to reassure, partly to assert how his cousin's family was fairing without the man of the household.

The shop was in a strategic location, smack in the middle of the burgeoning business area. Compared to the usual mix of bungalows type shops, some of the adobe style, other with cement wall, and flat roofs, this area was different from the other areas of Mogadishu for its western-type modern structures, several stories in height, with a large business premises all in glass on the street level.

Hoagsaday had his main business for spare parts for vehicles in this locale. The elder's driver dropped him right in front of Hoagsaday's shop, in one of the western-type three-stories, with the large window facades that enabled the passer by to see the whole store from the sidewalk. The elder saw Tusmo in the back and entered the establishment.

"Hayeah. Mahala chez gay."

"Everything is okay, Alhamdulilah. We are just anxious about my children's father Hoagsaday. Please let's go into the office where we can talk away from the workers."

The elder was greeted by all the workers. There was an air of respect in the way everyone in the store, assumed the importance of the visit.

By now, most of the immediate workers were well aware that their employer had been in some trouble with the government.

They sat down in the captive's office, as the little ones came in looking for their mother. When they saw the old uncle there, they also abstained from interrupting the grown ups. Tusmo sat quietly facing the elder in deference, trying very much to look with steal looks at what his eyes said with his voice. She did so in the hope of discerning the truth from what the elder would present despite the many layers of covering brought on by the standard decorum meant to avoid the excitability attributed to women. Although inside the clan by marriage, the woman was still on the outside of the clan based on her gender.

"First of all, Hoagsaday and Abukar are now both in the custody of the police, and we will soon know their fates. Our cousin the General has inquired about his case and is keeping the outmost vigil on this case. Apparently, they have accused Hoagsaday of collaborating with foreign elements to overthrow the revolution. When you left me I went straight to Beheyeah, and we as his fellow clan members charged him with the welfare and redress of whatever circumstance might confront Hoagsaday. We all are convinced that we will soon come to some productive head way, hopefully sooner rather than later."

"My husband is not in jail for what they are claiming he is. I think anyone who does entertain such notions knowing full well who he his is plainly misguided, or wants to be misguided. Rather that resisting a knife by holding it from entry, they chose to take the more cowardly approach. Your cousin was abducted in the daylight for all to see, by men who are Somal, wearing the shirt of Government. It is a tragedy Hoagsaday does not have the men behind him who would do what must be done to redeem his humanity. The others who did this would not be comfortable where they are."

"I know you are angry, but we can not unsheathe the spear without reason. No one has yet harmed him, and we are confident we will have him out soon. We are not blind, but there are things that are involved that need careful consideration. And this is why the matter must be judged by us men, but, rest assured, none of us are going to stand bye idly."

Tusmo was breathing fire at the elder, and also crying in pain. She said, "Why is he not here with us? Why must he be picked for something beyond him? What is it? What will it take? They know he is the cousin of the general, and in spite of that they have done what they have done. I know you consider womenfolk not to know too much, but I will tell you this – Hoagsaday must pray to Allah so that his clan has the courage to see the entry of the knife and resist it with and equal force."

"It is not what you think it. I know your children and know you want us to repay the disrespect and humiliation you are facing now, but I assure you we are not sitting by idly. We will have Hoagsaday back, and we not settle for anything less, by blood or by negotiation. Asalamu alaykum, I will be back as soon as possible. Please do not hesitate to come and see me either at the warehouse or at home. For now, calm down, and tend to the children and this business."

With that, he left Tusmo in the throes of her grief and frustration. She didn't notice her young daughter had come in, stunned by her mother's condition. The girl started imitating her mother's actions towards her daughter when she is distressed. She started kissing and gently caressing her mother, all the while saying "Stop crying, Hoyo. Stop crying, Hoyo."

The awkwardness of her loving daughter's attempts at playing Hoyo caused her to laugh convulsively and return her to her role as mother. Through all the tears, she laughed with the tenderness of a moment of innocence, void of the outside, a tenderness challenging the actual coarseness of this family's situation. Internally, she was again after this brief effort, warned by in her inner depths to be critical of how Hoagsaday's clan was handling the whole situation. Why not give them the benefit of doubt, she thought then. But was this even feasible in light of what has transpired? It is for reasons like these that she preferred the hinterland ways. A clan would have be squarely accused of transgressing the boundaries of Xeer in the hinterland, and immediately there would have been moves to address the issue. No one would be waiting for the nameless Trojan horse.

 NINE

Aesthetics

. . . .

IT WAS EVENING IN THE CAPITAL AND THE COLORS OF THE women's silk painted the scene around Beheyeah like a Cezanne. The multicolored pastels of the long translucent dears, and the beautiful head silks the women used to cover their hair – light blue, off tan, turquoise, jade, meandering blue – all accentuated the tall and handsome chocolate brown of the Somal women as they walked the capital in groups. Everyone did this after the siesta and so before the sun went down, Mogadishu came alive with the symphony of the pastels, the varieties of chocolate hues, the white of the beautiful smiles. This sensuous beauty stood against the background of the Indian Ocean which occasionally let off a breeze which blew the derahs closer to the shapely contours of the bodies. To behold Mogadishu before the sunset and in the early onset of the night, was to view an ancient town, in the contrast with the tropical beach and white of the earth, with a sky so magnificent and clear that each star was distinct. The whole sky looked as if a giant artist had loosely swished the distant between the stars with a paint brush leaving in wake a silver dust lining.

Beheyeah liked to walk in the evening in parts of the old and new city as a normal person would, dressed like the other men his age, and he usually did it alone as far as possible though there was always a retinue of his assigned guards in front and behind, but at a distance, so as not to disturb his evenings away in the crowds. He marveled at the mixture of Mogadishu's residents, the old residents were descended from the old settled pastoralist, and the mix of Indians, Persians, Portuguese and Arabs, merchants had settled and married the Somal during the many centuries Mogadishu was a mercantile hub, on the Red Sea.

Somals themselves were a seafaring people, plying their trade on the ancient Indian Ocean. Today, there was no city in what he saw. All he saw were the multitudes of people, but only barely. He was now contemplating the elder who had said that he should wake up to his place and time in this world, in the world he was helping create. Was idealism a dogma for him now, so much so that he could hardly see? What was happening around him? If indeed the elders were right, then what could he do? Was he blinded by an unrealistic vision of the world? Out of touch with the everyday life of his people? Still he was not sure about the report, it was incredulous, true, but that didn't dismiss it as a possibility. There must be answers, he thought, for himself, for the nation, and for his clan.

Yusuf, went home to Ali Deray's, where he stayed. He was familiar with Ali's contemporaries, they were from both the private and government sectors of the state – they were the noveau powerful. They had an avaricious single-minded pursuit of the spoils of state and it kept them together as a close knit group. They were generous in their consumption, and with those who consumed with them. As a group, they encompassed the people who occupied the positions of upper to middle management in the government. The was a thing called da'da, other then salary. This could manifest itself in a variety of forms, since the government was subsidizing all, and by subsidizing the is the sister called ration, and breaking this limits is where the da' da came in. The high ranking were not affected largely in the military. The people who where the victims of this were the public, who were always trying to get by.

The home of Ali Deray was the place these individuals gathered to partake of the afternoon chat chewing sessions, a popular mild stimulant cartha edulis. The sessions were part network, part entertainment, and here also was the mixing of the genders with of course the very present sexual overtones. Their gatherings were implicitly guided by greed. Their ears were to the ground, listening in on market movement. The idea was to make as much as humanly possible, and get all for yourself.

"I hear there is a shortage of cigarettes in the city, Ali. Do you think we can get a shipment through to the market?"

"Yes, I don't see why not."

"What about the government agent for cigarettes? You know he has the ear of the big guns."

"You saying there are bigger guns then me in this town?" "That's not what I am saying. You know what I mean."

Ali smiled having checked his friend. "This is the way I will go about it. I want the money and I will get you the cigarettes."

All the men were wearing the most expensive ma'wiss, they were leaning against the stuffed cushions seated on cushioned mattresses and placed around the floor. Fans were every where the women were dressed in their translucent dress, also chewing, and intermittently singing popular Somal songs.

TEN

Courtiers

. . . .

BEHEYEAH SENT HIS ADC TO THE ELDER WITH A CODED message to meet him as soon as possible, and the message was taken promptly to the elder's shop. The elder was to meet the General at his house. Once he arrived, the elder could see in the General's demeanor that something drastic had happened to the General since their last meeting.

" Beheyeah, you look sick. What has happened to you?"" Sit down. We do not have time for niceties."

"Yes, yes."

"I have thought a lot about the counsel we had as a group. I am going to get Hoagsaday to go home while his trail is still pending. What I want you to do is to arrange for him to be driven out of the country. You will need to be discrete with whom and

when Hoagsaday is transported. You will do it as soon as he is placed in my official military vehicle which is where the exchange should take place. I will try and stretch the time as much as possible. So make the necessary arrangements to let that vehicle stop anywhere until it reaches Ethiopia."

"What do we do with his family? There is no time. Plus, they will arouse too much suspicion before Hoagsaday gets anywhere. But, alright. I will await your delivery"

The elder walked out of the General's house quite disturbed at the consequences both for Hoagsaday and Beheyeah. When the word eventually got out, which it would, that they had secreted a clan member off to another country, it would particularly leave Beheyeah open to all kinds of problems. But the writing had been on the wall for all who could discern the unusual circumstances of Hoagsaday's arrest. They knew all along that something terrible was in the making. It was their only option, and now the elder was more inclined to this because he knew it took something insurmountable to sway Beheyeah to act against a government he help create and shape. Their agreement was for the family not to be notified so as to allow for less scrutiny from the authorities.

The elder prepared the vehicle and the driver under the utmost secrecy. Though he was very anxious about the General's position when everything would come out into the open, nonetheless he worked diligently towards his end. They would get Hoagsaday across the border no matter what, and everything else would just have to be dealt with as it came along.

The elders were gathered around a radio listening to its mundane programming full of speeches from the revolutionary leaders' wisdom and propaganda. There were titles announced, names like Knower and Father of the Nation, followed by the lengthy praises of unabashed lackeys, and then by a speech lecture that often took up the whole rest of the program. They basically covered him? everyday, all day. He was also plastered everywhere in the country on huge bill boards, with one of his aphorisms slightly modified, or sometimes verbatim from the rich source of Somal oral literature. At first he was liked by the population, with his single minded rhetoric against clannish nepotism and corruption. But for the real news, Somals relied on the short wave radio broadcasts from the BBC in the Somal language. The revolution was deeply committed to Socialism, from the Soviet Union, China and Eastern Europe.

The elder continued his plans to make the vehicle worthy for the journey towards the border. He knew he had first to find a driver who knew the terrain well. The roads to be used had to be off the track, and in any case they were mainly unpaved. He also had to acquire someone from the clan, for reasons of security, and this would prove difficult because it probably meant one of his beloved sons.

The elder was reassured by what had transpired with the arbitrary arrest of Hoagsaday. He knew they could and would come for anyone in the clan after the planned removal of Hoagsaday to another state but he fortified himself and summoned his son. "Hassan, come here. I need to speak to you."

"Yes, Abay."

"Hassan, sit down. This matter is very important. I am sure you know of your Uncle

Hoagsaday's arrest?" "Yes, Abo."   "

"You also know your other Uncle the General." "Yes, indeed."

"Well, today or tonight sometime you are going to drive Hoagsaday out of this country to Ethiopia. We have decided that nothing good will come out of his pending military tribunal. And I want you to know there will probably be some difficulty coming back. In fact, I do not advise you to come back here at all. Remain in Ethiopia. I don't think this county will be safe for our clan any more. Stay and help establish something for us there like we have over here. I know there will be more and more of us crossing over. If you do not hear from me, remember it is your solemn duty to help the clan prepare for terrible times ahead. Do not be weak, my son, because the times ahead will require all that you have in tolerance and fortitude. Please wish your young wife and children a good bye, I will send them to you later. As soon as possible."

With that, Hassan went to his family's quarters close by. His father went into deep convulsions after Hassan left. Both he and Hassan were devastated after the conversation. Everything they had built in the city – their shops, their buildings, their family – were all to be abandoned. As was the case in a clan feud, people left the proximity of danger from the other clan, only this time it was the government, now *the Enemy*.

The word from the General soon came, and Hassan was prepared to drive all night across the foreboding terrain, constantly avoiding towns, military outposts, and anywhere there was too much movement. The vehicle was carrying an extra 200 liters of fuel drums and a young worker, who serviced the vehicle in case of flats. Only later would he find out the destination.

Hassan waited for his dad to come back from the General's with Hoagsaday. The plan would be to pick up Hoagsaday after he returned to the General's house from his house, having conferred with Tusmo. Then at the opportune time, he would be picked up again and driven too the General's house, where he would finally leave with Hassan.

Hassan went to the General's house and entered the compound. He sat for a matter of minutes when the General came in with his uniform and shook his hand. Hoagsaday was right behind him they all went straight to the waiting vehicle. Hassan got into the driver's seat, followed by Hoagsaday, and astonishingly the General too slid into the front of the land rover beside Hoagsaday.

There were movements in the back of the truck where the drums of fuel and the young attendant was, and Hassan figured around three other men had just climbed into the truck. He said nothing and started the vehicle. It was late evening and just getting dark. The General and Hoagsaday were deep in thought. Hassan followed the main road out of the city and then got off driving into what seemed a vast and open wilderness.

After a long drive on the off-road, they stopped for a minute when the General asked Hassan to stop. They stopped in the middle of nowhere, and to anyone else this terrain would have been impossible to negotiate, but Hassan had been trading throughout this area since his early childhood. The others, the three men of the clan, all with their military gear on and heavily armed, now alighted the vehicle.

All the military men changed into civilian clothing, including the General. Hassan knew them all. Together they were silently determined it seemed for every eventuality. The terrain ahead was demanding for both the sturdy vehicle and its inhabitants. Hassan kept an eye on the wheel and on the any appearance of a military, police, or any kind of government encampment in order to avoid the inevitable armed confrontation that would ensue if there was a confrontation between the two.

The territory was heavily controlled for movement, for those traveling within or without, and there were all kinds of restrictions in place on the Somal nationals which made things quite austere during the period of this government's self-proclaimed revolution.

The wages were low and most of the jobs involved national service, not a particular favorite of the Somal's egalitarian disposition. But they were initially quite enamored with the nationalistic jingoism and military display of their new government's ethos. Initially the new regime portrayed a certain structuralism absent in the previous government's haphazard style of nepotism and corruption.

As the Land Rover drove at breakneck speed, utilizing the contraband routes used by the chat smugglers, the vehicle flew above the tracks, as if it was a small vessel tossed about by a tempestuous sea currents. Hassan and his passengers were extremely conscious of the tumultuous journey ahead. They were all on alert; each man was going through his own internal tempestuous in convulsions, not unlike the vehicle they were riding in. There was a definite air of finality involved in this sojourn away from all that they had known as a constant in their lives thus far – their loved ones and their nation.

Hassan was attached to his beautiful new bride. They had just had a son, and they were enchanted with each other. The driving eased the pain, but it was there in the distance trying to overbearingly prod through his mind's concentration, negotiating the journey, the tension of escape, and driving.

 ELEVEN

Rebel

. . . .

THE GOVERNMENT WAS CAUGHT UNAWARES BY THE DRASTIC action taken by one their most loyal members of the revolution, a party hardliner and ideologue. The news came through a BBC bulletin late in the evening a few days after the sudden departure of the General was already well known within the hierarchy of government. Their reaction to the whole thing was quite embarrassing. Though they were usually quite efficient at it, because of the international news' blanket coverage of the event, they were unable to contain it. What irked them most though was that the General was well known to the Somals as a man who was beyond the usual moral reproach. He had never engaged in the petty chauvinism of clan favoritism, and his soldiers loved and respected his fair and forthright manner.

But the news spread like wild fire through out the land of the Somal via short wave radio. The broadcast announced that a Somal general and members of his retinue had crossed into Ethiopia and were received by the head of state, and was granted political asylum.

The General was quoted as saying, "We are gathering forces now. Some are already here, others are joining the struggle on this side of the border to overthrow the clan-based autocracy that has been disguised as a socialist revolutionary government. The state of affairs in Somal today is no different or probably worse than the corrupt clan-based regime we had overthrown in a coup d'etat initially. I urge the

Somal people inside and outside the country to take up arms against this callous regime. They do not encompass or represent the true aspiration of the Somal nation, but are merely an elite clan portion of it. May the so-called Father of the Nation fall from the grace he has squandered on only a few of his relatives. May the regime collapse from the weight of its own injustice to the nation at large."

The government and the Father of the Nation were livid, they went out on a rampage in the General's clan area and killed, arrested, maimed, and created an atmosphere of siege around the innocent pastoralists there. Their rational was that these were probably the most ardent supports of the defected General and that they would teach the other clans, through the quelling of the General's clan, that it would cost them a lot to follow suit.

The elder was arrested and though Tusmo was not arrested, her husband's businesses, houses, and property were seized by the regime. All the close male relatives of Hoagsaday and the General, that is those who were not arrested, were already on their way from the capital, out to the hinterland or on their way to join the resistance.

Overnight, the country's posture had assumed one of high tension between the regime and a section of its people. There were summary trials ending with death administered by stooge military commanders. The government created an atmosphere of fear and mistrust of everyone by everyone. Fear of the government's arbitrary nature took precedence over the citizen rights of any member of society. The sense of entitlement of the ruling clan was clear to all from their swashbuckling bravado. They signified wealth and power beyond reproach. The Somal were aware of clans and clan disputes in their way of life, but in this instance there was no reproach. This clan government was already in a new paradigm of inter-clan feud. This clan was a government. And it was clear the head of the clan state was doing as he pleased – one day, entertaining clan elders with grievances against the government, paying some for allegiance; and the next, paying only lip service to some, killing others.

[What was clear to the collective outside of the ruling clan, was that the Head of State was a nefarious clan thug who was diplomatic in what he said to members of the traditionally powerful clans, but hardly so as he continued his agenda of consolidating power at the top of his clan arrangement.]

With Mogadishu assuming this new disposition of fear, the usual casual relations amongst the city dwellers from the hinterland had taken a turn for the worst. Quite literally affecting long relations between neighbors, schoolmates, friendships, business relations, and co-workers, the recent actions of open clannish behavior brought to the surface the clan identities of all the city dwellers. The ones who were related through bloodlines to the regime, although not all, were the few who were gallivanting about the city arresting members of society over some pretext or another.

The rest watched the wealth and power of Somal be emasculated, impoverished, and in constant danger of abuse from corrupt officials who had no bounds and no laws to restrain them. The city became a place of silent terror, broken relations, and negative assumptions manifest in the people's fear of their neighbors depending on their clan or associations.

It seemed overnight the country had been transferred into a nation of informants. The government tried very much to keep the city out of the skirmishes, but dealing heavy handedly in suspected regions were those who were anti-government, or those the government liked to term part of the retrogressive action against the revolution.

Naturally, the government was more reactionary towards certain regions while it would for other regions go through a brief love affair. But even those were in the end always bitten by the regime and bitten hard.

The approach of maintaining a semblance of a fair revolutionary state that had transcended the institution of clan, which it did by rewarding clans other than the ones the government was embroiled with, sometimes lasted for years, simply because other members of the clan were in such a rich honeymoon for individual gain, they thereby stalled the eventuality of its victimization. By and by though, no one was saved. Every clan was used and abused at the behest of a few people who ruled in the name of the clan bloodlines.

The elder was now facing criminal charges for crimes against the revolution. He was not allowed visitors and at seventy with lack of food his health began to deteriorate quite fast. The revolution was keeping a close watch on him. They knew this was a potential power keg, but they felt it was nothing they could not manage. The maxim was let them feel the power of the government. They went on a covert campaign of reactionary repression of the General's clan, randomly victimizing related nomads. The rest of Somal was aware somewhat, but it was not common knowledge that the military was now engaged in fighting its own civilians.

Tusmo was now in a state of panic. She was under guard in case some of Hoagsaday's clan members showed up to move her out of the city. They had earlier arrested or restricted the movements of Hoagsaday's male family members, and they took all the males visiting from the hinterland. They also instructed Tusmo not to venture further than the immediate shops. They had closed any business premises that belonged to Hoagsaday, the elder, and they had also arrested his sons, cousins, and likewise the house of the general was similarly visited.

Tusmo was virtually never alone. Helpless without freedom to move, she had since that fateful afternoon, effectively lost her world as she had known it. Nonetheless, under the circumstances she had to maintain some form of structure or appearances for her young children's sake. She was well aware of the government's position towards her husband and consequently all her clan networks for redress had just been torn asunder. They were the declared enemy of the state. She had no idea of what she was to do with no husband and no freedom of movement to go anywhere. She did not see how things would work in this extremely restricted confinement. She was hoping for some form of counsel, she knew it was ultimately impossible to either go home in the hinterland, to her mother and family, or to be reunited with her husband now in another country. She kept a brave face, but would break down in tears whenever she was out of the children's view.

TWELVE

Guerrilla Movement

. . . .

MOST OF THE SOMALS IN THE CITY DISCERNED FROM THE
BBC broadcast that the general was a traitor. What made them reach
this conclusion was based on that fact that he chose Ethiopia, a country the Somals vehemently disliked for many reasons, and there was
no love lost on the Ethiopian side either. They had just gone through
a massive war with Somal involving the Soviet block and with Cuban
and Yemeni soldiers fighting on the Ethiopian side. The Russians had
been the main Super Power partner of the Somal revolution, but had
just recently absconded to the side of the Ethiopians. The Somals were
now imbedded with the United States who were giving the revolutionary state only verbally an open check to defeat the Russians. Both
the strongmen of Ethiopia and Somal, cultivated this human loss in
the form casualties to their populations, both civilian and military, as a
plate form to increase their encroachment of power, under the guise
of nationalistic jingoism.

The weapons and monies to these regimes from the Super Power
rivalry served to leave both the populations of Ethiopia and Somal
open to the whims of these Stalinistic strongmen regimes with no
recourse from the international avenues because their weapons were
quite clearly supplied to them unrestricted, with the where with all
to violently repress their populations.

The horn of Africa during this time became the cauldron of human
abuses, gone amok. The radio service of the revolutionary state, now

a self-claimed democratic republic with the Father donning civilian attire and running unopposed, delivered one his now patronizing speeches hinting at the recent military-type tribunals that would leave no stone unturned in pursuit of the Ethiopian allied traitors and any communist sympathizers.

"They are a retrogressive group who want to send the nation back to the days of clan nepotism. Somal and its people have moved far away from such bankrupt ideas. We are now a nation that favors none other than those who have exceeded the others in self- sacrificing nationalism. This is the new breed that will lead the Somal into the future. With that the group of children mainly orphans called the flower of the nation sang the now well known reprieve, 'Father, Father, our Father of Knowledge, and revolution—" And with that, the broadcast signed off.

The General was welcomed in Addis Ababa with all the amenities his rank entailed. There were already a few movements under the support of the Ethiopian military junta. They unanimously declared an open ended fight with the [Father!] regime. There was a running radio station that was beamed into most of Somal by the movements. Their broadcasts were considered seditious in Somal to say the least. Anyone caught listening could face a stiff sentence or execution. However, those who were aware of the broadcasts were not very receptive owing to the group's tag of 'traitor lackeys' for working with a known enemy of Somal and the Ethiopian nation.

The General was now involved in daily talks with the those who were here before. They were all weary of the general, but could not deny his bold gesture of defecting to Ethiopia. This was considered a strengthening move for all those who had earlier been and were now still critical of the regime. Beheyeah being a stalwart of the ideologues and the most senior ranking member to remove himself from the regime, brought a lot of credence to the so far only marginal self-styled liberation movements. Initially, they were gathered around Somal nationalism ideals, that being the case before. They were slowly moving to a gathering of many organizations implicitly configured around the original clan relations.

This situation was frustrating for the General to begin with but it was the only thing available in terms of something viable enough to topple politically and militarily the regime they all despised in common. He now went about organizing relations with the de-facto clan heads who were at the top of these organizations. The meetings were focused on many levels in particular – like how to maintain and bolster the limited guerilla type incursions aimed at destabilizing the military might of the regime. So far they were comprised of small missions deep into Somal using stealth and spectacle as a way to affect the confidence of the soldiers posted at these installations, and to also embolden the nomads to join the struggle. But the actual damage if assessed militarily was very minimal. There was now a move by the leaders of these movements to come together for a more organized effort to solicit funds on the basis of clans diaspora overseas, in particular from the larger Somal populations in the Middle East. The appointed leaders from the ranks of the prominent clans were sent to collect monies for arms, rations, and all manner of logistics.

Beheyeah understood it was going to take a long drawn out situation. The old dictator and his clan and his stooges from the other clans never even considered these movements in Ethiopia as any form of a cohesive or even a viable threat. The government of Ethiopia was even actively providing these organizations with housing, arms, transport, and up keep for the ranking officers. Beyond this situation, there was the more personal story of his entire family and by extension his clan, who were now open targets of the very regime which had now joined the ranks of the previous pariah clans slated for covert and overt marginalization and brutal repression.

Earlier, he could not understand why these clans had chosen such an unwarranted path of opposition, but this was before, and Hoagsaday was the last straw for him. It brought some archival memories of incidents, actions, and behavior that he had not noticed or chose to ignore to the front of his mind.

He was walking around now with something hard stuck in his throat. He was unable to reconcile how his idealism was used against him. They had made a mockery of all he stood for. They took him for a ride, but no more would he let them.

Hoagsaday briefly enjoyed his escape from the clutches of certain doom. He was conflicted as anyone would be whose freedom entailed the sacrifice of a multitude of people, enjoining them to problems, late night or day light visits from the brutal ones, not unlike the one he had undergone. He was buoyed through his uncertainties in regards to subjecting the innocent ones to unwarranted scrutiny, only because he was also abducted into what was inevitably fashioning itself as a political response, with more and more commitment on his part, growing stronger daily. And he was quietly resigning himself to the position of been unable to care for his wife and daughters. Surely, the government would limit their lives considerably now they had drastically changed their positions from few relations to hostile interactions with the government.

He could not bring himself to see then the end of this nightmare's divide, between his family and himself, between the nationals and the nation, between what was known and now unknown. Unfortunately he understood quite clearly the road ahead was filled with unreason and violence, the only language the clan turned government understood. Hoagsaday's new separation covered his total existence, his position as father, husband and provider were now replaced with futile misgiving of what could and possibly would happen to his family.

The road ahead was filled with the apprehensions of encounter between the training guerillas and the regime they wanted so passionately to unseat. The apprehensions were largely about the brutality of the counter moves on the innocent nomads in the hinterlands, their family's being marooned and at the mercy of the thugs masquerading as government officialdom.

Hoagsaday was shipped to the training facilities as were the many others who had crossed before him. Their lives were strictly regimented, drilled and more drilled, to turn this type of unlikely revolutionary cadre from civilian to guerilla fighter in a matter of days. Hoagsaday, like the many others, was determined to see the end of this brutality, particularly in light of what he saw as a gruesome outcome which had scattered so many afar and near, personally fuelling him to heights of determined abidance in a worthy endeavor.

It was after the long grueling days of weapons instruction, march-
ing, tactics maneuvers, when the was mind deadened by fatigue, that
Hoagsaday would still bring to the forefront of his mind Tusmo his
beautiful wife and her distress when she told he was escaping out
of the country right after his release. Even then in the midst of such
terrible circumstances, there was beauty in the stoicism she tried to
show, even though it was obvious to him beneath the façade of her
feigned exterior, her eyes showed horror and disquiet in the inner
sanctums of her soul. She encouraged him and made everything not
quite so dire, despite the overwhelming uncertainties cast in their
speech, face, and movements. The danger that lay ahead looming ever
so large seemed, through her graceful exterior, fortitude to dissi-
pate into oblivion. They sat silently embracing – he assuring her of
a return to sanity, she affirming what they knew to be impossible
under the circumstances.

Hoagsaday had in a very short time moved from an upstanding
member of his society, a well known businessman, to now a state
pariah and burgeoning liberation guerilla. He kept his eyes on the
future where no one would be victimized again at the hands of an
autocratic state, currently run by a few disinterested in the humanity of their subjects. Things will have to change, he was certain, but
through force of violence! Yet he did understand one thing: those
in power were not mentally in a place to see the rationale of ideas if
they had no force of violence behind it.

They were collectively assured the military apparatus at their dis-
posal was unbeatable to them. Therefore they were ready to do what
it took to keep themselves at the head of the nation. For his children
and for his wife he was prepared to make the sacrifice. He was willing to place his life at stake, if need be. Hoagsaday's life had taken a
new urgency in the makeshift hardship life of a liberation guerilla,
fighting for a just ideal in the middle of the bush, far away from
the city life in the lap of luxury as a prominent man of means. And
Hoagsaday took on his new quest in the most humble of manner, he
neither complained about the new hardships, the terrible amenities,
substandard sleeping quarters in the open sky, and even worse, gruel
as a substitute for food. All things considered, he brought an air of

urgency to the struggle, and an exemplary disposition to such a hard circumstance.

The General was constantly in meetings, some with the other liberation groups, some with the cadres in his, and in others with officials from his host government. Hassan, like all others was at a loss, but he in particular felt the pain of a spiral of drastic incidents one after another, all beyond his reach. Hassan was not happy and rightfully so, but underlying his unhappiness was his apolitical nature, he was more inclined to the life of the cosmopolitan youth of Mogadishu, having come there from the hinterland at a very young age. His clan relations were more distant then the typical Somal.

Since the capital was a meeting place for the entire nation of Somal, people of Hassan's generation were developing a more of a neighborhood allegiance, but even in this there was still recognition of clan predisposition. Lacking the traditional severity, they established local friendships that were broad based. His wife was also non-traditional, a city girl attending school in Mogadishu, a rather modern practice for the nomad. Hassan and his elk had only known the nation in this way and believed deeply its capacity to modernize. Therefore with his Uncle Hoagsaday's victimization along bloodlines, his father's pending tribunal, his family's wealth and the sanctity of his entire life's meaning having disappeared, in a moment's notice, right before his eyes, Hassan was brought into the fold of the clan, a position he would have disputed a few weeks ago as a very unlikely position to take had he not experienced the anguish of such an intractable situation.

The elder's trial was held as a big fanfare with all the pretensions of a kangaroo court. They had even thrown in some obscure persons who had nothing to with the escape of Hoagsaday or the General's defection in order to masquerade the entire affair as strictly revolutionary business. The elder was paraded as a traitor and collaborator of the General and his relative Hoagsaday. They were all maligned in a propaganda campaign on the only radio station, and the daily party organ, the Star of October, who the silver tongued nomads had dubbed " dare you finish me." They were depicted as retrogressive elements harboring clannish ideals, an anathema to the revolutionary progress so far achieved by the all knowing Father of the Nation. The tribunal was now called a High Court, but the only difference from the Military Court was that no one was wearing a uniform, it was still a kangaroo affair all the way. They found the elder and his co-defendants guilty of high crimes against the revolution. The sentence was quick, as was the execution date.

They elder's public trial showed the public, that is, those who cared to see, the power of the state slowly running amok, with no such thing as a bridal to hold it back from visiting upon those of its nationals deemed public enemy. The elder for his part was resolved to meet fire with fire. He had no regrets, but rather was happy to help ignite a formidable resistance to a brutal regime. The details of the trial were soon known internally and externally, impacting the relations of the Somal Diaspora, and dividing and causing strife among inter-personal relations along the same lines as the internal clan alignments. Needless to say, after such actions, those in the Diaspora had to chose a clear position vis-à-vis the government's rhetoric and action towards their individual clans. Suffice it to say, the circumstances of the elder, Hoagsaday, and the General, were known prominent entities, and, what's more, they were known as a wise and moral group even by the begrudging members of other clans. There were numerous clan based groups who were organizing day and night now, collecting money mainly in order to help those on the ground resist this awesome military clan apparatus.

The two strongmen were actively trying to overthrow the other's regime. The father of the nation had his Ethiopian guerrillas in Somal. There were several leaders of liberation movements based in Mogadishu. He was training them and helped train the cadres. Each had there overseas supports and were financially supported by, in the main, their respective ethnic groups, extending to political activism centered the organization.

Tusmo was now under the pressure of raising her children under the new circumstance. The businesses were effectively closed. There was no money for anything for the children, whatever resources they were getting from the clan. There was a constant stream of neighbors some for sympathy, some to carry stories.

She was at a loss as to what direction to take. The children as young as they were knew a lot was amiss. She didn't say much to them but it was apparent they knew what was going on. If not the actual details, nonetheless they knew something important was amiss.

The elders, those who could manage to maintain some semblance of their old lives before the incidents, came to her to discuss what they were doing in relation to the government's position of appropriating the wealth of her husband. The government held steadfast to the confiscation of the businesses and property of Hoagsaday. Tusmo for herself was not really interested in the business without the owner's presence but she did not know how she could entertain living as before, when everything had changed so quickly, so drastically.

She tried to gather her nerves for the days ahead. She was certain her husband could not come back to her if she stayed in the capital. And if her husband could not come back, Tusmo did not see a future in living in the same place which stole her family from her, stole a father from her children. She made it clear to the few in her husband's clan that she needed to go somewhere, anywhere other than this capital that had become so cruel to her.

Though initially Tusmo did not much like the city, throughout the years before this interruption, she was getting used to the life of ease in the city. Abundant water close by, the shops and fresh milk without the work of milking. In these ways, Tusmo cherished the city, but the recent events overarched her acquired taste for the city's conveniences. She could not stay here with all the uncertainty surrounding her person and that of her young children. She did not see anything to look forward to other than perhaps more havoc from the state. She wished her self back in the simplicity of her beloved hinterland, where the land and people were open for miles on end, with no surprises, and where, if there were any problems, there was a place to address it.

All in all, she was resigned to do the best under the circumstances.

 **THIRTEEN**

Comprador

. . . .

HOAGSADAY WAS TAKING THE TRAINING WELL. THEY HAD been split up into small combat units to fulfill their surprise-attack missions on the military camps in around his clan's region. Meanwhile, to accentuate their brutally on the pastoralist's herd who could not sustain their livelihood without water, the military was poisoning wells. Their official policy was to scare, maim, and kill the nomads with minimal attention to the city dwellers so as to prevent, on the one hand, further support for the militias, while, on the other, to create tension between the hinterland nomads, and their leadership. The nomads were predictable in a bind, and the government was soon collecting virulent hate from the indiscriminate murder of civilians and the killing of their the prized livelihood of the camel. The nomads had to not only survive the harshness, but also to abandon more and more their homesteads, for there was no safety anywhere in the plains.

Homesteads were left to the women, children and the elderly. Rather than attempting to stem the tide of confrontation by isolating the immediate kin of Hoagsaday, the military went about a violent campaign involving everyone in the area affiliated by blood. Every homestead with a distant or close affiliation was accused of harboring guerilla attacks on the government. When a kraal happened to be in the close vicinity of an attacked barrack, the military officers would come to the homestead and raise hell. Their rationale was that these clan members were the ones sustaining the clandestine attacks. They were the ones, after all, who knew the lay of the land in the stealth of darkness, with all its unevenly jagged sand and rock formations.

The situation between the nomads came to a head swiftly, creating more and more hate towards the system. This military's policy only went further to entrench the resistance, filling the numbers of resistance groups with recruits in the clan repressed areas. It also incited the support of heavy numbers of relatives abroad – those who were already out for some disenfranchised reason or the other – to become steadfast in their resolve to overthrow by force of violence this unconscionable regime. Monies were collected from the Diaspora in earnest, giving much more momentum to the struggle based in the neighboring countries and much greater political activism abroad.

Beheyeah was coordinating both strategy and liaison work on behalf of the movement. He had trained some cadres in the many facets of a viable organization for his immediate clan, and acted as the nominal figure of all the clan-based configurations of the guerilla movements. In the evenings, he would still take his walks, contemplating the years of folly – was he truly that naïve to think that he was a marker for the Somals in the sense that he had transcended his clan? If he had the capacity to act in line with his clan then others would too. Sourly, this was not the case he was reminded of day in and day out, with the multiplicity of agendas each clan brought to the table. There were always long and much heated contentions about what clan should lead, and mainly the relations were based not on the interest of the clan members, many of who were nomads, but rather on their western educated kin. These so called elite were just in transit to the next government that might take over, so their rhetoric of blood was used in acquiring power through this political mode. They were for those who knew them quite a morally bankrupt lot, however, they felt a sense of entitlement when it came to leadership. It was they who felt, because of their western education, themselves qualified to lead the blind and primitive nomads, judging from their callous ways. With the lives of their kith and kin, the were always in flux – where they saw the most immediate bread was where they got the most butter. So therefore the pastoralist was not only facing internally the brunt of the military, they also handled an enormous amount of subterfuge.

Brathwaite was quite a natural at intriguing the State Department with its overzealous vigilance towards the Soviets [who was losing in the interim to the Soviets], and who became the de facto supporters of the popular movements within Africa, though elsewhere they were, it seemed, losing ground. With their unabashed support for their very greedy African counterparts, the people were well aware of the position of the West in relation to their countries in particular, as well as to the continental outlook at large. The days of independence euphoria were gone and the new so-called independent nations were now faced with the reality of the coups, nationalist leaders assassinated by mysterious entities. The message was very clear: play ball or else.

In other areas, the common welfare of the citizens remained by in large in the hands of a few chosen ones, aided by the power of the West and reactionary police forces, always in a hurry to lock up after severe beatings. Exclusivity reigned supreme in certain nations. Whether it was based on clans or on an ethnic group, it was the same animal. The fruits of the Independence were arrayed in front of all the nationals, but forbidden to the touch let alone the consumption of the mass majority. The genealogy of the government leadership pedigree was in this order: product of missionary school, member of a large ethnic group, and finally, and the most important, those who were progressive in relation to how the Western World moved. In plain African terms, you were greedy enough to eat an entire elephant and show no signs of the feast the next day. Whatever was left over, you stored away in foreign refrigerators.

This was the festering environment that Brathwaite drew his knowledge from, though, unfortunately, the Somal socialist ideologues would not have it. They were young idealists, and not your run of the mill African comprador in his natural habitat. The Soviets had placated their vision of true independence, and they provided whole sale help for the liberation from the West, which came in the form of a multiplicity of guns, training for doctors, hospital, roads, and so forth. They were also engaged in finding antidotes to the sphere of the West in the form of the United States' influence.

$\mathcal{A}$sha's $\mathcal{P}$reposition

AFTER THE TRIAL, THINGS GOT WENT FROM BAD TO ATRO-
cious. Tusmo was under heavy surveillance. Her moves were considered crucial in the aftermath of her husband's escape, and the
authorities were literally at her doorstep. They imposed without
imposition, but she was stranded in many other ways. The only saving grace was an insider who was closely related to her by blood.
Thankfully, the Somals were not usually given to seeing women
and children as worthy of the type of repression usually accorded
the males, but nonetheless, she still needed to rendezvous with her
husband and couldn't. This meant the clandestine removal of whatever wealth she could muster for the purposes of her travels, an act
which was proving more and more difficult by the day. Her former
networks through the clan had slowly disintegrated to almost zero
after the elder's execution, and no one, absolutely no one, wanted
to been seen at the home of Hoagsaday. It was just an open trap to
walk into. Tusmo was also not able to get transport from the city
to the hinterland. The roads leading there were all heavily-guarded,
and also there were now a multiplicity of military cops in the area.
Her beloved home was not habitable with all the wanton death and
destruction targeted specifically at her husband's clan. It clearly was
not the home she knew nor a place where she could run for safety.
What heightened everything to an almost frenzy in her mind was
the mere thought of what had or could have happened to her family

– her elderly grandfather Awowo, her father and mother, her brothers and sisters.

As she sat in the emptiness of her house full of furniture, remnants of a former life, empty now of meaning, empty of her husband, the father and provider of her girls, empty of freedom of movement, and empty of the knowledge of the way forward, someone knocked on the door in a soft and urgent manner. It was late at night and most people were in their houses for the night.

Tusmo was sure it was the authorities, so she went to get the door, but when she inquired as to who it was, an elderly woman's voice said in a somewhat muted tone, "Tusmo, Tusmo, open the doors. It's me, Asha."

She opened the door surprised to see that her neighbor, from the very clan that was hunting her husband and restricting her life in the interim, was at the door. She welcomed Asha inside, albeit suspiciously, and ushered her into the living area, quietly restrained

but extremely cautious at the possibility of what might transpire. She concluded, based on Asha's usually aloof manner during the long time they had been neighbors, that they had barely exchanged more than a sentence, despite their living so close and their two husbands having known each other through many business dealings. Tusmo ordered some tea to be prepared. "Bring Asha some tea to drink," she spoke to someone in the kitchen.

"No, please don't bother yourself. It is late and I would like to speak to you urgently. Hurry, please sit down. We don't have the luxury of time. I would like to let you know that I am a mother like you. I may not be as young as you, but I do know certain things, and I want you to know that I am opposed to the behavior that has been increasingly become a mainstay in our land. I might be of the ruling clan, but as a woman I know what it is when one clan uses is power indiscriminately without any regard to the rights they are trampling. I have sons and daughters, and I know one thing – it is not right for the government to reek havoc on any family.

"My daughter, although I have been rather quiet in my interactions with you through the years, it is because of my nature. I not given to too much talk, and I have my reasons, but I am here to let you know that we have not all abandoned our senses. I know that your time in this city has come to an end, and if one can not eat, sleep and walk in peace, then anywhere else will be better for you and your girls. There is no safety for you here, nor is there anyway way for you to get back to the hinterland for the roads are heavily guarded, and, not to mention the lack of safety there. I also know there is no way you can access your husband's money in the bank. I know the accounts have all been frozen.

"I have thought of your plight and I have a proposition for you, a way out of this mess. I have brought with me some money for you, and I have also asked my husband's driver to take me to the port city of Kismayu three days from now. I want you and your daughters to come with and from there you can slowly cross into the border of Kenya. It should be relatively easy because nobody expects you to go there. And from there, you can try to commence to Ethiopia where your husband is.

"I will be ready in three days, and we will leave from my house, where no one will question us. Do not take much with you, but take what gold you have – it will come in handy in Kenya while you wait to be reunited with your husband. I will get enough money for your journey. My husband has told me he has monies saved from a former transaction, and he is well aware of what is going on and also does not agree with his clan's victimization of you and your husband and your daughters. He is willing to create an interference with the officials until he is assured of your safe arrival in Nairobi. So from today onwards, start packing only the essentials. The journey will be long after our separation in Kismayu, so bear this in mind. What you need for your girls, clothes and things of that nature should be the priority and nothing else. I will take my leave now and see you at the house. Remember the journey beyond our borders will be full of the unknown. Remember the girls are young and will be a handful in any case. Anything you might need, you will have to buy. My husband has someone in Nairobi that he and your husband did business with in the past, so I will try to send you money for you to travel further so as to meet your husband."

"I am deeply moved by this gesture to help myself and the girls reunite with my husband." Tusmo said this at first without a hint of emotion, because she was stunned beyond belief. She had never in her wildest fantasies imagined such an outcome, and she never once thought that this lady and her husband might be her way out of this previously intractable situation. The person she least expected became the person she would lean on the most. The Asha she had known crumbled in her imagination to pieces into oblivion and was replaced by an apparition of some of the attributes she had known her mother for. Asha did not side with the madness that was going around her like a contagious flu, that was going to get everyone eventually. No, she said, No to all the madness of her clan. Within the air of the mighty or the weak, she chose the different way. Tusmo could not find the words to express both her disbelief and the wrenched relief she felt of finally settling on, in her mind at least, a way forward. Finally, slowly brimming, her eyes grew hot with tears, which had become too much to hold, and her lips trembled so much from emotion.

She let out a hesitant, "Thanks Asha. Thank you, Asha. May Allah reward you. May Allah bless you for your humanity. With that, Asha tried herself to comfort Tusmo, saying, "All is well my daughter, all is well my daughter," trying to sooth Tusmo to see her through this emotionally-charged moment.

"Tusmo, everything by the grace of Allah will come to pass. My daughter, it for us who will remain here that we should worry. When blood starts, the smell of it lingers as it engulfs all within its range. So don't worry for you and yours. Worry and pray to Allah for those of us who you have left behind to face the forces of irrational pride unchecked."

FIFTEEN

Jet Set

. . . .

THE MOGADISHU JET SET WHO CHOSE TO GATHER AT THE waterhole of Ali Deray now gathered to undertake the big and illicit dealings associated with the appropriations of confiscated wealth from the people that the state had accused of something or the other. They dealt with Hoagsaday's vehicles imported from overseas, which were now openly driven by Ali Deray's military drivers, a further display of clan arrogance within the subterfuge of government. And even then, somehow, the state was still considered by the majority of people to be an honest institution because they were not exposed to the violence the government exacted on the clans in the hinterland. Most of the populace were aware of clan nepotism, but only some suspected more nefarious clan actions under the guise of the state, those actions made in the name of the revolution or republic. These ideas were not common currency. Mostly, the people felt the state was still viable, if sometimes rather heavy handed, and they worked with it, both out of fear of the brutal example of previous dissenters and out of understanding that the state was also one of their biggest employers.

Ali Deray was summoned the house of General Kumanay. He arrived there and was ushered into the study of the General, saluted him, and sat down. This was not the first time for him to come here. He had come here on many occasions, the last time being the occasion to receive the classified and detailed report on Hoagsaday just before he was ordered to arrest him at his home.

Apart from being the General's favored enforcer, Ali Deray was a distant cousin of the General's. He was meticulously chosen by the General for reasons that were based on inadequacies rather than strength. Ali had been a "never-do-well," from the ranks of his impoverished kin, and his father and uncles had not had the wealth of camels. Despite this obvious disadvantage, though, Ali still had a nomad's arrogance of self import. He was very much aware that the president was a member of his clan, which only further exacerbated his already arrogant disposition. He was not very bright, but fortunately for him, this was not a quality that served anyone well in Somal. The quality that served him most was in actuality his inability to function in a modern state. He possessed no education as such, and he also possessed irrational greed, what Somal called, aptly, "dumb greed." These qualities made him a favorite with the General, who consistently moved from rank to rank until he had become a very powerful colonel. The wisdom of this relation, above and beyond his clan loyalty, was that Ali Deray was always beholden to the General for his rising him from a lowly illiterate camel herder to a high ranking member of the ruling elite. For this, Ali would literally piss an ocean if the General asked him to. He was never going back to any such station as he had occupied before. He had moved up in lifestyle as far as he was concerned he was not moving back.

It follows that he was also very insecure when he encountered anyone who had even been to kindergarten, whether they were from his clan or not. He kept all those he knew from before, unless they were already in the mix of things, very far from the corridors of power. No entry was his resolution if he could help it, and thus he became nefarious for his glaring inadequacies. The General cultivated the calumny of Ali Deray's weaknesses, but the General was also vicariously beholden to Ali for his knowledge of the about the town gossip and its potential hotspots.

Some suggestions Ali merely created to feed the insecurity of the General, who spent all his time masquerading his true identity, rather than accepting his proffered one of enlightened fairness beyond the quagmire of clan nepotism. The General was in reality a sociopath not unlike most politicians, killing with abstractions with no remorse what so ever, and unfortunately, he was the most powerful second to the supreme leader, the most trusted, and the most deceivingly nefariously brutal of all the elite. And he carried this in a very deceiving sinister package of gregarious humility.

SIXTEEN

Safari

. . . .

THE THREE DAYS THAT COMMENCED RIGHT AFTER HER neighbor Asha left her house for Tusmo were overshadowed with an urgency blanketed by the fear of a journey that seemed mired in certain peril. She tried very much to hide her inner uncertainties with her usual unemotional disposition. The fear was very much that the news carriers might, in the blink of an eye, gather that something was afoot based on any large or minute irregularity that Tusmo might reveal — a suitcase here, a household in the midst of abandonment there. The very disarray of things might give them the ammunition to report a possible escape by Tusmo and her girls. This would be a great loss to those who were in power, the ones who had the household under siege, and, not to mention, the more and more people who were part of an ever-widening net of injustice.

She did everything she could in broad daylight not to arouse suspicion by stirring shadows within the house at night. Her drapes were not heavy in part because the compound in the times of normalcy had a tall surrounding wall and no one would be out there looking in, and if they were, it would be very conspicuous in the trees adjacent to the house, or on the wall itself. But as this made everything easily observable from outside, she did things quickly and around the time of afternoon siesta. The sun kept everyone inactive for those hot hours during the day, and it was during those hours that she gathered mentally the essential belongings, heeding very strictly what Asha had told her, "Take all the gold and clothes for the young ones." She tried to get things packed in order of importance. The gold, and whatever money she would carry on her person was first, and the next thing was to find two or three changes of clothes for the children for their journey into the unknown.

She would try and put them all in a pillow case so that she might easily store it without anyone noticing. Most of her many servants had left during the previous fiasco - they were too weary of being bunched together with whatever their employers were accused of – and, of course, they had seen and felt the tension of the missing husband, they were there when he was taken, and had seen the military truck filled with soldiers. Tusmo had instantly dismissed the ones who made her doubt their allegiances, and she had done so with the very real reason of loss of income. The ones that remained were loyal and related to the family and could be counted on to stay and help out through this uncertain period. But even still she kept a vigilance over herself and the girls, guarding their eminent departure.

She thought it was unnecessary to burden the servants with any knowledge that could either compromise their sudden exit or be a point of conjecture in the aftermath of their departure, for their complicity in harboring their escaper. She knew they would surely be detained and questioned when and if the flight was discovered.

Like this, Tusmo went about trying as much as possible to seem as normal as possible. In the wee hours before day break where all but the cock would crow, her mind raced through the possible encounters with the coercive forces along the large expanse of the road to Kismayu. She was wondering how the children would hold up given the fact that they were children, innocent of where they were going or what they were doing. She was sure of one thing and one thing only: there was no alternative to where they were now. This escape, however foreboding, must be embarked on.

What remained to be done now after the end of the third afternoon, was for Tusmo to go to the neighbor's compound with the children ready with whatever she had gathered for succor, emotional or material, for the flight to Kenya. She made the girls sleep a bit longer than usual in the afternoon, so that they might stay awake for a while during the night, before they ventured to the next compound.

She had already sent most of the stuff over, piece by piece so as not to arouse suspicions. And she had the girls go over with a servant, and then she finally joined them, under the pretense she was going to get them. The guards outside did not look in the direction of her neighbor's compound; they could hardly believe that a prominent member of the ruling clan would aid and abet a family targeted by the clan. This to them would have been an absurdity. What they thought was that there were neighbors, and that Tusmo was there to ask for some assistance from powerful members of the ruling clan to hopefully gain the release of her husband.

Tusmo was greeted graciously by Asha as she was the final one to get to the house. Asha tried very much to conceal the risk she was taking through the sort of smile that hung forced on her face. She was not much for laughter nor for talk, but she did want to assure Tusmo not only that is was not a trap, but also that she had not changed one bit since their encounter three days ago. She had, after all, accepted everything conspiring against her own household to keep, just as Tusmo did in her own house, everyone away from her trip. The trip planned by Asha was told to everyone as a trip to go and see a certain sheik known for his healing prowess and spirituality. This was what was to go, and she was leaving at night to make even more remote the possibility of discovering her wanted passengers. Asha had requested her husband have a member of the military, their cousin, escort them in the vehicle all the way to the major port city of Kismayu.

The vehicle was ready and so were the passengers, and they made it out of the compound gates amidst very little ceremony. They zoomed out of the gates and headed towards the outskirts of the city very early before the cock started his premature crowing, to announce that the day had broken.

The girls and Tusmo were in the back of the hardy four-wheel drive Toyota, very popular and as rugged as the camel the nomads used not so far back past, and a status symbol too, just as was the camel in the past for the pseudo-urbane nomad. They were sitting in the back seat with the girls fast asleep. In the front was the trusted driver and Asha's cousin the military officer. They sped through most of the controls and went forth toward the very quiet main highway towards the Southernmost coast city of Kismayu.

Along the way, the landscape was greener than any Tusmo had seen. Her part of Somal was the harsh plains that changed green to some extent, but nothing like what she was seeing now, with the beauty of the land heightened by the slowly rising sun. The differences were stark, and there was a lot of farming going on as they progressed further and further away from the coastal city of Mogadishu. The subsistence farmers were busy tilling the land, with their womenfolk alongside them, babies strapped to their backs, earnestly putting their backs into to the work before the glaze of the sun's heat began in earnest to slowly burn their backs.

The sky a clear blue with an abundance of green trees, farms, and the spots of the farmers plowing here and there sometimes with the help of a donkey. You could see for miles how the beige color of the earth dominated between the green. This open expanse worried Tusmo, even though she should have been quite secure in the company of this powerful entourage. She was always worried one military hot head or another would give them a difficult time. Along this large openness of land, it seemed, they could show up from anywhere, and worse, Tusmo feared, their Toyota could be seen from very far off. But this made her, more than anything, markedly pensive as they moved along the way. The vehicle was alive with the chatter of the children who were getting more and more exited as they caught sightings – in bits and pieces – of animals single and in groups, darting about the place. The girls were city kids and didn't see much wildlife other than the usual domestic animals. But here, already, they had seen deer, warthogs, ostriches and numerous other birds. They were excited by the farmers and their clothing, which seemed to them not up to the standard clean fare of the city.

Meanwhile, the men were engaged in somber conversation. It was clear they were a little groggy from setting out at such wee hours. They were not very communicative as was Asha, who was quiet as usual, engaged this time in incantations using her prayer beads. She repeated over and over, "Alhamdulilahi, Alhamdulilahi. Graciously thankful, Allah. Graciously thankful, Allah," so very quietly that one could only see the movement of her lips in time with the fingers moving one bead simultaneously. She continued there in her seat, vigilant and attentive with her eyes to what was going on as they passed the landscape and as the children mentioned the names of the animal, sometimes getting it wrong, making Asha break in to an uneasy involuntary smile.

Tusmo was getting less and less pensive as she was now caught up in the thinking of what was ahead of her both inside the border as well as beyond it. She knew she could rely on Asha's stalwart protection until the town, but there were several other towns before the border, and though Asha would no doubt make some arrangements for when they got there, it would be another country that was entirely different in language and culture and religion. Even more frightening was the uncertainty in terms of their wanted destination. What would Tusmo do when the real journey commenced in this territory? She feared for the girls because their guide and mother was, in this case, completely in the dark, having never gone anywhere away from Somal.

The vehicle was making brisk headway, and they passed a great many small- and middle-sized villages, some with only two mud shops at the center of the town, some with more than forty, but mainly the landscape was dotted with small farm huts and farmers in the business of tilling their land. The vehicle stopped at a mid-sized town for lunch. Asha got out for her ablution for prayer, the rest for food and use of the bathroom.

The men were also getting excited to get started chewing their mild stimulant, and they left the vehicle to walk around in search of the souq, usually to be found in every main or small sized village town. After their purchase, they arrived at the restaurant where Asha and Tusmo had ordered lunch, and said that they would be soon ready to go on with the journey. Tusmo and the girls had already eaten and used the bathroom, and Asha had also finished praying. But she still sat there without a word, only breaking her incantations to point out something now and then to Tusmo about the girls.

Then, they all got into the vehicle and were soon off, resuming the brisk pace the driver had started the journey with. Now, though, the two men at the front were smoking cigarettes incessantly. They had had a flask of spiced tea with their chat at the station, and the women watched as their whole demeanor of grogginess quickly faded, as they grew steadily more animated and joyous. The music from the car cassette deck was blaring popular Somal music. They talked about each song's artist and sang along. After sharing the ritual of chat, the military officer was now very casual with the driver, and though the driver and the military officer still maintained some form of hierarchy, there was an unconscious shift between them back to the pastoralist's mode of equality, a return of their individual humanities.

Music in this period came from a popular play, it was a cross between Shakespeare and the added poetic penchant of the Somal, a music whose songs were later as popular as the play had been. So a song would have all that connotation apart from the highly idiomatically-conceived lyrics based on the experience of the camel herder. This was the language of theater and song, layered, and more and more esoteric to the city dweller youth, but vastly popular to the majority of the Somal.

Tusmo was observing the front of the vehicle as was Asha, who continued her murmur of incantations while she looked at the men. The men were totally oblivious to the marked change in their behavior towards each other and the rest of the vehicle. It was now late afternoon and running past the window was a thickness of vegetation around the river Juba. Tusmo could see a very fertile area with trees larger and more abundant than she has ever seen, trees of the fruits she had consumed with glee when she first devoured the sweetness of the mango from this part of Somal.

The bananas she had grown accustomed to along with the bananas they had with the various meals for lunch all came from this papaya region of the lower Juba. This was also the former home of the large settler plantations of the Italians in Somal. The people of this region were also distinct from the rest of Somal, largely sedentary and from Bantu stock, a group highly discriminated against by the pastoralists from the Hinterland. They were discriminated against in terms of racial difference and positions of power. In fact, these people were pretty much left to the Italians' mode of dealing with the Riverine people, or Gosha, who used their labor without much remuneration.

The government was now in charge of the former Italian colony, and while it tried with rhetoric to wipe out the racial distinctions by verbally destroying the clan system, in reality it used the system as a power base. There was certainly more school enrollment and expanded positions held during the Great Father's so-called revolution, but the disparities lingered in the stark under-developed mode of almost slave labor manifest to anyone traveling through this lush and rich region. In general, the region's very poor inhabitants existed in a near medieval state, being hardly versed in the slight modernization of the capital or Kismayu close by and living, it seemed, as if stuck in a bygone era of small two-shop villages run by the Yemeni's long domicile there. The sense was that here, time stood still as did the camel and its herder in the Hinterland, for both of these modes had not moved with the time of the rest of Somal.

They arrived late in the evening at the small town of Jilib, a very old settlement with the main road and shops in some modern style architecture in the form of Bungalows. It seemed the men would have carried on further had Asha not asked to stop for the evening prayer and the night. But, obliging her, the driver looked for a hotel and found one quickly.

The government had created a tourist hotel comprised of a larger bungalow building, a hotel restaurant, and a general entertainment area where alcohol produced in the Somal was served, usually to local government officials from other regions on duty at this outpost, and this is where one could imbibe without guilt or undue scrutiny from the majority of the Muslim public that just thought the worst of anyone who drank alcohol, particularly their leaders.

This became the site of one of the clashes between the new and the old. The officials, stemming from long stints in officialdom where they had all worshiped at the altar of this modern Somal adventure also enjoyed the Western entertainment in the form of drinking liquor or beer, but mainly alcohol. Since everyone was from a nomadic recent past it seemed they were falling all over themselves to drink so as not to be accused of not being a city sophisticate, because sophisticates drank their heads off.

They entered the hotel and walked through to the sleeping areas, slightly removed from the goings on of the tourist hotel. Such areas rarely ever saw actual foreign tourists, but rather the closest thing to that, the local foreigner, in the form of the local police chief, the governor, and the bank directors, all with exclusive regions within these hotels.

Then there was the junior staff who were also in quite a big hurry to shed their primitive skins. These groups were constantly at watering holes like this one, in search of this ever hangover-ridden ritual of modernity.

 SEVENTEEN

Stock Exchange

. . . .

THE HOME OF ALI DERAY AS USUAL WAS THE HUB OF THE
city's jet-set not because he was this brilliant conversationalist, but
because he was a magnet for making money, and a lot of it. They said
it flowed through Ali, and he was the money flow because he was the
interlocutor between the always elusive officialdom and the eager,
very greedy sell-your- mother type of entrepreneur. It was a pretentious lot that gathered there, usually bearing gifts for Ali's voracious
entourage who could possibly make everything crumble into a 'no
deal' if certain overzealous gestures were misconstrued as negligence,
or worse, a sign of disrespect.

The treasure of these gatherings were the very beautiful women
from most any and everywhere in the nation of the Somal. These
were free spirited often stunning representations of the kaleidoscope
of the Somal's legendarily unique and unadulterated natural beauty.
Depending on the position they occupied in this patriarchal society,
these women were articulate and highly opinionated in such irreverent ways that they pushed Somal's already egalitarian tradition. They
neither sanctioned the institution of marriage in a society built on
this particular notion of fidelity, nor were their interactions with the
men around them ones of equality.

These men sought solace and feminine engagement beyond the
much defined gender roles that were largely subservient. Often,
these successful males did not marry this type, but, on the other hand,

practically did. They spent most of their private afternoon hours in the women's company, sometimes individually or as a group. There was a heavy tone of sexuality in the ambience at these closed door sessions in what was usually the private residence of one of these women.

Music and musicians, and all manner of artists joined the gatherings as well. There was an interesting interaction between the normally feared officials and the artist whose power lay in articulating the mood of the masses. Dissent was, in this era as much as in the yesteryears, dominated by revered poets and their poetry. This form of lyrics put to music was, though very much hidden in the idiomatic subtext of the rural nomad existence, a conceptual wellspring through the centuries of Somal existence.

The afternoons started off with the heavy scent of the burning of perfume. The traditional frankincense and myrrh mixed with a combination of perfume baked into a cake and burned on a charcoal fire, creating smoke which enveloped everything the body, the clothes and the whole environment.

Their afternoons in this ambience of ancient lure scent and the beauty of women accentuated by their loose translucent bright pastels and brave long dark complexions and set with a luxurious mane of provocative, unruly, glowing curly hair. The innuendo of their shapeliness less than concealed by the see-through pretentious barriers of very flimsy silk, the men adorned by the multicolored ma'wiss skirts slightly more soberly colored slick, both dazzled in this indoor attire suggestive of the gathering's opulently cozy ambience.

Everyone showed up here with the customary bundles of chat, stimulus for the artists and greedy, ambitious deal-seekers alike, and great also for animated conversations at such an intimate gathering of a very few choice people all connected by different pleasures. They sat together in very close circles, pairing off in twos and sitting on the lush cushioned carpets surrounded by tea, the perfumed smoke, and the gentle wind of the sea breeze from the Indian Ocean.

Since the Somals were naturally newshounds, here in part was where Ali gathered the latest news from the previous nights' rendezvous – here, at the elite watering holes where a lot of discussions on all types of concerns – political, clan, personal, on prominent people's mishaps and embarrassments, and so forth. The crazy atmosphere at these tourist retreats, especially when induced with the reduced inhibitions of the already uninhibited Somal disposition, made for rambunctious evenings heavily doused with inebriated congeniality, all stoked by the blaring inflective rhythms of the live band couple with a wonderful cool sea breeze, a great apology on behalf of the sun, by the ocean.

Ali came into the gathering amidst smiles and salutations from the cozy group who had already started their chat session.

"Warya, Ali. Man, you are so busy running this town, you are late."

Ali strutted in with an air of great self-importance. "Yes, you know how it is. I was kept waiting by one of those young ignoramuses from the Hinterland."

Four throats agreed with a loud reassuring, "I know, I know."

"Yes," said Ali, "the idiot was a young clan member, so fresh you could smell the camel odor of his ways, and he didn't know anything, yet he insisted he should get a great paying job because he was my clan member. He said he didn't want the job when I offered him the regular jobs he was qualified for. He arrogantly declined, said it seemed such a preposterous position when the entire government belonged to him."

"He queried what was the use of the President appointing me to this position when I was not really helping him, a clan member, get a job with all the perks deserving of his noble lineage. He became increasingly agitated and as the conversation continued along a path he saw no gain in it. You should've seen this nomad. He never saw what he looked, nor saw any of his shortcomings. He just didn't see any of it as his own serious inadequacies. He really took offence at my sticking to him some crazy rules that I made."

"He even once was so disgusted by me that he said he was dumfounded that I, such a weakling, should be anywhere near 'the clan's business.' After besieging me, I quickly decided to give some him money for a few days, and told the driver to take him to the clan. I also guided him to see an elder, because I simply could not make this guy an officer in the military nor give him a position he wanted without causing too much strife. What I did do was basically got rid of him with a bribe."

"I told him he shouldn't worry about such a position at the moment, but to first get acclimated to the city ways. I insisted on this, although he was not convinced of the wisdom of it. In his eyes, he never wanted to be anything like I was. I wish you could have seen his facial expressions. He was so disgusted with me, he just thought I should be shot at first dawn."

Everyone present in the large expansive living room gathering was teary-eyed throughout Ali's narrative. There was so much laughter at this character, they all knew so well, seemingly, the great oppositional differences between their world-view and those of the people of the Hinterland.

Ali then laid the stuff he was carrying down, and went to take a bath to wash and cool his body from the relentless heat of the day. The others continued laughing and expounded on this incident with anecdotes of their own. This, after all, was a favored topic of the city dwellers as it elicited great consternation about the behavior of their uncouth kinsfolk.

The conversation was then directed by Ali on his return, he was all refreshed and ready to tackle the forthcoming chat session with a much-savored anticipation. After sitting down in his luxuriously prepared space, with every little detail taken care of by instructions to the maid by the women of the house, he sat on a small mattress covered with perfumed sheets. Immediately in front of him were his cups of spiced tea, an ashtray for his cigarettes, and water. He had already changed into a sleeveless tank top, and next to him sat his bundles of this ancient plant, wrapped in a wet towel to keep it alive by lessening the rapid dehydration which makes it lose its potency.

It was such an extravagance when you looked at the time and related things that went into the creating of this ambience. There was, underlying all this, a great and almost spiritual reverence, and this whole gathering centered on a certain religious type of feeling. They literally brought themselves together primarily to go on this induced journey of the mind. This stimulant released the more acute conservativeness involved with issues of gender, primarily sex.

The artists — be it playwrights, poets, or song lyricists — were frowned upon in this society, ironically revered for the magnificent work they put out. This stemmed from a religious idea that such endeavors were, at best, foolhardy. They were also contra to the harsh camel ways of arduous work. The society enjoyed the intrigue of the lyric and sophisticated symbolism involved in the choice placement as posed within this arduous life of the Somal.

Suddenly, one of the women broke into a much loved song of the past about a camel breast when it is lactating and full of milk and the work of milking done by two men. Everyone joined in on singing the well loved camel song put to music. The descriptions were detailed and deeply involved with the landscape, the special conditions of certain plants in certain seasons working as an allegory to Somal.

The conversations assumed a more reflective pace as the afternoon wore on and the chat starting taking its effect on the gathered. The tones had become more modulated to the intimacy of the interaction between pairs of males and the females next to each other. But everyone was now moving towards a larger session discussion, and simultaneous discussions within earshot of the first person very close next to them, sometime breaking into a communal singing of a popular tune, or one in the stages of composition.

The news of so and so was also freely filtered in, but by in large this was a group trance, with connotations of business dealings and power corruptions moving within. The male standing within the society in relation to private enterprise was largely a misnomer, for the women wielded influence for those ones who wanted to get ahead financially in the city or even elsewhere in the nation. One could easily say they ran a great deal of interference in the world of government and senior government officials.

This group was sought after because they could break stringent walls erected for the consumption of the public. Those who were in the know, in the group of those who could make things happen, could virtually circumvent the rather inhibiting laws of the land, and the thus the definition of a criminal was actually quite its opposite.

Later, after the chat session was complete there was the later rendezvous around the expensive watering holes of the large hotels which catered to mainly to Somals domicile overseas and the few officials of the usual international organizations. Every group had a favorite spot that they frequented to drink and be merry as in Robin Hood, but this time the poor stole along with the rich and kept themselves there.

This is where all those who were in need of Ali's assistance – be it business or otherwise – would meet him in Somal, and he had an associate, like his own small limb, who would arrange such appearances at this or that lush venue, in part to see the seriousness of the inquirer and also to sort of economically ascertain to some extent the depth of their pocket, for they usually picked up the tab.

Also, most of the wealthy were in the ranks of traditionalists so they had their younger relatives in this milieu, both trying to break out at the same time paying their dues to the family business.

For Ali today, the great well-known watering hole of Taleh awaited just such a visit. He had headed there right after dusk and was ushered to a table in the inside but open air. He was familiar with most of the Somal around and he stopped at these tables on the way to his, chivalrously engaging in laughter about something or the other. He then requited himself at his table with his assistant, briefing him on the nature of the business that was to be commenced shortly when their expected guests arrived.

Meanwhile, the waiter brought the usual drink for Ali Deray – a bottle of rum distilled from Somal cane in Jowhar, not too far from Mogadishu, and dubbed with a feminine name Asha Wal, the demon Asha, for obvious reasons.

Every foreigner who was ever brought this rum as gift from overseas, which happened whenever the visitors were from around this general area, they would inquire on how they could possibly replace such a pleasurable drink they had run out off such a long time ago.

The business guest had arrived and was now sitting with Ali and his small limb. The matter at hand was started with a slight clearing of the throat by small limb.

"Ali, this is the smart young man I had been telling about. He has been very anxious to meet you, and I was telling him how you're very smart yourself in such matters. I think the two of you will do wonders for this city."

Ali took all this in stride and smiled a knowing smile of self-acknowledgement, clearing his throat as if to say something.

"Please, let's start with what you are asking Ali to help you with."

"Yes, first I want to run it by you so that once you understand the issue, then you can give me your input. The State has been receiving a lot of food from America and other Western countries, and the Government has appointed some state organs to distribute this food stuff to the public. The shipments are already arriving as we speak and all of us merchants will feel the pinch once the rice and other grains are out. A number of us merchants are in this situation and are aware how this will affect our usual market. Once this hits the stores, the price will dive down so it will make the price of our market price really dive way below the initial buying price we paid for. So this is the problem a group of us foresee and it is the reason I am before you here today. We are very willing to make all that you require from the gains and whatever separate fees you come up with to resolve this issue. As you know, we are talking a great deal, based on the quantities we traditionally import from outside."

Ali listened attentively, looking engrossed, imagining how this would move him up a further notch within his circles. He was beaming, as was his smaller limb, as they all partook of Asha the demon. Everything was beneath his feet in the world as he saw it. He could not imagine anything, no matter what, stopping him. People he could dismiss and liquidate as he had done in the past if indeed they even dared pose any type of obstacle in any way, shape, or form to him. He would just send his brute cousin Yusuf to visit them with all the power of the State.

"Of course, there were the more cautious of the ruling circle, who kept on advising, and disapproved of my ways, but those against it, like myself, were many. If people like him were left to their own means then we would have been out of power a long time.

This nomad, as my senior, knew no mercy, the only thing they subscribed was fear, and I am the symbol of that in what I do in many ways."

He beamed slightly, feeling the juice of Asha, smiling contemplatively at extra limb, and then at the young entrepreneur. Now Ali, looking after the most dramatic effects to enhance and conjure this elusive spring of great power invested in his person, spoke very succinctly, stressing each syllable, "Listen, I will talk to those concerned. I am sure there is some solution to this problem. Matter of fact, rest assured that I will handle it."

We that the meeting was postponed, once Ali had said he will handle then who could question this. We that the group indulged in the pleasure at hand at this very lively spot filled with music, Asha Wal and the beautiful fairer sex, all making merry camel style.

 EIGHTEEN

Safari Continued

. . . .

ASHA WOKE UP BEFORE EVERYONE FOR HER REGULAR DAWN
prayer which she made in the room while Tusmo and the girls were
still sleeping. The prayer call could be heard from nearby minarets
creating some rumblings of the sound of those who awakened to
catch the prayer at a time when sleep for most was at its sweetest.
Asha sat after prayer on the prayer mat silently asking for a safe journey forward to their intended destination.

She prayed for the safety of the little ones and Tusmo through the
many perils of encounters, and that the family would be reunited
wherever that may be. She prayed, "May Allah make it possible and
without harmful incident for the girls and Tusmo."

The men, true to form, groggy again from staying up into the wee
hours were nonetheless inching their consciences to the awaking tasks
the journey demanded of them. There was no radio, just the sounds
of Asha's incantations at barely a murmur under her breath, but loud
in contrast to the silence inside the vehicle. Tusmo was anxiety-rid-
den at this point, still believing – no matter what – in Asha's power to
secret her from one end of the country to another. She was now more
attuned to the irrational, such as had happen to her dear Hoagsaday.

Everything like this trip was normal until – Bang! – just like that,
everything changed forever. This great hole in the tapestry of the
norm would not leave her still. It was as if someone or something
within was lying in wait, and knew all about the escape at every

bending corner, every small settlement, or hidden within a distant cluster of approaching trees. Tusmo sat in the car next to Asha this morning, but was already, in her mind somewhere quite tense and very far off – somewhere ahead in the journey.

The eyes of the men portrayed their long night in reverie. Their eyes were blood shot and puffy from the lack of rest. The girls were asleep still, but were soon to wake up and, as children will do, break the ordered silence making the vehicle hum with their active little lives when they greeted the landscape and nature with the great exclamations of joy just to behold Nature which they expressed by the loud calling of the known or unknown names of the animals or birds or trees they saw. In doing so they at once showed their enjoyment of such simplicity, for grown-ups have rather excruciating boring reactions to the splendor and balance of nature. On the other hand, in the vehicle, for the first part of the journey, the men were preoccupied with getting to the time where they could imbibe their chat so as to lose themselves in the movement of time. The ladies were each occupied with other reverences, one to God, the other to fear.

They made little stops in the wilderness. There was an enclosure of the light hard cloth of a burlap wrapped around skinny dry posts. Dark colored tea in transparent glasses heated over open hearths in the back somewhere, along with the tasty meat that tasted as if marinated or sautéed for hours with delicate spices, added at watchful intervals by a great chef specialized in the preparation of meat. What is amazing is this delicious meat bought in the middle of nowhere is really devoid of both a chef's watch and spices, the meat is naturally scrumptious.

The lore of the village tyrant was experienced here in the form of the driver and his many exploits at the various little towns where he had a slew of women who urgently awaited his arrival from time to time, at the exasperation of his passengers who were always left far a ways from the driver's exploits. The passengers knew they were far from there intended destinations, with no other form of transportation. This of course resigned even the usual hotheads into calm, but internally agitated patience for the drivers' impossible behavior on the many stops along the way.

There were several different places of reprieve from the hot sun. Yusuf, like all self- respecting city-dwellers, had a place to go to for the popular indulgence of chat. His was more low budget in that the women at Yusuf's waterhole were slightly less pleasing to the eyes. They had been in the scheme of things for longer, they had been at the business of pleasure much longer and there were, of course, the draw backs that come with the wear and tear of time on the human body, especially on one that has gone through life burdened by terrible rest between the wee hours; and a life of imbibing this mild narcotic too had its ravages.

Yusuf's spot was frequent for the ones who didn't have as much as Ali's group and who were often indebted for their bundles elsewhere, but who were also somehow trying to maintain the lifestyle identified with manhood in the city, which is defined in the city by the consumption of chat during siesta time.

Hawa even in her middle-age was a stunning lady – vociferous, articulate, and gruff in the sense of her worldly, impatient wisdom that suffered no fools, only in her case she would if they indeed had what it took to be around her and her dwelling. She kept everyone on a very short leash – the other women and men who gathered there. She, in essence, knew exactly what she was looking for, and once she got you, you were dismissed in a hurry to make room for the next victim.

Yusuf was dropped off by a military vehicle as was his custom since he discovered, from Ali Deray of course, what real men do during slow hours of the hot afternoon. Yusuf had an adulation for Ali bordering deity worship, and with this fetish came a burning desire to posses whatever Ali had in every sense, whether it was material, business, concerning acumen, power, or even his behavior. In all this, Yusuf aspired to be Ali. However underneath all this, Yusuf was also consumed with envy, and jealousy, seething with controlled hatred and contempt for his idol.

He knocked the door to the Hawa's, and was let in by one of the girls there. Yusuf cleared his throat, adding a little deliberate stress while he stretched his steps placing his feet from side to side, signifying his importance as he made extra noise with the sound of his shoes on the plaster cement finish floor of the bungalow, saying and announcing his importance simultaneously, as he made his way to the gathering area.

Hawa made a fuss at welcoming him, and all the women under Hawa's charge announced in unison, "Oh! Oh! What a pleasant appearance, Yusuf! Welcome, welcome! Oh you look like you had a very tough day today at the office."

Hawa immediately cleared a spot for him very close to her. Hawa shouted to one of the girls with a great deal of heightened performance in her voice, "Where is his ma'wiss? Didn't I warn you just yesterday to have Yusuf's water, soap and towel ready for him? What an idiot you are! Must I remind you how important this man is? Don't you know he opens and closes this town? How many times must I tell you to be very careful with our important guest? Do you want him to go and mingle with more important people, because of you, he is doing us a favor to come here and take such insolence from you. Now, hurry, get his stuff underway, and make haste!"

Yusuf, if you could see him now, was literally ballooning with pride like a bull frog in full croak. He was just gleaming with self importance as he looked around the room as if the men and women gathered there were not people but flies.

Hawa ran around buzzing with activity – getting a flask of tea, perfuming Yusuf's spot. Her fat proportions, particularly her extraordinarily large buttocks, in a land where generally large buttocks were common, were jiggling with a vengeance inside her rather voluptuous version of the translucent derah, usually meant to accentuate the suggestively hidden youthful bodies, rather than the outrageously plump Hawa.

"Oh Yusuf, come now and rest yourself. Yes, come close to me here. Sit. Sit here," she said, looking glaringly at the men sitting with the women next to them, sitting along the wall on mats, leaning on the hard stuffed pillow, with water in a jug, placed on a tin tray along with a flask of tea.

The group was comprised mainly of people with some education, most with a secondary education from many parts of Somal, most working in paper-pushing positions with not much authority

beyond their immediate offices within their governmental depart-
ments. They made what they could of the living, charging here and
there what they could from the public who needed this or that
bureaucratic paper to live in some way or other.

Most of this was, on the books, a public entitlement, but if you were
to somehow feign that you didn't happen to know that it was just in
the books and not in practice, no one would make you the wiser. The
government workers would just role-play along with you until you
either lost whatever you wanted the papers for or they would quickly
see through tremendous stalling. If you knew or, more importantly,
had a powerful clan relative, and it goes without saying if you were part
of the ruling clan yourself, than you could easily wield the fear of what
would or could happen if anything you wanted was denied you.

But, luckily for the middle officer group and for administrators,
most of the public were neither powerful nor part of the ruling elite
clan. According to them, they simply made ends meet. This, of course,
was not the consensus. Many thought they lived way beyond their
means, and expected the public to foot their extravagant lifestyle, a
lifestyle in excess of everything.

This was the group who came to at Hawa's. They couldn't afford
the more pricey gatherings with various young, demanding, and
sophisticated beauties who were under the patronage of their supe-
riors. They tended to steer clear away from such places or chance
confrontations. This could mean a very quick transfer posting to the
middle of nowhere far away for the comfort and life of the city.

Each man knew his place and bided his time accordingly. The
rational was that in this land, where there was constant shifts in places
and positions, the only safe thing was within the circle of the ruling
clan elite. There you did the replacing not the other way around.

The thing was if you had the uncanny capacity to socialize in these
circles through ever-innovative ways to skim the public treasure,
then the doors would be opened to very powerful benefactors who
might know the value of your particular talent, if indeed it was not
a one time fluke. The idea was that it could all be cultivated easily without you, but if you kept moving quickly, and with a much
smaller share of the spoils, you had a chance of staying in power, and

you might indeed become, in time, regardless of your clan, one of those who shaped and formed, in certain ways, the powerful sea of things because you had, in time, accumulated quite a lot. And those who were recently important wanted to also accumulate through an already wealthy partner in crime. This is the ultimate position for those who were at the moment making due at Hawa's on their way to the big time.

As the journey continued toward the final destination of Kismayu, where Tusmo and the girls would journey on further towards the border between Somal, and Kenya, Tusmo wished Asha would be a little more of a talker. She never misused a word. Every word she spoke had been contemplated deliberately and placed in precise order. She was not one for wasting breath, words, or time.

She just sat in the vehicle, consumed in the reverence of worship, here and there breaking into a great smile that betrayed her austere seriousness. The girls with their laughter in their realm of fantasy play forced her to partake of certain humorous moments. Tusmo, however, was anticipating the immediate future, always suspecting a rude stop was imminent. But, so far, nothing had occurred, and they had covered a great amount of the journey. There was almost nothing left of distance.

This time, when they stopped for the night, it marked the beginning of the end. They were expected to arrive as the sun went down in Kismayu. Asha had not told her anything. Perhaps she was waiting for a final talk after they had rested in Kismayu, perhaps then she would reveal her plans for Tusmo and the girls' journey forward from there.

The men were now very cozy, having had their rations of rice and meat, and were now quickly shedding their hangovers from last night's chat session. They had opened up their bundles and the spiced tea they had gotten from the pervious stop. As usual, the stereo was blaring with the soft tones of a famous female singer with a large bass behind her, including some strings. In the current song, she was in a give and take with another very popular middle-range male vocalist. One was in love the other was not, this time it was the women who was smitten by the man, and he was playing hard to get. '

"My desire for you has no description. It is more than the earth at the moment of the scorched dry season, yearning for the sky to open up and shower with the love of a deluge of water, sustaining the love of replenishing life," the female singer would say.

"I am neither in need of such enveloping nor for the skies to open up this shower upon me. I have a well of water from the previous rainy season, and I yearn for nothing nor want to be drenched with this excess of water," the male would say.

This went on back and forth between the singers. The men enjoyed this witty subterfuge tremendously. They had by now become very familiar with one another, and the rank and status stuff had become passé now. They were loving the journey in the sense of their camaraderie based on the situation and the narcotic.

They were both eloquent. There was no shortage of eloquence and even a heightened wizardry with the word. This characteristic transcended the Hinterland/City divide. They talked famously as critics of the musical plays, as connoisseurs of Somal Hinterland culture.

They were deeply cultural as was most Somal, a sort of a contradiction given what they wanted from the new. With how much they cherished the old ways, the wisdom of the philosophical symbolism that endured and would endure as lessons on life based upon past experience of life itself. This was the biggest contradiction in society, but somehow this love affair with words, set in the idiomatic language of the Somal, refused to go away, and the city dwellers, despite their favor for Western ideas of progress or pretensions of it, loved this because it spoke to their being in everyway possible.

The driver and the officer continued their journey in this manner. The girls and the women were oblivious to the front and the men, and the front occasionally looked back at the girls in their constant consternation with nature as they moved along the journey.

They made sure that there were enough stops along the way for the little girls to relieve themselves, and they made longer stops for themselves and the women in the major centers where there was water and bathrooms for the women. As the vehicle progressed and the routines consolidated, Tusmo could see approaching lights from a distance as they continued their journey after a dusk break for Asha's prayer. As the vehicle went further, the lights of the settlement increased and her heart started palpitating in anticipation of things to come. She was both glad and afraid of what lay ahead, but her whole being was now bodily involved in this worry. The palpitating turned also into a mild trembling of her legs.

It was uncontrollable, and she tried very much to cover what might seep into her facial emotions in the darkness of the back seat from Asha, who was, as usual, too buried in incantations to notice any change in the woman seated next to her. Tusmo wondered why at this juncture was it happening in this way. She had been worried all along the way, but it was now an unstoppable crescendo – a unity of the pensive overload from a while back encompassing both body and soul, and affecting her hitherto resilient management of her outward façade.

The luxury four-wheel was now in the city of Kismayu, heading to the somewhere towards a home Asha had spoken about initially. It was around nightfall when they started now in the midst of the milieu of this midsized town. Like Mogadishu, it was an ancient port city on the Indian Ocean and there was a certain similarity between it and old Islamic ports of calling, be it Mombassa or some other port along this vast and ancient sea route.

Like Mogadishu, the residents of the city were out in all their splendor, the women in a symphony of pastels, walking in large groups, the sea breeze, the contrast of the white colored sandy earth in the moonlit of early evening in Kismayu, shadowing the low level façade of the white bungalows, and the multitude of colored minarets, now calling over the speakers the adhan a call to prayer. The ravishing scenery was lost on all but the girls, who were mouthing the name of this fascinating town laying in front of them.

Tusmo, however, was now better controlled and the quivering had subsided. She was more in control of her physical attributes. They arrived at a large bungalow with green iron gates, there were three well placed trees within the compound that gave good shade to its occupants during the hot slow days here, the trees gave linger to the breeze that came in from the sea.

People came running out of the main house, a women was rushing almost crying in excitement, crying as if she was bereaved, "Hoyo! Hoyo! Hoyo! Oh, my mother is here! Oh, my mother is here!" and she carried on with such an intensity, hugging and kissing her face and hands as a mark of respect. Nimo, who Tusmo was now looking at, resembled Asha, just a lot younger.

This cry of unification was continued by the grand daughters, who chimed in "Ayeyo! Ayeyo!" but at a much faster repetitive pace. Soon, they were all hugging Asha from every corner of her being.

The daughter was soothed by her more serious mother, "Now, what is all this crying? You would think someone died and this was a funeral wake. Now please, Nimo, stop this minute and let's attend to the guests first. They have come through a long journey.

"Yes, please. The girls are tired and need food, a bath, and to go to sleep. They have been driving us crazy with their rambunctious energy." This was the most Asha had said since the journey commenced. Tusmo saw a softer side of her now in the presence of Nimo. She was almost teary-eyed herself from the joyously loving welcome she received from her daughter. The daughter Nimo looked like the spitting image of her mother – beautiful, slender, and tall. She was a rich dark brown in complexion, with raven black hair, with proportionate milky white teeth. She also had two daughters like Tusmo, and they seemed to be the same age, give or take a few years.

The men were busy unloading the vehicle of the belongings of mainly Asha. As instructed, Tusmo did not carry much. The night was, for Tusmo, a little settling because she now had what seemed a very secure place for her and the girls. She again thanked the heavens for Asha's intervention. This was truly divine providence. For the moment, with all the animation involved in seeing Nimo, and all of Nimo's making them comfortable, she decided she was going to get, as far as was possible, a good restive night's sleep and to keep her world of endless worry at bay. She would try for a few hours at least. Then she will set out without lingering to the border when a good safe opportunity was in the offing. How she would discern this, though, she had no idea.

She was shown to a comfortable room with her girls. They all laid down to sleep. The girls grew excited as to what the new day would bring in the new environment, and their mother tried her best to keep the worry of the future at bay.

NINETEEN

Assignment Hinterland

. . . .

TONIGHT, ALI DERAY WAS GOING TO SKIP THE LINGERing HE usually did at the chat session. He had to have an urgent face-to-face with his commander and mentor. His vehicle entered the large walled compound amidst a buzz of large expensive later-model vehicles on their way out of this expansive, walled mansion. He stepped out of his vehicle and told the driver to find a parking place in the space between the ends of the large red metal gate, while he commenced inside the large gates through the door of the sentry. He knew most of the high powered personality in passing, and worked with a determined rod-like gate through the enclosed path leading to a cordoned area in the very back of the acreage, where the general entertained his regular high-powered guests.

Ali was sweating slightly even though he had just taken a shower. The sea breeze that usually cooled him did not tonight. He saluted some of the visitors as they passed astride him, and he recognized them as officers higher in rank to him, even though they were mostly attired in large shirts with pockets, a Kashmiri shawl tapered over the shirt, and a silk ma'wiss. He proceeded through the cemented pas-sageway, all with a red tile rafter canopy over the polish, to a fine, fin-ished cement walkway, slightly raised above the rest of the enclosed surface.

The night was brilliantly lit by the stars ever so near you could touch constellations of them, clear and distinct with conjoined sparkling layers of star dust accentuating the early evening sky. Ali Deray went to the end of this middle passageway where the general entertained and held court within the inner sanctums of his vast and sprawling estate. He sat in a comfortable waiting lounge area on one of the doors that faced the office.

He was slightly uptight as he normally would be in the proximity of this powerful general, and men of his elk. As he sat, the large wooden doors of Kumanay's study opened and exposed the office to him. He unconsciously internally reinforced his posture through his stomach muscles. He recognized the man leaving as one of the members of the supreme council.

His back was turned to Ali who was facing the now open door, he was engaged in hearty goodbyes with his friend. As Kumanay was stepping out, Ali turned towards the entry to the pathway back to the cars, stood up, and saluted him as he passed. Kumanay smiled absent-mindedly, only slightly turning his head towards where the salute came from.

His smile seemed sort of plastered where it was, but there was probably not a reaction in his inner thoughts. Ali sat back down even though he could see the General's large study was empty. He waited for someone to summon him. This would normally be the General's ADC, who was of equal rank to himself.

The ADC came in abruptly and took a kid-glove approach to Ali because, all things considered, they might be of the same rank but Ali had the inside track to things. You see, he was the General's cousin, so he was a clan blood affiliate.

Ali followed inside the office after the stiffening of a crisp salute, and he was casually gestured to sit down on one of the couches.

"Hello, Ali. How are you since we last met? How is everyone doing?"

Ali answered in a deliberate, almost forced way. "All is well, Commander."

"Well, what is going on in the town, Ali? I have an assignment for you. You are now to move on to the National Security Services. You will report there as of tomorrow. I have already sent dispatches to your immediate commanders, so you need not worry about going back there for a while. Leave your official vehicle at your regular office. You have been assigned another one more fitting to your new line of work. I have changed a few things in terms of gathering information services. I want you to be very vigilant and aware of your surroundings when you go about town. We have a lot of envious groups who are eager to take our hard-won position. What do you see when you go about on and off duty?"

"Well, the town seems to be very much under control. People do not like the groups in Ethiopia. They see them as traitors and antinationalists. Furthermore, they are also very skeptical about their designs for this country. They are seen for what they are – very

much clan-based. However, you know that regardless of the ill conceived ideals, they will have support from the majority of their clan, except those who have a lot at stake in the capital and in doing business with the State. The nomads are, as you know, to a man behind their General, however". He will be a tough sell for other clans. In all honesty, I think we should now continue to make them feel the power of the Government and, in very subtle ways, of? the rest of the Republic. We will keep an eye on Senior Officials in every branch of Government, keep them stranded at the top with no power to speak of, but keep everything on the up and up.

Ali, don't worry about this so much. I will take care of this problem. Don't worry yourself in this regard. I will address everything in due time. I have a special assignment for you that you will be briefed about when you assume your new position in the National Security Service. You will soon be commanding a very crucial operation in the Hinterland. We are to engage the rebels, who are making sneak attacks and causing minor damage to the military but damage that is of very high value in terms of propaganda coups in the Hinterland. If there is anything else?

He paused ceremoniously waiting for Ali Deray to make a response, and then extended his arm for a goodbye handshake. Ali first saluted then took the outstretched hand with both of his and shook it with a mixture of awe and reverence.

The General said to Ali as he was about to leave, "I expect nothing but a very successful mission from you. Goodnight."

With that, Ali let himself out and back to the passageway. On his way back to the front, as he neared the entrance, he was quite preoccupied by the sudden turn of events.

He was not at all aware of what mission he was intended to undertake, and he was more than worried had he never been on such a mission clearly of high-ranking import. He felt sick to his stomach and very far from his usual arrogant self-confidence. He had one thing on his mind and that was not to fail. No matter what happened, he would not fail.

He walked briskly through the long passageway lost in time. He crossed into the large carpool area and saw a vehicle flash him a beam from the darkness of the many cars that were parked in this area. He went toward his vehicle and got in. "Take me home," he instructed the driver. The driver was surprised at this early venture to the house. It was indeed a very rare occasion when Ali did not keep extended hours at the usual waterholes.

The driver was quiet all the way to Ali Deray's residence, unusual for him too, his nickname being motor-mouth. The driver dropped Ali at his home and was thankful that for once he could go home early, instead of waiting for his boss parked and in the vehicle all night till the wee hours of the morning, nodding off on a flimsy mat thrown on the ground, just like most of the other drivers who drove the up-and-comings and the big-shots.

Ali Deray woke early and went straight to the office. He presented himself at the reception area, and was led into a plush waiting area. He sat there, taking in the office where he was seated, and what he was about to embark upon. The National Security Service had quite a reputation in Somal. Largely, they were feared and avoided to a fault. They were the local James-Bond-types, and were largely a country onto themselves. No one knew exactly what they did, but they had, from their practice of daily intrusions and interruptions in the lives of the common people, an aura of almost mythical proportions. For the work they undertook, the people had come to the realization to stay as far as possible from this nefarious institution.

Ali contemplated the improvement of his public persona. Now people would know him not only as a powerful military man. This new persona would overnight add a certain edge of a more tangible power, in the sense that one could immediately disappear like a genie for any reason, and right there and then. Unlike the military which really was a defensive force and preoccupied within its own largesse, or the police, which was much more accessible to members of the public, with this force, once one was in the clutches of its long tentacles, there was no reprieve in either knowing much about what exactly one had committed or about one's whereabouts.

This information was not required of them. In other words, they were a law unto themselves. People had to reconcile their actions as if they were within the higher rational of Government and National Security, and thus they were beyond the pale of the pedestrian understanding of the people.

He sat there abstractly viewing his new persona with a smile, grinning at how much more power he had accumulated with this new appointment, and at his own fashionable image, his youthful force complete with designer sleek sunglasses, his being always up and about in equally sleek later-model vehicles everywhere in the city. He could see himself in and out of uniform and in these type of scenarios around the city and outside in the region.

A man came to get him from the reception area and took him behind a pair of transparent doors heavily fortified and manned from the inside. He went in the door and through to a well-lit corridor leading all the way to the back. The gentleman ahead of him softly knockeded the door, but he did not wait for an answered, then turned slightly to look at Ali, gesturing with his head in a forward motion to Ali to follow him into the office.

He then motioned Ali to sit down as he himself turned to leave the premises, with another brief gesture of a narrow smile as a sort of welcome.

The office was full of papers, loose in stacks and in folders; there was also a clutter of photographs and a lot of communication equipment, such as, telephones, and walkie talkies. A large dark man sat there lost in these folders. He had a pleasant almost handsome face had he not been slightly less rotund in some proportions. He wore a light short-sleeve shirt, an expensive watch, gold in color, that gleamed in contrast to his shimmering dark complexion. He was engrossed in reading something in his somewhat organized mess. He grunted towards Ali while he continued looking at these papers.

He abruptly took a handkerchief from his behind pocket, agilely lifting his humongous behind, belying his weight and size. He wiped beads of sweat from his face that were trickling down his forehead. His head was a tuft of curly, soft, jet-black with a rush of startling bright white at the crown, and side burns. There was a tray of cups and a flask of tea on the coffee table next to the couches on which Ali was now sitting. The man stood, towering over the large swivel chair, moved towards where Ali was sitting, and sat next to him.

"Please have some tea." With that, he lifted the flask quick and effortlessly pouring Ali and himself tea that was already premixed with milk and honey sweet with an overdose of sugar. This was another thing everyone agreed upon, not just in the city, but anywhere in the world where there gathered two Somal.

"Ali, you have been assigned on special detail to quell the guerilla incursions into the Hinterland areas from across the border. Since you are familiar with this area, you have been assigned on a mission to root out their local collaborators inside our borders. There will be men and logistical information available at your movable campsite in the Hinterland. The mission is top secret, and, as you know, the people who've chosen you for this mission have a lot of faith in your abilities."

"I've occasioned such missions in the past, and I can tell you from experience, to get to the heart of the matter quickly: your men will look for any signs of indecision on your part and it will lead to the questioning of your authority and the possible mayhem of bad morale. You will meet the men in your command when you arrive at your posting. Are there any questions? I will coordinate the operation for you."

 TWENTY

Transgressor

TUSMO GOT UP EARLIER THAN THE GIRLS DUE TO A RESTLESS
night of thinking. Her time was of the essence. Asha's husband could
only keep the authorities at bay for so long. She was hoping to keep
her anxiety under wraps for at least as long as Asha would broach the
subject of the journey further across the border. Asha presented the
idea as a fait accompli, so she knew what she was doing.

It was just Tusmo's fear of having now left on a forbidden journey.
She had now moved from wife of transgressor of the law to fellow
transgressor of the law. She sat in this beautiful large room with the
balls of her feet touching the ground and the rest of her leg almost
dangling.

She was now painfully aware this would be probably the last
comfort of the familiar. From here on out she would have to rely
on her wits, and quick decisions on the move. She hoped to hear
news of what Asha had planned for her and her little ones; she
needed a moment's rest before going forth into this wilderness of the
unknown. Nimo brought them breakfast in the room. The girls were
out playing in this new place of adventure and exploration. Nimo
was still bubbling from her excitement; she continued this endless
chatter with interludes of harnessed laugher. She was quite different
from the solemn Asha, steeped in her visions of the afterworld.

She sat and ate with the other women. They ate a traditional Somal
breakfast close to crepe, succulently spiced with onion-marinated

bits of liver placed on top of the anjhero crepe fried with a butter extract, with a large flask of spiced sweetened tea.

"Stay. Eat with Nimo."

Engaging the two women in a conversation how she grew up in the city, Nimo elaborated on how she had just recently moved from Mogadishu. "Had there been any new film theaters? Buildings? And had Tusmo seen or was she planning to see the new popular play at the National Theater?"

Unfortunately, Nimo's bubbly questions were quite far fetched for Tusmo and Hawa, under the circumstances. To say the least, they tried to answer, but it was with much difficulty, since they were unclear about what was going on. Tusmo could see quite clearly Hawa had chosen not to confide in her daughter the real reasons for her abrupt visit to see them. Tusmo tried her best to convey some of what she knew without letting on that she was conflicted in a bad way. What Nimo was concerned with was as far as the distant horizon to the traveler lost in time and space.

TWENTY ONE

Flying on Earth

. . . .

TUSMO BYPASSED THE BANTER GRACIOUSLY AND PROCEEDED
to cover it all up with uneasy pretensions at laughter, awkward at
best, scary and stiff at worst. Tusmo wondered if she had betrayed
her uncertainty. She never wanted to burden anyone with even an
inkling of what she carried in the vessel of her body and soul.

Asha sent Nimo after some matter or the other, and asked Tusmo to
come closer. Tusmo was silently relieved that it was about to happen.

Asha said, "Alhamdulillah, we have reached thus far with the grace
of Allah only, and I hope he will continue to protect us as he does
every day we live on. I have made arrangements for you to ride in
a vehicle that transports goods for my husband. This lorry will take
you to the border where the driver will arrange for your journey
beyond the border.

"The owner is a respected member and is generally well known
in the area, so, inshallah, it will be a safe journey for you. He knows
his way around and will be of great service to you until you cross the
border. It is tonight, in the early hours of dawn that you will set out.
He will be here at that time to get you and the girls. My daughter,
I will pray for you so that you may be protected, and, inshallah, it will
come to pass."

Tusmo was relieved -- lingering for even a minute more necessarily brought her great worry and unease. After all, every town in the nation was at very close hand to the roaming masses engaged in counter-intelligence. This might mean anything, but more so than not, it meant groundless unpredictability for the person in every aspect of life.

Bearing all this in mind, Tusmo was only concerned with the motion forward in the fervent hope of eluding the Government by reaching another destination, far off in miles, creating an ever growing space between herself and them.

"I was really worried and still am about getting to Nairobi, and I am very clear that it is your kind will that has gotten my girls and me thus far. The measure of your good will and your act of humanity can never be repaid by me to you, however much I would be in the position to do so in the future of our existence. My heart aches with compassion towards your gesture of good will, which you acted out instead of remaining with the majority in silent witness of false persecution. We thank you! We thank and hope for you an internally righteous life on this earth and in your journey to the next, eternal bliss. May Allah quench your soul with the everlasting springs in Jannah."

That evening, they slept outside. At least the children slept soundly until the wee hours of the cock crow, then Asha, Nimo, and Tusmo stirred the house. They woke up the little girls. Tusmo packed the little things into the pillow case. Asha was busy with preparing tea and breakfast for the children and their mother to cushion their stomachs through the journey.

They soon saw lights at the gate and, way before that, they had heard the unmistaken cacophony of a large diesel engine puttering. Tusmo and the girls hugged and kissed their hosts saying an emotional goodbye. Tusmo bid farewell to Asha, who had thus far become her mother, her only relation to the humanity of her past, her sanity that they were wronged in her unwarranted persecution. She was only naturally lost with the loss of this bedrock of sanity in such an insane mode of the world she was in. She said her goodbye tearfully sobbing, but trying very much not to alarm her children. She was determined to do what a mother does, protect them both physically and emotionally by being as constant and normal as possible under the circumstances.

The gates were open and the driver, a man of about fifty with loose-fitting pants sagging, exposing his behind due to his larger pro-portioned belly, came down from the high position of the cabin, on the step just under the cabin door, with great effort, finally reaching the ground and commencing to where the ladies were as fast as his body could carry him. He graciously met the ladies, said his somber hellos. Meantime, there was a kid of about fourteen or fifteen who swiftly came out of nowhere. He was skinny with wild dry black curly hair. He had a cigarette half-consumed dangling from the side of his mouth, like you would see with old chain-smoking men in the city. He had a greasy, worn shirt open at the chest, exposing his chicken-like chest, partially covered by a tank top.

He spoke to the older man grabbing—almost pulling—the little pillow case from Tusmo. "Boss is this the only luggage?"

He said this in a an unsteady voice that was still in search of the resonance of a complete timbre. It was a crackling voice, a voice still in the process of becoming. In little movements, he belied a certain brashness in his ways.

The older man was very curt with him, and responded, "Take that to the front of the vehicle in the cabin."

He then led Tusmo and the girls to the passenger side of the large truck. He lifted the girls and helped Tusmo onto the step to climb into the passenger side of the large cabin. He then closed the door behind them, and attended to his own cumbersome ascent. The boy had disappeared somewhere in the rear.

With that, the vehicle commenced on its slow journey. In the din of the diesel, the outpouring heat from the engine filtered into the cabin. The truck wound its way around the early morning lights of the city. The changing of the gears was just as cumbersome as the driver himself. Everything to Tusmo was winding into a slow cum-bersome grinding movement, but at least it was movement. However slow, it was momentum, and this was all that mattered at the moment.

In her mind, Tusmo said a thousand further goodbyes to Hawa. She recalled her delicate beauty in spite of her age, her weathered dark chocolate skin. Her haunting eyes accentuated her great silent intelligence, her sharp face, chiseled but round in features, and her silky flaming dark tan-brown off-orange hair, tufts of it exposed at the edges of her tight colored-cloth wrap. There was also the presence of natural white in the under growth of the new hair not yet touched by the regimen of the henna dye she used.

She was preoccupied within her thoughts, and kept quiet to her self. The big-bellied driver was sweating already. Even though it was still very cool and the day had just broken, the cabin was literally on top of the large noisy engine, protected from its heat only by a thin cover. Unfortunately, this was an already worn and old vehicle. The use of that cover barrier had long since dissipated, but in this part of the world, such vehicles lived way beyond their naturally allotted machine years by the sheer will and tenacity of the individuals who owned them.

Vehicles were a rather large investment, and were kept going with not infrequent makeshift, local mechanical interventions when one could not find parts or trade-ins with ease. The vehicle roared on in the open expanse, drier than the dense green that made most of the way along the great river up to the coast. This was more of a low land, and there were nomadic encampments in the middle of nowhere, a mark of arid land as they continued in along with more light and a rise of temperature as the sun commenced in its axis of ascent.

The rains had recently hit this area and the girls as usual were delighted to see the magnificent variations on the beige tan of camel coats in the midst of all this growth from the rains. They were bewildered by this large yet slow vehicle at times, but at the same time they had their heads almost poking out of the window, past their mother who was seated between them and the large cabin door. The driver was pleasant and patient to them, unlike the other men who were either hung over or into themselves. He seemed aware of the girls, as he kept his attention on the road, when the girls exclaimed their joy at seeing this or the other. Whether it was trees or wildlife or the family encampments, he would go out of his way to explain these things to them, paying very close attention to bringing his language to a level the girls could enjoy and learn from. He seemed to really enjoy talking to them.

Tusmo thought this a little weird because most of the men in the city were more like the other two men during the previous journey than like this one. The men in the city were all men of big affairs. They were not very serious when it came to anything about children and women other then their obligation to take care of them and treat them with kid- gloves. Despite their definite positions in the running of things within the family construct, males had their respect only for their wives, their mother, and the daughters. The oppression of their household through maltreatment of his own was considered by the Somal as cowardly and unmanly behavior. The affair of rearing the girls, the household, and, as it were, the local government were all the bastion of women. Men who entered the affairs of the kitchen were considered quite beneath the pale.

The children now referred to this older man as they would any other Somal, as their uncle, their Ad Her. In this manner, he continued with his sensitive conversation with the girls. He did not say much to Tusmo who was non-committal for her own part. She had a lot going on, and at this point there was no telling what she did or did not want to speak of. He, on the other hand, did not ask much other than the usual Somal identifying questions – Where she was from? What part of that? Who was the children's father? And, if the regime had not made it unlawful for the public to engage in this age-old tradition, he would have asked directly what the children's clan was, rather than their geographical route, which gave one a roundabout way to ascertain a person's clan along with their accent of speech. The driver then informed Tusmo of the answers to pretty much the same questions, giving him a very good idea of who she and her children were.

The young worker was called Ki-rish boy after the type of work he was engaged in, which was everything that had to be done on the truck. He looked after the truck during the slow travel checking the cargo, slept in the truck when the driver was out gallivanting with the amorous women he had all along the route he plied.

Drivers in these stops brought modernity to the doorsteps of these remote places scattered far off from the capital. They brought people and things that were often new and unheard of in these places. The smaller the town or village, the higher the celebrity status accorded to the driver of this massive machine that carried all manner of things in its belly.

Even the Ki-rish boy was liked for his irreverent city ways and his rapid talk, inflected with the modernisms of the city – an Italian word here, an English one there, altogether a much spicier, rhythmical Somal, which some in the periphery thought was just amazing. Particularly for those who related the city to progress, wealth, and a connection to a much larger universe, drivers were a door to imagining what was heard on the international shortwave broadcasts from the B.B.C Somal Service, long since incorporated into the fabric of the Somal's life. The Somal driver was the precursor to the pilot, and, like the pilot, he maintained a certain aura and general mystique that makes a very attractive figure for the ladies, and a subject of much discussion and envy amongst his fellow nomads, who he had seemingly left in the dust of ages, motionless in time.

The large vessel of modernity had now been in motion for a while. It was almost noon, and the sun was cast overhead scorching the already very hot cabin in the furnace of the diesel engine. The sun was also taking its toll on the vitality of the girl's excitement for the wondrous landscape dotted with surprises just waiting for them to see. The vessel turned onto a side road a little off the main road, and into a small town. Tusmo was on pins and needles all along, waiting in heightened suspense for the eventual interruption of her journey by the authorities.

The driver continued his playful banter with the girls, explaining the name of the town, and that they were stopping for food and something sweet for them if they finished their food. Tusmo was really appreciative of the gentleman's preoccupation with the girls. It was clear to her that he had a lot of experience with children, and she wondered what the reason behind his taking sympathy through entertaining the girls was – if he had some idea as to what was going on or if he was just a kid buff.

The truck stopped at a small hut-like of hotel that had an open air extension to it. There were several elderly men sitting outside sipping tea. The truck came to a halt in front of this small adobe type structure with faded light green paint on the top half and white lime plaster on the bottom. Outside of this structure sat the men on tables and chairs, with transparent glass cups of sweetened spiced tea with milk, the other staple in Somal.

As the vehicle came to a halt, some men stood in some form of stirring recognition, others just continued sipping their tea nonchalantly. The driver was someone who it turned out was well known and welcomed by the elderly men. The owner of the little establishment fussed over him, loudly calling to arms whoever was in his service to prepare a large portion of goat meat for the traveling group, shouting out orders to someone or some people that were yet to be seen by the travelers. Then, all of a sudden, as if from nowhere a group of women and men joined the girls and Tusmo along with the driver on the now-cleared tables. The old men had moved to standing positions around the retinue of visitors. Some were pleasantly listening to the to and fro of the conversation between the driver, some of the men who clearly knew him well, and the owner as he went along his business of catering to the new stream of arrivals.

At the head of the other group that appeared out of nowhere was the lanky youth talking in a crackling voice very rapidly saying, "The food is great here, the meat is only the best." "And the prices!" he said with a sharp whistle to emphasize the many incredible points he was making to his audience.

All of them were much older than he, but this didn't seem to cower him in the least. He took charge as the knower and city guy who had traveled many times to this place. He recommended the choice foods, while the grown-ups became quite comfortable with this ad-hoc arrangement, there was just a few of this crew that ignored him and sat elsewhere and ordered their food. All these travelers were actually in the back sitting on top of the load the truck was transporting to the border – of sacks of rice, and other items such as sugar from a closer destination.

The driver asked for soda for the girls; while Tusmo protested, in a way, she didn't mind. She was not interested in all this, and was more in tune to what might happen in terms of who she might know or who might show up in this small town. Every village had a replica of the State in a more provincial form, usually much more powerful than their counterparts in rank in the city. She was just waiting for the normal to happen because there was no way the small government outpost in this town would not notice the large vessel carryng goods and people, a veritable endless moving violation of many, many obscure laws both real and manufactured. She knew they would come to this rather large event sooner or later, and she kept vigil for the signs of them. Eventually, this ruined her decision to eat something so as to keep up with the girls and the rest of the trip.

The owner started placing a rather huge portion of meat on tin trays with a few cutting knives. He placed some brown rice along with a lot of knives for individuals to cut the meat into eatable measures. The boy was now gorging himself with the group of adults he was with, and he had oil from the meat all over him. Tusmo half-heartedly ate with one subconscious eye open for the village officials. The driver was also busy eating and sweating from the exercise of having his lunch.

The girls just thought of this whole affair as quite splendid. Sometimes gawking at the young boy's very mature ways, they would stop eating and just stare. They somehow discerned that what he was doing was not normal. They knew from their home life the difference between how children his age acted and how this guy had mature ways even for a young man. They continued in this way until the shadow of a uniformed man came and stood in front of the driver as he ate. He flashed a smile, and greeted the driver by name. There was an all around return of his greeting, after which the driver started to speak with a mouth full of meat.

He called to the owner as best he could, "Bring some more meat for the Officer. Forget about the rice. Just bring meat, a portion for a lion."

The officer convulsed with roaring laughter at the prospect of being called a lion and spoke to the driver in very friendly terms. "Stop joking, you know if we go according to what and how much one eats, then you are the one who is a lion."

This he said with a roaring laugh. The elders were slightly less animated as were the rest of the passengers. The uniformed man seemed to cast a subdued feeling to the previously animated conversions. The owner looked on wide eyed and betrayed a subtle caution as he looked on at the interaction between the uniformed one and the others. Somehow this uniform unsettled everyone except the captain of the vessel. The restaurant brought another large quantity of meat, the entire side of a goat cut into large pieces and set it around in front. He also washed his hands in the water basin while the owner poured water on him, and he rubbed his hands before and after the soap.

He continued to talk. Taking the place of others who had been sitting on the other side of the Driver, he was now facing the girls. He played a little with the girls who were all around their friend the driver.

"Are these your beautiful girls?" he asked the driver pretending to be quite pleased with the girls, though everyone there could see he was faking the rather awkward dialogue he attempted to have with the girls in a playful manner. The words came out in quite the opposite of what he intended. The girls lost attention almost right after the first word.

"No these are my relatives. They are traveling, going nearby."

With that, he also lost interest. He was more interested in other things – like whether the driver had brought him the better quality of what meat? they had in Kismayu, as he normally did when he passed this town. The quality in this small town was atrocious because there were not many clients here. Tusmo looked at this man very sparingly out of the corner of her eyes. To her, the uniform he wore seemed to merge his humanity into a grotesque thing beyond her control. She noticed he was a one-stripe private, but he hardly had the gauntly look of this position of poverty.

He was large and very well fed. His Private's uniform was well pressed, the top khaki was shinning from the press. He carried an officer's stick, usually carried by commanding officers, under his arm.

His tunic shirt fit him very tightly. The buttons around his portly midsection strained to keep the khaki tunic wrapped around his stomach. The buttons looked like they could pop at any minute into the eyes of the diners, finally losing the battle to his pot belly. In essence, this was a man of power, non-negotiable power for those who came through this little village whose only claim to fame was that it was on the way to the border. Tusmo pretended to eat, keeping her head down as she hoped the village king would forget himself in the meat. She knew very well that if he was so inclined he could frustrate all the travelers at the drop of the hat. She was trembling inside. Inevitably she cast fate to the winds of the driver's wisdom, in the hope that he would prevail over this greedy official.

The lunch went on with a two-person conversation and only minor interruptions from the girls and the smacking of mouths enjoying themselves. She sat there almost paralyzed by the prospect of what could happen in the blink of an eye, and under her breath she murmured incantations to Allah for deliverance from this potential misery in the form of a fat overfed one-stripe who seemed just above the bottom of ranks but in reality was the king of this village.

Though nothing moved without his approval here, he was powerless as soon as you stepped out of his domain. His power lied in the waylay, in the remoteness of his location, where no one could assail his power, however misguided. You just had to deal with it within its moment of exercise.

The officer dismissed everyone but the driver. He ate and chatted pleasantly with him and him only. Everyone might as well have not been there.

"Everyone to the truck. Lunch is over," the Ki-rish boy announced, consumed with his own authority. "Everyone who is riding in the back of the truck, let's go! Let's go! We need to make good time, we have taken too much time for lunch. Okay everyone, onto the truck. The time for those who want to answer nature's call is almost over. There will be no stopping once we get started on our way."

The passengers started moving towards the truck, one by one. The boy's crackling brashness was the most pleasant and stirring Tusmo had heard since Asha's admission she was going to help them get out of town. Tusmo took the girls and washed them in haste. She deliberately tried to avoid any facial or verbal contact with the busy eating private. She had her eyes on covering the small distance between the eating area and the safety of the cabin, where she thought she would be out of the gaze of the officer, and as close as possible to the moving away from this town toward the safety of the unknown. In perpetual motion there is the hope of evasion sort of carried forward. She finally got the girls and herself to the safety of the cabin.

All the previous sweatiness from the internal heat of the engine coming straight into the cabin was not even a consideration now. She got there and sat in tense anticipation as to when the driver would restart their journey back. In the fervent hope there would be an escape from the king. She sat there for what seemed to be hours but was in actuality just minutes, maybe ten, maybe twenty; to Tusmo this seemed an endless reserve of grueling expanded sections, each seemingly longer than the other, from an endless reservoir of expanded sections. The driver finally got up from his extended eating fest and washed his hands deliberately.

The officer also did the same, and they commenced toward where the restaurant owner had his wooden drawer, which was his register. The driver paid for the bill for the officers, Tusmo, and the girls.

Then the driver yelled to the boy, "Bring the wrapped bundles where we part the fresh chat, bring the whole thing here."

The boy quickly brought something wrapped in soaked sack cloth, over large fresh banana leaves, tied with dried strings also from the banana plant.

The driver handed the officer the whole soaked wrapped bundle of chat and said, "Special choice of the big shots. Take your pick. That is enough for you and leave some for me."

The officer received the bundle as others would receive some very important mark of distinction; he celebrated with every part of his body. His eyes seemed to be dancing around, his being seemed to exude a joy, and he was constantly keeping his mouth in check from wide open gaping and the attended drooling while he examined and opened the bundle of proffered treasure.

He was standing with the driver somewhere off at a little distance from the eyes of people at the restaurant and the truck. The uniformed one's roar of laughter could be heard punctuating the animated staccato verbal back and forth between the two. Tusmo watched and listened from a distance, physically looking away acting as if she was nonplussed.

The Private slapped the driver on his fleshy back as they now started moving towards where the truck was, still engaged in conversation. The wrapped chat was now securely tucked under his armpit replacing the officer's ceremonial stick. The driver laboriously climbed the little mountain between him and his seat in the cabin behind the wheel, while the official went around the other way, stone-faced, looking straight ahead, looking scantily at her in a huff to get to the back.

The Driver started the vehicle somehow not concerned with the official who lifted himself up by latching onto the closed half door which exposed half his body to the passengers, and gave himself a head peak into the canvassed enclosed area of the large flat bed with long wooden benches fixed to the edges of the flatbed. He greeted the passenger to a quick look around with his eyes and the let go of the half door dropping himself back to the ground that was about four feet in distance. He then went around to the front where the driver was and motioned him off with gesturing waves, as the driver took his cue and started the slow paced movement toward the main road.

Tusmo kept her composure belying the trembling shaking her from the inside. She was still ambiguous about relief because the man was still within distance of catching the truck. The driver was busy exchanging his by now usually familiar voice with the children. He was now getting ready for the festivities of the evening by slowly opening the chat and chewing on the slender stem of deep red and green. Tusmo was glad he was preoccupied, otherwise he might have noticed her heightened sense of nervousness. Instead, he told the girls to take a rest so that he might engage in his chat session without too much noise from the girls' enthusiasm.

He wanted to start this part of the journey in silent reverie of the stimulant. Tusmo began to believe in the possibility of escape more and more as the cantankerous vehicle made its slow gains further and further away from the clutches of this lowly official who in the environment had morphed into a much higher ranking official, very powerful and what was worse was that he only had this aggrandized self image for counsel. It was not bad for himself, rather for those who where grasped within his greedy talons.

Tusmo had gotten used to the slow metallic grinding force of the truck's movement coupled with the heat and the smell of diesel during the now many hours before the stop for food and the call of nature. But at this moment she wished more so than before that this snail pace would abate, leading further and further away from that puny official, she wished the truck would merge itself to the distant horizon, out of reach from the overfed one.

She was thankful to the turn of events and mumbled her dually graciously thanking Allah for the good fortune. The girls, weary from the heat of the afternoon sun and slow burning temperature of the cabin, were lucky to fall so blissfully asleep, Tusmo thought. Their cheeks looked flushed from the daunting combination of the sun and the high combustion diesel engine, of the over ten ton vehicle.

The vehicle was finally at a distance Tusmo approved of, and she forgot the official, only to get lost in the things that were possibly laying in wait for her. The scorching sun was slowly sinking by and by, as the time rolled by gruelingly slow, and as the truck plodded along forward determined to reach its final goal-the border, if you will. The border got closer as the sun became less potent and the light of the day began to fade; the driver continued his chewing taking one green stem after another lost, it seems, to the unfolding world.

He was happy the girls were asleep and probably hoped for them to stay that way. The two of them became fixed on the long road ahead them, one not noticing the other, but bound together by the circumstance of time.

Tusmo's heart pounded as she saw a distant light that resembled a light bulb in the wilderness of darkness, and as they moved on there were more and more lights pushing out from the darkness. It looked like a good sized town or village, and from that deduced that this was the town before the border that was her final stop before she embarked on her journey further.

The girls had long since awoken and were silent with the intrigue of darkness that enveloped everything to mythical proportions for children. They could see distant lights, and once in a while the truck's lights would, very quickly, flash a herd of deer, or the girls would see luminous eyes from a distance, the red of the meat eater, and green of the herbivores, this both scared and excited them into a further vigil of the mythical enveloping darkness. They were up on their knees and gawking through the large window of the truck as it moved along the wilderness of the night. Their mother kept an eye on them as they had their heads plastered to the closed window, revealing the vanishing tracks of their moist breath.

The vessel started winding around as the lights became brighter and brighter and as they came very close to entering this village town of sorts. The lights turned out to be a multitude of kerosene lamps dangling at the front of establishments, outdoor-type tea drinking places, homes, and shops that had a much more powerful light made from a paraffin-soaked filament that burned with the brightness of a hundred watt electric light bulb.

The village was alive in the early evening hours. The residents looked on at the large vehicle as it passed where they were spending their evening. The driver as usual had his place that seemed to be in the heart of things, there seemed to be more prominent buildings concentrated in this part of the village.

The driver who had remained silent for most of the journey broke his silence to speak. "We have arrived, there is a place here for you and the girls. This is my home. There is plenty of room. The wife will arrange it for you. You can get down now. The boy will show you the way. I have some business to take off, but please you and the girls should feel as if you were at your own home."

With that, the brass boy chewed the curd he had gathered on one side of his face, stretching the limits of his thin cheeks to its outer extremities. The glowing cigarette butt was in its usual place dangling from the side of his lips. He opened the large door and his head

appeared on Tusmo's side as he stood on the step. The driver gave him
instructions to first take Tusmo and the girls to the house, and then to
hurry back to the truck.

"Yes, boss," he said with his crackling voice. With that, he quickly
helped Tusmo and the girls down the high seat of the cabin, and carried the little pillow case along with him while firmly grasping one
of the girls. He led them at a fast pace along the narrow alleyway
of the border town. He was deft in how he negotiated their way in
the darkness, he moved with just enough speed so as not to lose the
young girls and Tusmo in the process. He always knowingly looked
back, and kept silent all the way there. They entered a light doorway
in a yard enclosed by a hedge of dry thorn bushes, and there was a
large hut type of house in the middle of this compound.

There was a light coming from inside the house, as his brashness
called out to the people he knew were inside, "Auntie, Auntie! We
have arrived! We are here!"

Tusmo, who was behind his brashness, could now discern some
movement from the interior. She now heard the voices of children
and a woman's voice instructing them to
go back to bed. She came out of the door to meet them, and welcomed Tusmo and the girls without too much ceremony. It seemed
to Tusmo that she was either tired or was just used to sudden intrusions from the complete strangers her husband housed there from
time to time.

"Welcome," she said, and she took Tusmo's belongings in a pillow
case from the young boy, without any questions, only asking one
herself.

"Where is he?"

"He is in the town supervising the unloading of the truck."

The driver's host led Tusmo with the by-now groggy with sleep
girls through the dim, dark tunnel of a corridor with a dim, flicker-
ing light of a lantern coming from inside one of the rooms.

They got into a deceptively comfortable room, clean with white
and multicolored draping on the bed and windows. The room was

very cozy and well-lit considering what the circumstances were. The lady told Tusmo where the bathroom and water were and told her to remove the sheets she had spread over the bed for decoration and to use whatever sheets she needed that were spread underneath the colorful spreads.

Tusmo thanked her hostess and began the business of preparing the girls and herself for sleep in what had become for her a familiar strangeness of other people's houses. There was not much sleep to be had here as in the previous places, and Tusmo was now also getting used to the fitful nights of no sleep thinking about the unthinkable prospects of being caught in the act of absconding if you will.

She had another fitful adventure of sleep, ending with her running from something, out of breath, with the creature in hot pursuit of her at only a small distance away. She had this recurring nightmare where some grotesque creature was in hot pursuit of her, for what seemed a great eternity. She sat there immobilized in a version of the dream in which she had fallen down during the chase, and could not get up from the paralysis of fear. She would scream, but there was no sound even though she was screaming at the top of her lungs. This dream sequence, which had kept with her so far, imitated the real and further imagined pursuit.

Tusmo was awoken from the nightmare with what she at first thought was part of it, an almost inaudible voice calling "Tusmo, Tusmo" growing louder and louder until she was awake enough to realize that it was not the nightmare but rather the woman of the house trying to wake her from her nightmare sequence calling her name. Tusmo woke up, startled by the woman's attempt to wake her up. Now, she tried to focus her attention on what the woman was saying.

"Get up! It is time to leave. The boy from the truck has been sent to take you across the border. I know you are wondering, 'Why at this time?' But this is the best time. It is very late in the night and there is perfect moonlight which will make it easier to get across. The girls will have to manage the distance on foot. It is not much for an adult, but quite a distance for a child. Hurry up! Let's get the girls awake to go. Now is the best time to cross the border. The guards on both sides are busy and well into their chat sessions. They will not move for anyone or anything other than a very extreme emergency. Make haste! Let's get to the boy who is outside waiting to guide you there. Hurry, hurry! Make the most of this opportunity."

His brashness was all quiet at this time. He carried a flashlight with him. The girls were now at Tusmo's side. They were as ready as they were going to be, half asleep and all. The journey started in earnest with his brashness in the front increasing the pace that was getting faster as they left the sleepy village town and encountered more and more space with huts, lights, and human or animal movement. The bright moonlight made the distance and the road ahead glisten with a natural floodlight quality. This illuminated Tusmo's vision who was a pace or two behind his brashness. He kept looking back to see where they were with each advance of his quickly accelerating pace. He was in a hurry as usual.

Tusmo upped the tempo to keep up with him. Still partly asleep and burdened with the shocking suddenness, at least to her, of this trip across country lines, Tusmo did not much question the rationality of this journey. Especially when it came to getting the girls at this time to walk as if they were adults, she knew this was really a lot to ask of children. She had never had to do any of this. There was nothing in her childhood that could measure up to this rapture of movement toward an unknown place, language and people for reasons beyond their comprehension.

Tusmo thought about this as she nudged them both on with a strong clipped verbal instruction, and a little physical tug, pulling their hands. She kept the tears in her heart and forgot herself in this process. His brashness, true to form, kept up the pace. Without relenting, he just kept looking back at the women behind him.

For them he had even stopped his perpetual smoking. He knew quite well the burning red of the head of the cigarette could be seen from a very far distance in the open space across the border at night. He weaved through an unknown path he followed knowingly. It seemed to Tusmo as if he had, even by this tender age, traversed here a thousand times, he was so sure of the road, granted, in the flooded light of the moon. He did not show any form of hesitation or fear for this expanse of wilderness. Tusmo took his cue, fighting to hold the fear that consumed her whole being. She urged herself in stoic fortitude for the hope of the other side's equally unknown terrain. She kept the girls moving as he maneuvered the moonlight travelers on this well trodden path to avoid detection of their crossing, against the law, imaginary lines splitting one country from another.

Ahead, they saw some distant lights that reassembled the one headlight of a stationary vehicle very far in the distance. At times, this light seemed as if it were a light bulb propped up on a lamppost far off in the dimness of the distance. In the vast loneliness of the wilderness, they could hear the distant howl of a hyena.

The girls asked, "What is that noise, Hoyo?"

"Oh, it is nothing but a far-off dog," Tusmo responded with the intention of making sure the boy did not offhandedly tell the girls what it really was. In the moonlight, Tusmo could see the land ahead of them clearly but could not discern any clear direction from the many directions offered up by the multiple narrow footpaths that all seemed to be leading in the same direction, crossing each other at various points along the footpaths.

The night was a dead silence apart for the animal noises from some dark distant corner. The very loud braying of a donkey carried much further in the stillness of the night, and even this sound was now in the environment of an expansive sameness, accentuated by the already very tense fear of Tusmo, although she was familiar with the harmless braying from the donkey.

The boy did not lose his pace, keeping just ahead. Unlike the previous times where he had been talkative, this time he chose to be very quiet and purposeful, it seemed, to get them to where he was assigned to. In the distance, you could now see more dull lights and the sounds of transported snippets of human voices that seemed very far off and directionless. The wind carried voices that were getting closer and closer, and the lights of what seemed like a small outdoor hearth's red coals submerged in a heavy blanket of ashes were now visible to Tusmo. She knew instinctively that they were approaching their destination on the other side of the border. Tusmo saw his brashness stop, and his waving for her to stop with his hand.

He then pointed to the direction of the voices and the camp fire, and said "Askar," in almost a whisper, very almost touching Tusmo's face with his, so close she could smell his pungent cigarette breath.

They took a downwind turn away from the still distant but visibly smoldering campfire and the voices. Moving away at a more deliberate and slower pace, he motioned to Tusmo by placing one of his fingers on his mouth that was expanded by the large curd he continued to chew. Tusmo understood what he meant very clearly and she whispered firmly in the ears of the girls, now confounded by both exhaustion and the night, not to make any noise, adding that they were almost there.

The other side of the border was asleep. The Ki-rish boy took them to another house amongst many such houses and walked into a thorn-fenced compound by just moving a large wooden door that served as the entrance, propped up by a wooden frame.

He ventured passed the entrance quick and gestured them into the darkness. She followed him with the girls, barely making it. They were met by an elderly man first, then a woman. The boy had jus been roused out of sleep. They took it all in stride, as the boy informed them in his crackling voice who Tusmo was and passed on the message from the driver that he had sent them here. Tusmo did not hear much of what was going on. She really was preoccupied by the now very tired girls, hoping that they would soon get a chance to rest from this rather awkward journey to nowhere they knew and in the light of the moon.

The couple showed them to a dimly lit area that was part of the household, and told to rest the children and herself here. The room was too dark to see more than the silhouette of the bedding in the moonlight. She neither cared nor considered it much, her mind was on the girls and their rest, in the hope, as little children do, that they may forget what had just transpired with rest. She also ironically looked forward to the momentary safety of convulsive subconscious sleep in this unknown border town.

TWENTY TWO

Ali's Return

. . . .

ALI DERAY IN THE MORNING WAS READY TO ASSUME HIS new position as an internal intelligence officer assigned to the Hinterland on a mission. He left his usual khakis to wear a stylish outfit of a tight-fitting shirt draped over the waistline. The top buttons were undone, the shirt hugged the body, and he had a concealed weapon tucked somewhere in his pants. The outfit was accentuated by Italian designer sunglasses, Persol; the glasses completed the espionage persona.

He went to the gate where he was taken to the new office to collect his unmarked vehicle, and proceeded to the assigned mission. He went to the yard and offered himself up to the personnel manning the area. Showing the required ID, he was shown to a waiting area where he waited for the vehicle. While he waited, he thought to himself that he much enjoyed the scary power associated with this organization of which he was now a member. He was a little discouraged that he had to leave his city business interests, but he hoped to finish up his mission as soon as possible and return from the backwardness of the Hinterland and its environs.

He was particularly aware that, if he left the city, he would provide some other less connected upstarts the chance to fill the vacuum he left. The filling of this vacuum would probably happen with the urgency of his former partners who always had something or another to facilitate through the government or from the state to the people.

This, he sadly recognized, was a moment that could never be stopped by any one individual. The greed needed to be fed and others would step in to fulfill this need. He had by now just gotten to know, from the small to middle-size hucksters, the more respected ones. They only knew whoever was able to deliver. Such was the method were the big guns, the very big ones, got their palms showered regularly with grease.

All the middle government men had the same backer or backers, without their knowledge. They sometimes played one against the other, without their knowledge, and then let whichever side, after the prices had been driven up sufficiently, slowly back off from the other. They who operated at the higher corridors of power were a more cohesive unit internally then the more divided outward appearance they cultivated, which was better for business. They somehow worked things out to their mutual benefit. The likes of Ali were mere enforcers of an equilibrium they had no idea existed, other than their crude premise of power through clan.

Their ultimate blind spot and source of power were one in the same thing. But Ali did not see these more complicated things, he just knew he would lose his day-to-day accumulation of steady wealth and power if he left the city. His was also thankful he was the man chosen by his mentor and backer for this mission. He looked at it this way: he could not afford to second guess the inherent wisdom of Kumanay, the man who had thus far sustained his quick rise to ascendancy within the circles of power in the city. In other words, he owed his fortune and prestige in the city to this General.

This reality was not lost on him; he knew he was less than adequate, particularly with regards to the standard fair of formal education, and the tenacity to rise through self- education in the process of training.

As the vehicle moved further with the little traffic of large transport vehicles overloaded with people and animals, he got a glimpse of his early life in the Hinterland and the manner of things going towards the capital on their final stretch.

The images he had of his father were not as a man much in the power of things. He had barely managed through his own father to pay the bride price. There was a large drought that had consumed the livelihood of everyone in those years called by the name Haramo Une.

The father left from the death of Ali's grandfather had not been of much regard. He was not particularly eloquent, and was not considered a man of wisdom when he became an elder. His lack of wealth and eloquence doomed him in a society in which the two were the markers of success. Granted, he was born during a tumultuous time into the already tumultuous and harsh life of frequent natural shortcomings. But beyond this, there were his relations to Ali and the other elders.

They often recited poems during this era of continuous strife based on nature and from the Ferengi who had come from far away seas and had interrupted the Somal. Before the appearance of the Ferengi, the Somal roamed with his herds stopping only for water, but as Ali's grandfather would say, "There was a very strange man, white in complexion."

In silence, the vehicle continued further along the journey towards expanding the blurry images in Ali's mind of a past he wished to forget as much as possible. Behind the dark sunglasses, the others in the vehicle kept away from what they thought was his gaze at them. But Ali on the other hand was busy fighting off these fragments of his former life in the Hinterland as they drew more and more flesh, amazingly in sync with the vehicle as it got closer and closer to the Hinterland.

The bits and pieces of a forgotten past began to conjure up in his imagination, going in and out of his consciousness but coming back more whole, more formed, and finally with a vividness of his previous life that was clear and sharp. He could see his father a broken man, gaunt with distance, haunting eyes, mirror of a life of just barely existing. The image made him consciously shameful although it was from far away and of another time. The man after all was dead, and as the Somal believed in looking at the good side of the departed, Ali still felt a deep hatred for the dead weight of his quiet whimper in life and in death.

Ali saw a direct fall of his line from a grandfather who had made it on many occasions into the Somal psyche and had remained there through oral archive with frequent mention of his greatness in the manly things of the Somal, wealth, eloquence, and wisdom, along with many brave exploits against rival clans, attesting to the greatness of Ali's clan lineage.

He preferred to skip mention of his father when speaking boastfully about his heritage, always happy to elaborate on his grandfather, consciously avoiding his father's less significant life or death.

His father was born to opulence. In the Somal sense, his father had acquired a lot of wealth at a young age, inheriting from his progenitor a good amount of prestige from a successful life as a man who had wealth in camels and many sons. His father was also known as a god-fearing, wise old-man. All this was passed on to Ali's father who exemplified the Somal aphorism that a lion begets a pussy cat.

He had many brothers from a different mother who managed to keep their standing in the community as the contemporaries of Ali did in his time. Even though his father was the eldest of the siblings, and was the chosen one to assume the mantle of his great forbearer, the younger ones being stronger both in mind and eloquence were able to out maneuver Ali's father-when faced with seasons of endless draught that were the last straw for any semblance of wealth in the form of an increase in livestock. And as his luck went, the little he kept without much increase was completely devastated by a long and enduring drought that eventually wiped out the few camels and goats they possessed.

What could have saved his dignity and spared him in the group of men who were a force to reckon with based on the exploits of bravery or eloquence and wisdom? Abyan, his father, had none of that, so that he did die heavily compromised as impoverished, as someone who could not be counted on for sound advice in relation to his age and leadership.

Ali now remembered the pain brought on by such inadequacy and how his cousins, the sons of his uncles, were treated because of their wealth, a wealth, Ali knew --had his father had the presence of mind--would have been his, but this was unfortunately not the case. This is what formed him in the Hinterland, even with the developed fierceness that comes long-term in wilderness. Fate decided for him early where he stood in the scheme of things nomadic. This is what ultimately made him go to the city to seek the redemption of his clan's heritage of greatness.

Like so many others he had heard, through the relentless passing of information from mouth to mouth, which reached every corner of the Somal, that the city was a place where one could find opportunity, and even perhaps change of one's future beyond the bad hand history had dealt him. The Hinterland was aware, through these networks of small sedentary communities of men gathered briefly for tea and for the citified chat sessions at the wells or in the small sweetened tea shops, of the goings on of the wider world of Somal and beyond.

The ancient cities along both the Red Sea and Indian Ocean had always been centers of much confluence. There was always someone who was returning or on their way back from a long sojourn in this port city or from such far flung places as South America, North America, Asia, and Western Europe. This type of movement to the nomad just seemed a longer and much easier extension of their already transient relations with the earth. Those who went eventually found their way back, though some never returned from their rather lengthy sojourns.

It seemed to them in this case they were in search of the pregnant rain cloud across a much larger earth, always with the concept of the camel as the reference of wealth. Money in the form of wages—to these mariners—was recalculated into the number of camels as an exchange rate.

Ali had come to the city after he had learnt the exaggerated tales some of the older men had a penchant for, showcasing their mastery of words and image, and an inherited proclivity for embellishing the dull, dry landscape in contrast to the elegant features of the human form that dwelt in this region.

His almost magical trip from the Hinterland came by chance, in the form of a sick uncle that was in need of physical assistance to get to the main hospital in Somal. Ali's father could not say much. His rich kin had asked for his assistance, and, his situation being what it was, he had agreed upon the receipt of a financial favor with the promise of his son's speedy return with more from his assistance of his wealthy uncle.

Ali with his Uncle in tow had boarded the truck. The old man stretched in the back with the load, and Ali looked in on him from askance, the distance of the long flat bed in the trunk. There were many items cluttered, each imposing on the other —humans, goats, and other articles for human consumption. The stretcher that the bony-with-sickness body was sprawled on was a narrow canvas bed, and it was placed in a tiny wedge on top of a styrofoam mattress, and then placed on the flatbed in part of what was the congested back of the truck.

The people, things, and animals were all in one space. Ali was sitting on one of the two long wooden benches that spanned the flat bed, running from where the cabin of the truck stopped to the closed small barrier door that was meant to keep everything from falling out of the flat bed. This group of travelers brought themselves together in close proximity. The seasoned business types, the first-time Hinterland mothers, grandmothers, aunts, brothers, and fathers making their journey in search of the relatives the Hinterland had long lost to the ease of the city.

Some had prepared meals such as large morsels of dried meat carried in large decorated dark wooden containers, some carrying milk, others carrying large morsels of preserved succulent meat, made from a strong but malleable dark wood that grows in the Hinterland. The milk containers had a charred inside with a surface of another medicinal tree, burnt to a coal, then used to treat the inside of this type of vessel by rubbing the charred limb. In this way, the pastoralists pasteurize their camel milk. The milk assumes a light, smoky, pleasant taste, such as the barbecue grill leaves on meat.

Ali thought this first journey was a mark of divine providence that marked a sort of agreement from the heavens that he should embark on the journey to seek his redemption in the city. The tacit acceptance of his never-return after his rich uncle was situated was a far gone conclusion for Ali Deray, a tall gangly youth of about eighteen. He held forth to his ambition to revise his statue and get his family name back in its rightful place of honor amongst the very great in his clan.

It was uncanny what he speculated of himself based on this ideal, and all of it based on nothing more than the nonchalant tacit resignation of his father's station of poverty, juxtaposed with the prosperity of his siblings and their offspring, paraded at every well encounter with him and his puny herd of two goats -- them with their handsome large herds, and almost just as many sons in tow.

The herds proudly wore the brand of Ali Deray's great progenitor. With the exception of a minor difference of detail — a split in the left ears of their camels and Ali's stock bearing a left ear intact, all other markings were the same: the large brand of the entire clan; that of the shared sub-clan; the shared progenitor's; the individual family's; and on further to differences identifying the different siblings' herds.

The markings, branded on the coats of the camels while they were still growing, served many purposes. They could not be removed, and thus hardly every concealed. Even distant clan affiliates could identify the ownership of lost or stolen camels across very great distances and then proceed to launch a claim on behalf of a very distant relative to the hierarchy of clan agnation.

Ali sat in this congested milieu of animals and humans, attentively overseeing that his charge did not get mangled in the tight space and the convulsions of the corrugated gray dirt patches that kept everyone on the flatbed in limbo between where they had secured a tiny place to seat themselves and where the truck's underbelly of wheels threw them upwards, no sooner, then, gravity pulling them downwards. The old man had been secured to the flat bed as best as possible. Even though he was laying down, you could hear his sickly weak moans, almost inaudible from the constant fight of his body against the grain of gravity pulling him down. Ali wondered what he could do to make things a little better for this live amulet that had brought him the chance good fortune he had being dreaming of – his way to the great city to finally seek his redemption and glory.

As the Hinterland faded into the ever further distance, he wished this would be also a symbol of the difference between the life he had just left in the Hinterland, and the new one. He wished himself toward the distant horizon – toward the city and toward life as it would never be again.

Ali had concealed his resentment from all those around him during the stops to water the animals, or during the seasons of plenty when the young men and women gathered in song and dance, celebrating the plentiful season of rain and reprieve from the long hours of thirst and gastronomic fortitude in the dryer, less bountiful harsh dry seasons.

He listened attentively in the Hinterland for news of the compadres he knew he had cut cords with forever, and always the news was filled with great superlatives of how so and so was making it very big in the city. Ali told no one, and concealed his unhappiness with his station in the Hinterland, masquerading himself in an exterior mask of even pleasure with his allotted position as a nobody in the Hinterland. They arrived in the city where, thankfully, the old man convalesced for months at the house of one of his sons, Ali's first cousin.

The old man was revered and so Ali attached himself to him as if he was part of the old man's body. He took to sleeping near to him, within earshot of his now sickly faint calls for whatever he wanted. He had, through the journey to the city, created an indispensable position in relation to the old man. The old man in his mostly delusional state from high fevers and pain, got to a point where Ali was the first and only name he could recall. Ali milked this at the homes of his relatives, who were so touched by how this very young person was so caring in contrast to their own children who were so busy with themselves.

Ali took this in stride and embellished his stories at every opportunity he could. He usurped giddily this good fortune of assuming a position of reverence vicariously through the guilt of the old man's children having a lot to do with not looking back at their homesteads in the Hinterland. He also showcased his pastoral wizardry for words as he related his closeness to their sick father who could not protest the lies while lost in the delirium of his deathbed. He made it seem that he was inseparable from the old man, and loved and enjoyed taking care of him, while none of the other cousins even bothered with his needs.

The old man had lived most of his life in the city and had decided in the dusk of his years to go back to how he had once known life after the passing of his one wife in the city. The children liked to oblige the family patriarch even in his more senile decisions. They let him go, he had been a great provider, a man of big clan affairs, he was one of the wise and just men of his elk, a position every man sought and cultivated for others to say when they held forth judgment about them in the courts of public opinion.

The old man was one of those who did not have to cultivate this. He was a god-fearing man and steeped very deeply in the traditions of his ancestors. He took the Somal code of laws and the ideal of just behavior from his religion as an ideal to strive towards, which he did for most of his life. He had never contemplated when he was sound of health that such a supine creature the opposite of him would ride the glory of his life's work as a decent human being. Ali, after all, was always faltering of the side of the better side of a mere mortal.

Ali completed the charade with a just-acquired theatrical religiosity. Complete with a faulty moralizing he had mentally recorded through the years related to him by the nomads in the setting of the remote one shop shack teas houses. After the night prayers, the gatherings would stay up longer than usual, because they spent their days in fasting without eating or drinking anything during the day, a month that reinforced abstinence to the pastoralist who lived it not as a maxim to strive for, but more of a reality of everyday life as it presented itself from the very beginning to the end.

Ali was quite fortunate for the slow and hard days, weeks, and months of the old man gradually losing his form, decreasing in physical presence to almost a blurry silhouette of his former physical imprint contoured beneath the sheets of the bed.

The signs were there for all who wanted to see: the old man's days were not long on this earth. Absurdly, the bed became an abyss that made more and more of the moral progenitor disappear. As this happened, the image of the old man was fashioned through Ali Deray's skillful imagery with choice words. He lionized his own image becoming almost inseparable from the image of the children's father now dying in front of their eyes with all the helplessness mortals encounter on such morbid occasions.

The narrative of the great old man during his short sojourn told of a man driven by nostalgia back to the Hinterland, back to his genesis where he was everything to all at once. And there was Ali at every turn making the old man's tasks that much easier, taking the place of his rightful assistants in old age, his children. This was the introduction of Ali to the city and the city to Ali.

The old man soon passed one morning and there was a great funeral that took place where a large congregation of folk – young and old - formed – a solemn mass gathered around the gravesite, though they arrived not just for him, but at least in part to be at peace with their own unavoidable fate.

Ali was a little unsure how long he would last as part of the center of attention once the old man had gone. He went back to the house with his relatives looking for signs of his possible withering away from the associated status he had cultivated diligently in the hearts of the old man's children. He knew he would have to act fast before such a thing presented it self unceremoniously.

The atmosphere of uncertainty did not last for long. Everything remained the same, and even got better because now Ali did not have to pretend to hover around the old man– he was dead. One morning, the son of the old man announced to Ali that he was to go in with him to work that day. The man was the eldest son of the dearly departed, and he seemed to Ali to be some sort of well to-do military man.

TWENTY THREE

Misleaders

· ·

AFTER HIS ARRIVAL, BEHEYEAH WENT STRAIGHT TO WORK in an already semi-established group in Ethiopia. He worked diligently towards undoing some of the disaster he had helped to create in the apparition of this brutal Government. He went to the Headquarters, furnished by the host Government, and tried to get an idea of what the reality of the operation was as opposed to what was released on the propaganda radio that the Front controlled.

Initially, he was welcomed enthusiastically for leaving at the height of his power and name, and his actions were not lost on those exiles with very large ambitions to overthrow the powerful State apparatus. He was accorded immediate leadership of the Military Wing, and the overall direction of the liberation struggle. He was respected across clan lines for his nationalistic fervor that transcended clan bloodlines.

Most of the exiles were people, not unlike him, who were former stalwarts of the Revolution. So there was an air of failure in relation to their shared naiveté; together, they were accomplices to creating this crazy powerhouse of a few.

Hence, the atmosphere was always charged with the second-guessing of the motives of each and everyone. The major question was not liberation for most, but 'don't get suckered all over again.' As far as they were concerned, a Somal was not capable of transcending himself, the clan creature, and even if he did by some spectacular event, his society would not let him. So this is what in essence put

Beheyeah, at heart an altruistic leader, at odds with his own. He knew most of the people in exile, especially those who had held high positions back home.

At the meetings, he came back to his lodging exhausted from trying to get a point across, or, more importantly, from getting anything to move out of its deliberation phase into action. In practice, it was becoming more and more difficult to deal with the inter-clan mentality of the officials he dealt with. Those around Beheyeah were very different from him, though, granted, he knew he was an exception when it came to his outlook.

What really irked his soul was that he could smell the banality of their type of evil. They pretended to speak for all Somals and assumed that leadership was obligated to their person. In other words, they felt that this was their rightful position at the helm, and even this Beheyeah could rationalize, but what he was sad about was that they were really a nefarious lot who only saw themselves at the helm of a full barge, though in reality despised their fellow clan members, as backward and lesser; they always reminded everyone they were there to represent these people whom they really abhorred.

He was becoming more and more frustrated by the collective of this group. They were busy with titles overseas, soliciting fellow clan member for funds. Some of these funds, the low end of them, got through to the militias, the fighting men that Hoagsaday was part of. They had very little in terms of food, equipment. They spent their nights in the wilderness, each day living in the harsh reality of water, and foodless combat skirmishes, usually engaging a well-fed, well-equipped foe.

Everyday, more gruesome reports of violent repression came from the Hinterland. The nomads were catching the brunt of the Government's repression because of the open exile insurgency. These reports tempered Beheyeah's every move. He felt very committed to serving those at home in the Hinterland who were experiencing havoc, while the elites like himself were safe in their government-provided hotels.

Like in Mogadishu, Beheyeah took walks, but not in the streets – instead in a well-protected enclosure. He tried very much to think through this stalemate of inertia on the part of the elites. It was clear to him that the collective had assumed a splintered platform, with clan interests riding high behind the official protestations of a unitary non-clan movement.

It seems that when the groups adjourned for strategy meetings, there were always other sessions in secret that were undertaken by the few different clans represented. This made a collective front very difficult, coupled with the sociopath-like disposition of the self-styled brain trust of the Somal whose education was based on the Western system. Learned in their language and in most cases as an adult, most of them juggled numbers, and the rote formulaic teaching of the sciences with hardly any emphasis in the humanities.

Beheyeah could not in good conscience represent his country or people in this way, trying to make the best of an ill-begotten premise that was the original sin. He also grew disenchanted with the manipulation of Western ideologies which maintained a choke hold on the continent. Yes there was independence, but as far as this was done within the Western vision, if that was not possible a friendly oppressor of his people, each time there was the overlooking of the aspirations of the people.

The elite were pregnant with ideas of Western progress. They imbibed what was passed on to them by the global loan shark, and other such organizations and represented this same very rich, very powerful few, resplendent with native informants, educated in their ways, walking around with sanitary napkins over there brains as if to sanitize themselves from all home-grown ideas, thus inoculating them from the everyday reality of the pestilence they sanctioned and helped create.

He questioned every one of his Marxist leanings because the Soviets decided in the last minute to abandon Somal and move shop to Ethiopia. The collective arms from both superpowers was what created a proxy war between the Russians and Americans for control of the horn of Africa. This entire region was flooded with weapons and neither party cared what nefarious reactionary was the recipient of the weapons that killed a great deal of innocents, each fighting the other on behalf of this or that slogan of nationalistic jingoism.

Beheyeah was completely at a loss – at the brink of a nervous breakdown that might not be reversible. His entire life was put on the coroner's post-mortem table. Everything he had believed and adhered to lost meaning, and he had no answers that were ready and near. All he could think about was his arrogance based on what he read and knew. He had thought he knew what his people needed most, and that was enlightenment from the West, but, in doing so, he disregarded the other invention that came along with this, weapons and the history of this gentile soul, underbelly of avarice and greed, always synonymous with the brutal savagery of wanton death and destruction.

He could not sleep and stayed at the local bars in Addis drinking himself to a stupor over the turn of events. His family was secure in the U.K. where he had gone to the Royal Academy. A man of ideas, he had suddenly become a victim to them. He took it very hard that what he believed was not what was around him in the world, real politic, and his finer points of thinking failed miserably in the wake of the African reality. He could not see how to move on from here. The hyenas he saw around did not think past their names and by extension their own interests.

He was sick of this arrogant self import – how they never thought for a moment of the harsh consequence of their overriding greed of ambition. The most dangerous and innocuously insidious thing was that they were chosen by virtue of their education in the Western sense. But this hardly made for a path out of the deep morass of ignorance, because their training or certification created a supposedly finite wisdom of things ingrained in other ways of doing things. Somehow Beheyeah knew that although he was not one of these self-enchanted types, he still saw himself as a beacon for ideas hashed out in the West, ideas not transposable past differences of culture and outlook.

This realization was brought home to him again and again throughout his interactions with the so-called group of elites during the struggle to free Somal. This group continually baited and believed in the folly of the clan as a worthwhile pursuit, never able to transcend their selfish inclinations nor through education come up with an ideal based on their own terrain. And they were only further compromised when it came to outside forces. They were merely interested in being at the head of the table and that was the means to the end, what leadership was obligated with was not a concern, but rather a non-issue. The people were obligated to the leader.

The General grew disillusioned with what he knew of life and his outlook, and drinking became more and more his companion of misery. He had cast away at a very young age everything that was not modern or progressive, believing advancement and wisdom came from the texts and teachers who had reached great leaps in advancement in the West. He cast away his heritage when he had seen no movement there in relation to the advancement he witnessed in the West.

In a benign way, he wanted to replicate the good fortune of man elsewhere and bring it to him, to the Somal nomad. This is why he cast away his heritage for a better one. Now sitting on a bar stool in Addis Ababa imbibing in one of his advancements of leisure time, he was a witness to the passage of his personal history in contrast to the last tumultuous years of rapine bloodbath in which both the nomads and the Ethiopian peasants had caught the brunt of the unloading of massive weapons in this region.

He was here and was busy trying to win a war for Somal over their brethren across the border. Now he wondered what for? Why did this apparent center of enlightenment give this kind of power to such reactionary strongmen? The answer was that they were not enlightened, but brutal, self-centered savages worse then the average nomadic council. He was haunted by what he had believed in with every atom of his soul.

He was dumbfounded that it was not so. The ideal was possible and the better world might yet come, but it would come not from borrowing whole things from interested parties, but from a self that is paramount in focus when consideration of societies are at stake. What is yours will always be yours, but others can borrow from it, partake of its merit. Nothing can come from another terrain without specifics for the local work.

Beheyeah's despair came from the realization that he had started a futile attempt in the larger context of history. He knew the State was more organized, and the citizens were still under the delusion that the Government was not clan-centered, which made for an ad hoc unity of Somals under the State as one force in the military and in the arena of public sentiment. The major cities were confined to blissful peace, and no one was under the impression that in the affected areas in the Hinterland the government was engaged in a full-scale war with its civilians.

Add to this the continued support of the Western World, and the lives being lost began to increasingly appear in Beheyeah's head. He was broken by the remorse of a mortal's discovery that the arrogance of always knowing and prescribing was deep in the folly of arrogance. He spent his days wallowing in booze, and he went back to smoking, a habit he had left a long time ago. His inability to rationalize his past ideals when confronted with the reality facing him and everything he ascribed to in the form of ideas and ideals washed away to the wayside while he drank.

Beheyeah was coming closer each day to spending most of his waking hours either on his way to getting smashed or smashed. He could not face himself. Sometimes he thought of himself as a criminal for so choosing open hostilities against a very powerful foe. The end result is more death to save your own initially, then the others.

He also knew that his fate was right next to Hoagsaday's, had he not taken the escape route. At least this he had some answer for.

He slowly, through his drinking, left the hot seat of battle, and kept away from all who would be surprised at the General's current, unkempt disposition. He had forgone the etiquette of concealing his habit of drinking alcohol. The Somal being a majority

Muslim thought the worst of this habit, and thought even worse of those who had the need to consume it. But because Beheyeah was undergoing literally a nervous breakdown from the effect of losing what his soul believed and lived for, these considerations were not important to him in the least. The only thing he did was sleep and wake up to do the same.

He hardly said anything to anyone. Whenever someone or the other came to get him for his liberation functions, he just roared at them to leave him alone. He would only commiserate in silence with the bar tender, who knew to keep his drinks going, and to keep him away from others who would disturb him. He was a man who finally had come to suspect everything he had done in the past, and he was surrounded by the futility of his life. This went on for months, until he had successfully made it clear he wanted no part of the liberation, nor anything else for that matter.

His wife and children were summoned by a concerned relative. Somehow he caught wind of it and disappeared overnight, to a remote area away from the city. He caught a bus in the dawn rush and found himself a place in Jijiga, a town which was ethnically inhabited by Somal in Ethiopia. He got off, found a hotel, and spent the night in the midst of a lot of travelers. The rooms were divided by two to three beds, and he decided to find and rent one for two people by himself. He had some funds, but they were sure to run out.

He just wanted to be away from himself, but this could not be accomplished by running away from his family and the city. It was his past he could not deal with, and his search for a replacement for his soul had led him here, away from the awakenings of his past.

His was woken up early by the crow of the cock, somewhere very close it seemed by the way it rang in his ear. His eardrums went through a further explosion of raw sound coming from the enclosed courtyard of the hotel where the adhan called all the faithful to the dawn prayer.

The sound of the adhan disturbed the General's sleep. He tossed over still dizzy drunk from what was a turning into a extended binge, covering months. There was something in the adhan that harkened him to his childhood, family, and how he was raised, steeped in the ways of the Somal.

He disregarded this call to youthful memories his mind was inviting him to. He was determined to keep this part of him as inactive as possible. He didn't want to revisit anything – not now, not ever. He wanted the heavy sleep induced by drinking to come and chase the demons that possessed him from his past, away with silent sleep, all in

the hope of pushing further from him the eventuality of them coming back with a vengeance during the waking hours.

He managed sleep and decided to go out to find a place to drink.
He took a shower and had breakfast at the now buzzing hotel. There
was the din of a large space with high concrete walls and very small
windows. The din grated on his fragile nerves. There were men sitting and drinking tea and eating breakfast, talking. Most were wearing the colorful ma'wiss shirts shawls, and some with Kashmir shawls
draped over their shoulders. He sat down, ordered, and kept to himself by looking only at the plate before him. He had ordered liver
cooked with ghee and marinated with tomatoes and hot green pep-
pers with sweet tea mixed with goat milk.

He hoped no one from this group of people either knew him or
wanted to engage him in endless banter about who he was and where
was he headed. He wanted to be apart from many such intrusive questions, but he knew this would happen at one point. He was just not in
the mood at the moment. He wanted to be left alone.

This was what he wanted – something a bit much to ask his com-
patriots, who considered it their given right to know everything
about everyone they might encounter within eyesight. It was not
considered rude, but just the opposite to inquire about one's well-
being and so on.

Beheyeah paid and headed out of the hotel into the street, and,
taking note of its location, tried to get as far as possible from where
the hotel was. He did not want to be seen drinking, here it seemed to
matter to him more. In Addis Ababa, one could get lost in the crowd
of Ethiopians, but here the crowd was Somal.

He finally ended up far off with the aid of a cab he caught from the
hotel. He got off and started his ritual misery. He asked the cab driver
how to get back and then commenced his silent drinking. The bar
was less crowded than the city bar he liked to go to, but he found the
quiet enthralling. Away from the Somal, he was happy for a second
then went back to his brooding, trying to fill the vacuum in his soul
with booze.

He neither forgot nor remembered. He was always in between
when he drank, but he steered clear of solutions for anything. He did

not have any for himself let alone for anyone else, and drank on till he could not anymore. He asked for a cab and went straight to his room on arrival. He kept the door shut until the next day when he was awoken again by the same sequence of raw noise, one from the cock, the other from the miked adhan caller.

After the latter, he was not able to return to his comatose sleep. He laid awake in bed changing positions restlessly until he was tired from both the recurring demons of his past that haunted him every waking minute, and the buzz of activity just outside his room. Behind the door was the courtyard where some of the residents were sitting drinking tea or coffee. Some of them continued their worship in their silent reading of the Koran while others were already starting their morning banter. It was too early for the General to go anywhere. He waited for an opportunity a bit later when he would brave the seated crowd and enter one of the bathing cubicles at the end of the courtyard.

He had asked the manager to heat his water every morning to be ready for his shower at 8am. He would then take the bucket to the bathing cubicle and draw warm water from it, mixing it with cold water. He put on his ma'wiss and went to the shower with a towel over his muscular shoulders and chest, another reminder of his former regiment of rigor. He was light-headed from his more recent regimen of alcohol, and to that added a short circuited temperament. He caught himself frowning at everyone and no one in particular. While everyone of the faithful he passed greeted him with the customary acknowledgement of 'How did your day break?' he would just grunt and move on.

This routine hardly changed for a while. He neither contacted his family nor anyone else. He had lost himself and with that a host of other things his former self did. He developed a stand-off with anything from his past, and this included his wife and children. In the moments he gained some reprieve from the demons that consumed his being, he would be afraid to think of anything. He tried very hard to keep himself blank. He was tired of the remorse. He was tired of losing himself, and he was tired of living in this condition of running from himself with the help of booze to sedate his painful existence.

He knew the vacuum had to be filled, but how that was to be done was not in his sight, growing further, and further away into the distant horizon perhaps never to be achieved. This scared him sometimes even more than the demons that tormented his soul. He wished for an out from some remote corner of his brain. He continued his daily bar ritual returning to the hotel always late to avoid the people at the restaurant.

He was sure, as Somal were known to be, that they were already quite curious about him, not having been with them for a month. His saving grace was his gruff behavior during the mornings in the courtyard. The worst time was when he was woken up by the crowing rooster and the adhan way before daybreak.

In Addis, no one could find Beheyeah. Hassan, his nephew, went to see his wife and told her the problem when she arrived from the U.K. He said that he was probably around but had gone underground for some reason or the other. No one told her that prior to this the General had taken to doing nothing but drinking.

He did not want to increase her worry, but assured her to go back, and that he would send word as soon as he got it. He also emphasized that he was not captured by the region from anywhere in Ethiopia. Hassan was very convincing and she took her flight back a little reassured from great panic. She was also none the wiser when it came to the drinking part. She had no idea how much her powerful husband had changed for the worst.

Hassan together with a few of his clan men were left with the task of playing the middle men between the larger clan outside, and the ones fighting using sneak attacks as the number one and only strategy. Hassan solicited everyone abroad for the upkeep. He had become the new official in charge, and he was breathing fire from the naked persecution he felt. He went from city boy with no clan friends just friends, to someone who lived and breathed the politics of clan.

He was not going to allow this clan masquerading as a Government to continue their focused persecution of his clan right after the Hoagsaday debacle. His business skills came in very handy. He turned all the money into bigger money as he distributed what he could to the militias in the stretched out position sprawled between Ethiopia and Somal. He could not have imagined this life prior to the day everything had changed for him. He lost contact with all he knew when he crossed that border – his beautiful wife, his righteous father. The laughter with friends from all over Somal he had known all of his life.

He was a natural when it came to things that had to do with money, and he represented the General in his absence and found that he could get things done better this way, getting his stamp on every idea that he came up with. He could somewhat understand what had so frustrated the General, the many interests within interests of the large sub-clans, always changing constantly with the latest arrival of one of the former champions of the now abhorred state.

Hassan got a very close look at the type of individual that formed the so-called brain trust of the Somal. This group had been used by the colonialists to circumvent the natural hierarchy of leadership. Leaders were originally cultivated with the qualities that the Somal revered most – just in deeds personal and public, self-sacrificing in the face of religion and his fellow man, and with a deep, hands-on understanding of those he led in deed.

None of these qualities were required from this new group of leaders. All they had to do was be anointed from the self-sacrifice of passing standard exams which moved them on to the ranks of the colonial administrators. Others had the fortune of getting a first degree from the West. These you could still count on your fingers. This was the genesis of the brain trust now assembled without Government or colonial sanction for the first time.

Hassan, because of his dealing with both the militias on a regular basis and their leaders, quickly understood that there was a great deal of blind faith in the brain trust by the nomads. This was cultivated by the elite under various kinds of subterfuge. The trump card was life no longer involved the savior fair of the Hinterland.

Even if you had had no encounters with modernity to make you a post-camel man, there was an ironically cultivated open ridicule towards the people and their traditional intelligence transmuted through the centuries. Having experienced the power of Western weapons and their administration through this heavy-handed persuasion, the pastoralists believed, through the inculcation of time, in the power of those the West had chosen because they could read the West's magical text.

And so, these differences and the power of large capital finance, helped create this concept of the superiority of these few. As the white colonialist ruled from his outposts at centers of the nations it had empowered, so too, did his creations. They were those who replaced them, and were the only ones deemed equipped and ready to take over by them. As much as a colonial can accept the idea of a native being ever ready to govern.

The first generations of this group did indeed believe in the process of self-determination and worked diligently towards the Western ideal of progress, taking seriously the mandate to their brethren in the same way as a burden for a progress that was truly obsolete in the scheme of things. They had a lot of integrity, and respected their old forms of egalitarians relation, and were also steeped in the ways of their fathers.

These comprised the majority of the intelligentsia until they were steeped with new appointees of a very ruthless kind. There was never a thought at self-criticism except to gain more in the material sense;they bent whatever came with their positions for their personal use.

TWENTY FOUR

The Abyss

· ·

BEHEYEAH WAS WOKEN UP EARLY AT DAWN BY THE USUAL suspects. He had gone further and further into an abyss of nothingness. He was out of the real world and not happy in the ruminations of this new fogged one he had no idea of. The mysteriousness of the depths of uncertainty awaited him each passing minute that turned to hours then days.

He was fighting the unknown with a great deal of drink. This was the best he could do, he thought to him himself, subconsciously wanting to be with the brutalized dead he felt responsible for. He took to longer and longer stints at the bar in silent mourning over his lost self.

He got up the next morning and went on his way out into the courtyard in a huff to the cubicle. The people seated in the courtyard were engaged in their after dawn prayers, dua'as (present term earlier), asking Allah for forgiveness, some by reading in passages from the Koran in low-tone rhythmic hums, other transfixed in deep worship, reciting their gratitude as they moved the tisbah beads in a quick rapid motion forward to the already counted and said beads on the string.

Their faces were religious, in shining radiance, and exuded bright and crisp cleanliness for their nearness of worship and the multiple cleaning rituals a day. This picture of spirituality for some reason struck Beheyeah with a mercy that entered his soul and filled him with an almost weeping desire of joy. It brought him back to his early life in a vivid dream sequence as he sat back on his bed in the secluded room, as if he had just crossed the courtyard for the first time.

He forgot to dry himself, just sitting and thinking of his father and mother and where and how he had grown up in a outpost city at the crossroads between his tradition of pastoralism, and the culture of the now-embedded white man from across the great seas. He remembered his early teachings in the Madrasah, where he was taught the wisdom of his forbearers.

They learned Ma'alim. The Koran and its related subjects were taught in a stern way, but there was always a smile from the infective emotion released by the triumph of a pupil over a particularly difficult surah. This was his first introduction to the written word.

He suddenly was overwhelmed by an image of his grandfather, a man of great wisdom, a man who lived long enough to be part of almost a century of Somal history, a man lucid in old age with a memory so vivid and eloquent in narrative, that he always had Somals captivated in the suspense of his extraordinary life story, told in a way that was sometimes unbelievably fantastic.

One of these events came quite vividly to him as if his grandfather was at his bedside in the hotel with him. Beheyeah had returned to the scene of his childhood, sitting one evening in the enclosure of his grandfather's great yard. There were great men of the town lingering a little before the dusk prayer of Maghrib. This is where his grandfather, Sheikh Qassim al Muhajir, held court and disseminated to the faithful religious wisdom along with hagiographies of the Prophet Mohammed's companions, well-known scholars, and the great men and women of Islam in history.

In his daydream, his grandfather articulated a low, firm voice as the vision of his childhood unfolded – the structure of the mosque at the home, the men in attendance, their names, who they were and how they were known to Beheyeah.

His grandfather had started these evenings when Beheyeah was a young boy. In between his scholarship he had been sent to the thriving port of Berbera after several decades of an agreement with the

Gaal. Berbera was then was under the administration of the British who had earlier taken the port from the Egyptians who had administered the city briefly and were now taking over from the traditional Somal ruler, one who had been the indigenous ruler of the area for centuries. It was in this ancient town, at the time when his grandfather had gone to take care of family business on behalf of his father, that he had a chance encounter that was life altering.

Berbera served as a merchant center for centuries catering to Somal sea-faring trade on the famous Islamic dhows and navigation systems, plying all the popular routes in that day all the way to China. The ancient Egyptians called this part of the world the land of the Gods, "Land of Punt," and it was here on this coast that Hatshepsut the mighty queen came with her state of the art armada.

The port town of Berbera had a diverse population from all over, as was indicated by the names given to some neighborhoods. One was called the Jewish quarter, the other was the Indian one. And there was of course the Yemeni one too.

Sheikh Qassim al-Muhajir, a youth of medium stature with very bright eyes and a voice of an amazing soothing timbre just between the very low contralto bass of a tenor voice. The timbre was shocking for his size and was a genetic trait inherited from his forbearers; his father had an even more captivating voice. His complexion was a golden brown and he had wispy, darkish-brown hair which he wore in the style of the scholars, hidden in a wrap except for the long curly bangs that flowed on top of his shoulders.

The city of Berbera was a modern outpost compared to the all Somal little settlement that the young Sheikh Qassim had come from. The British were strategically here to guard the sea routes to their imperial jewel in the crown Indian, and they had a military garrison on the adjacent side of the Red Sea in Aden, Yemen. They stationed mainly Indians soldiers who required rations of fresh meat, which the pastoralists had plenty off, and this port city became, after a decade or two before the turn of the twentieth century, one of the premier ports of its time.

Sheikh was a lad who was, at the time, home from the ancient walled city of Harar, an ancient center of scholarship in Somal, where he attended to his scholarly endeavors under the tutelage of many prominent Somal men and also of men of other nationalities who had journeyed there in search of Harar's prominent men of letters. The city was known throughout the Islamic world as an ancient center that produced excellence. Qassim al – Muhajir was sent there, as his father had been sent there before him, to seek knowledge.

Qassim was not a neophyte to the ways of the city – the dazzling items from far away spots on the globe. It was a far cry from his usual solemn solitude in deep contemplation where nobody spoke in a loud-self conceited tone. Even the Alims who were well-known throughout the world were the most humble in mannerism. They exuded what an individual could attain in terms of the simplicity of the modesty of great knowledge and patience.

After a few errands in the souq, attending to the exchange of live-stock for their sprawling wealth in the Hinterland – their small and larger settlements – Qassim lingered on after the asr prayer in the late afternoon during the sun's descent in the furiously and exceptionally hot weather of this Red Sea Port.

As the oppressive heat went on through the night and became a little cooler in the wee hours of the morning, just before dawn prayer, the people took to doing a lot. Sheikh Qassim had heard from people in Harar that there had recently landed from a long sojourn at Berbera a Somal scholar. He tried to seek out the man after getting information on him from acquaintances who lived in Berbera, and he was guided to a non-descript mosque with a little congregation on the outskirts of the main city.

He hastened there after his work was done for the day to see and hear this Sheikh who had caught the eyes of some discerning students whose opinion Qassim greatly valued. After the prayer and the dua'as were made by the small congregation, a man of strik-ing appearance stood tall in the front. He was of dark, vibrant, shin-ning skin sparkling with its smooth dark tone of color. He had large observant eyes that seemed to take everyone in their sweep.

He had a well-shaped countenance – sharp, aquiline, and round at the ends – with lush lips and long, thick, curly hair grazing his powerful shoulder blades. He wore an immaculate white thobe at the bottom of which was a trace of the silk ma'wiss' purple borderline that came to almost the top of his feet. He wore an embroidered black vest from South Asia, popular attire for the Sheikhs in this era, and his coarse, curly beard was long, full, and groomed meticulously. His appearance arrested your attention before he opened his mouth. There was a fire aglow in the depths of his large, brown eyes.

He started by greeting the gathering, "Asalamu alaykum."

He addressed the group. They promptly answered in the standard, "And may peace be onto you, too."

"My brothers in Islam," he said, "I greet you today from the multitudes of your Muslim brethren in Arabia, Sudan, and Kenya. I had left this my homeland for many years in search of knowledge, as it is required in the religious path of our great prophet of which he said, 'One must seek knowledge even if it is as far away as China.' When I returned I found my beloved city of Berbera, as other places under the control of the infidel.

A few days ago, I met some orphans in the city under no one's particular care at the time. I asked them who they were, to which they replied, 'We are in John!' I was shocked that they had chosen to adopt the padre name as their lineage. The shock of this is still with me. I wonder how we have allowed our children to be adopted by strangers with even stranger ways. This, my brethren, is just the start of more things to come, because of our weakened personal faith.

Our sheikhs in this city have chosen to rely more and more on this stranger, and even help them collect money from the Somal to help this Gaal further change us in our very old and sacred ways.

The whole Muslim world is going through a period of weakness brought on by our very own sheikhs who have worshiped the Gaal and the worldly inducements to him. For this our children will have to pay, like the orphans, and the many more who will follow their misguided religion.

I have wanted to say this to you today: I am here to lead the return to the right path of pious Islam and to dismantle the collaborator sheikhs who are full with the treacherous ruin of the devil. Join me my brethren in Islam in ridding our land and people of a foreigner who wants to make us slaves to him and to his religion.

With that, there were shouts of "Allahu Akbar, God is Great. Allahu Akbar, God is Good," and the Prayer for the Maghrib prayer was now called. The exhortation from the fiery Sheikh was very different from the scholars Qassim had heard speaking at such gatherings during customary Friday sermons. This Sheikh did not skirt about the issue most of the rest were inclined not to say anything about, in particular about the collusion of the older Sheikhs who, it was true, were very much part of the new order, with their new monthly stipends from the British, and post-Islamic judges in the Sharia Courts which ran slightly lower than the District Commissioner's court.

Most of Qassim's group was much aware of the once powerful Islamic Ottoman Empire falling bit by bit until there was hardly any of it left to speak off. The younger man was convinced that something would have to be done for the Somals to continue their God-given right to practice their religion without the supervision of the British and their appointed lackeys.

The Sheikh was soon reported to the British administrator of Berbera. Qassim decided very quickly that he would follow this great Sheikh onto the calling to liberate Somal from the vice-like tentacles of the Gaal.

Without a word, the Sheikh, who came from a small sub clan which had not been the traditional ruler of the much larger clan collective, settled in the Hinterland with his mother's powerful clan who allowed him, as a man of God, a free hand. At first, he was appreciated by the colonial administration for curbing banditry in the area, but soon his band become a subject of great consternation to the British, the Ethiopians, the French and a large cross section of clans who considered him an infidel for going against his leadership, and joining forces with the Gaal.

Beheyeah was pulled away from the daydream by a loud conversation outside in the courtyard. He left the vivid daydream to find himself sitting at the old mosque.

He went outside for breakfast and came back to his room rather than heading out to the bar as usual. Something in the daydream kindled some of the spirituality of his formations. He just sat in his room feeling some relief after the daydream from the usual torment in the waking hours. The demons today were nowhere to be seen.

Beheyeah knew this was a sign from his grandfather to return to the ways of his forbearers, something he had shunned with Western education as retrogressive. He felt his insides welling with a spiritual calmness he could not explain to himself. It was as if his grandfather had come from the other side to help him out of the his doldrums.

TWENTY FIVE

Marital Bliss

THE SUN FILTERED INTO THE ADOBE HUT WHERE TUSMO was resigned, announcing the day had broken. The girls' faces seemed so happy with an almost suggestive smile though they were dead to the world in deep sleep. Tusmo remained quiet in pondering as she contemplated the journey forward. She was momentarily safe from the immediate hands of the Somal government, having now crossed into another country. She had both some requited joy in getting out of the madness in her own country, but, at the same time, she knew little or nothing of this land she had fled to. She awaited for the day to fully break for her to know what had been surely organized by the Driver's contact who was now hosting her.

She could hear a women's voice and an elderly man engaged in a conversation she could not make out. She got up, leaving the girls to rest, and ventured outside to see if she could help make breakfast for the girls. She stepped out of the narrow, dark passage of the large house built in the style of a hut, making it outside to where the voices were drifting into the room. She stepped out of the front door of the house, which seemed to be in a slight depression lower than the courtyard. The voices came from underneath a large tree, under which the woman and man who welcomed her last night were seated under the large branches that covered and shadowed a great deal of this courtyard.

She approached the woman who was facing the door of the house. The man had his back to her, as she approached. He turned to look at the approaching person behind him as her feet rustled the large dry leaves on the ground, which cracked under her weight. She was straining to find her bearings, she had no idea of her surroundings.

She had not been able to discern much during her very brisk walk in the moonlight in the night. She could see the silver light of the moon shine over the scattered bushes and trees in the open spaces, as well as the silhouettes of the dark mirages of the night, moonlit images of the enclosures that did not quite enclose the compound from the passing public eye. The women greeted her as she sneaked glimpses of the lay of this village from the inside of the house. It was close to other such houses, which seemed to all look alike: mud exterior, thatched roof and some with corrugated iron roofs, most mud brown with wooden doors and large wooden shutters that opened out into the courtyard.

From the back, Tusmo could see the dry, dull, white-grey color of the earth. Firm with a sheen from a firestone underlayer, the topsoil made the dull white sparkle from the metallic rock fragments aplenty. She returned the greetings from the lady of the house who was sitting on a short goatskin stool of a good height to work on an open hearth with the pots all placed on the large stones.

The man smiled and asked the woman to pour some tea. She seemed very busy, already sweating from work, although the spot under the tree she had chosen for her open fire was much cooler especially in the morning hours than the rest of her enclosed compound or inside the house.

She managed to quickly pour some sweet tea, then she placed a crepe type breakfast sprinkled it with sugar, and gave it to Tusmo who was now seated on one of the stools near the man and woman in their open-air kitchen. She continued to look around the house which seemed to be built at the end of a cluster of similar houses and compounds that ran in a sort of encampment on a slightly elevated part of landscape.

From the compound, she could see little foot paths marking the separation from the others with short, mostly shrub-fenced doors, and a wooden door joining the circle of the fence. The doors were hardly suited for their purpose of outside cording because they dangled on their wooden frames without the support needed for the door to actually work as a barrier.

Tusmo tried to be very polite and respectful to the elderly couple, who seemed not to have any grown children or otherwise anywhere near, unless they were still sleeping indoors. She made small talk. The usual was asked – "Where are you from? Who is the father of the children?" – even though Tusmo knew that the driver had told them everything about her.

She still wanted to know, just to pass the time, whether the old man was going somewhere, because he kept telling his wife to hurry. He had to go into the main part of this settlement for something or the other. Right then, he left after a few forced, loud sounding attempts to drink the blazing sweet tea. He gave that up and disappeared through the flimsy leaning door, and went into the clustered maze of endless fences.

Tusmo sat quietly observing the old lady who had now stopped her earnest frowning into the work of the fire. She poured herself a blazing cup of sweetened tea, and some of the sugary crepe with the butter on top. She still was nonplused about the guest who was eating and drinking her coffee in silence. It was as if Tusmo was not there. She looked bedazzled by the blazing cup of tea, by the way she clasped the hot drink with both hands, bringing the glass to her lips, sucking up the very hot tea until her lips vibrated in a slurping buzz sound.

Tusmo did not understand this silent treatment or the old lady's dazed preoccupation with the tea and the glass. After making the full vibrating sound of the woman's lips cheating the hot liquid from burning the insides of her mouth and throat, she placed the glass now that it had cooled a little. She then placed the cup, still very hot, on her temples and closed her eyes in a transcendental moment, and then went back to sipping her tea.

Tusmo was really surprised at this reception. The lady said nothing and did not give any sign of acknowledging Tusmo's presence beside her. She thought what a contrast from the silent but very hospital and caring Asha. They were about the same age, but Asha seemed to have aged a little better. Living on the border, she had been over this routine over a thousand times it seems. The travelers were invariably uncertain: they were like fish out of water. Still they had dreams of leaving for one reason or the other.

When she was younger, the old lady wrapped herself in the dreams of the travelers, and she cried with them during the uncertainty of their times. When they were stranded without money or goodwill from the drivers who expected to be paid for their transgressions against the law. They came through there and stayed, some even becoming de facto family because of the amount of time they stayed. They had attempted to make it to the modern city lights on their way out to great fortunes overseas.

Through all this, she had learned that most of them, as humans go, were prone to forget their family at the border that gave a lot of attention to their forward movement. She found it very hard at first never to receive any news, or "Salaams," from the city some of them had become prosperous in. She always heard from the drivers who came back and forth about such and such a person, but it was always news from those who saw them.

It was strange that these very humble and gentle souls on transit could be so un- callous when they got to where they were going. This is why the old lady became nonchalant with travelers, and made it a rule to be disdainful of any personal involvement with any of the transients.

The old lady cleared her throat and spoke to her, "My husband, as you could see, was in a hurry to leave. He wanted to see if there were any vehicles in town setting out of the capital eventually. I would like to warn you about this village. Let these huts not fool you. There is here, hidden in this place, not open to the public eye with the compound's flimsy wooden doors, enough crooks to rival any major city.

This is a border town and, as they go, it is the home of the deceptive carrion that feed off of the insecurity of the wayward and vulnerable traveler. The weaker and more gullible the traveler, the more satisfying the conquest. For years the people who came through like yourself were immediately caught right here in this compound the very same morning of the very same night they had come in."

"We suspected our neighbor," she pointed to a compound next door, winking at her, "but the border police kept coming long after the person we suspected had passed away. This town is one of a collection of transients themselves who exemplify all the horror stories you ever heard – and more – of border towns. Keep yourself and your girls indoors and as quiet as possible. My husband will be back later with some information on when you will leave. There are two ways to leave. One is by the truck you came here with, but experience has taught us that this method rarely gets anyone to Nairobi, unless the driver is a man of honor, a rare commodity on the open road, with so many check points between this border and Nairobi.

These checkpoints are manned by the greedy police the legal scavengers of humanity. To avoid all this but at the risk of injury at best and death at worst, the chat vehicles are fast and driven by maniacs at great speeds often turn into projectiles of greatest velocity as they hit the uneven and corrugation of the secret dirt paths to avoid the police completely, and many roll and kill all aboard. But this is also the way to avoid the hardship of returning to the beginning of your journey or to do jail-time. If you are apprehended, no one can get to you in between here and Nairobi. The only consolation of this mode of transportation is that the maniacs will take care of you if they avoid the common hazards of the trade, and will get you there very, very fast and, otherwise, safely from the authorities.

They will also let you ride in front with the girls. Rarely do they allow ladies with young children to go on the bare flatbed of the flying land cruiser. They might be crazy, but they are Somal men, and would feel shamedfaced if they let the girls and you ride in the back. They know there is no sitting whenever the truck is in motion – everything on it is also in perpetual motion."

Tusmo listened intently and thanked her host for such an honest narrative of the perils of the journey. She made up her mind to follow the no-frills lady's advice, and take the crazy men to the city of Nairobi. She finished her work and kept the girls as busy and quiet as possible. She quite daringly awaited the news upon the return of the old man of the house.

. . . .

It was in late in the afternoon before the old man returned from the heart of the settlement town. The no-frills lady had prepared a place under the big tree's shade, on which she first sprinkled cold water to subdue the rising of the light sand layer of the courtyard and also so to further cool the area that was already shaded from the sun. She laid out a long mat, placing pillows and cushions, raising it from the ground with the bedding. She then leaned some of the pillows against the giant trunk for the old man to lean on.

Then, she prepared the aromatic black sweetened tea that went with the occasion of chewing chat, and laid the hot liquid out, ahead of this ritual affair, along with a tray with a jug of water on it. She anticipated his return at the same time almost everyday. He was quite an unusual man, he preferred the company of his elderly wife, rather than the company of his male friends as was the standard practice.

For this the community considered him weak, and called him names behind his back. But in his own defense, he would say, her company was more stimulating than any of their repetitive stories about the same things over and over again, just like a broken record with no one around to stop it. After a while, being by himself under the tree, the old lady woke up from a brief siesta and joined him after a shower, filling her room with the aromatic, homemade musk she burnt on a small limestone urn and wallowed in, covering every inch of herself with the perfumed smoke.

Tusmo knew this ritual amongst women in the traditional style. She smiled at the old couple's behavior akin to that of a young married couple at the threshold of their amorous adventure as newlyweds. She waited in the room with the girls who were quite good given their confinement in the little room of the house. She hoped sooner or later she would be summoned or the old lady would come in and disclose whether the crazies had arrived, or whether there was a no show in town. And considering the danger of the trip with the crazies, she felt that escaping the authorities was well worth the very dangerous trip there.

She fell asleep as she watched over her sleeping young ones worried for them and their safety with the impending danger of such a treacherous ride non-stop at breakneck speed. She slept waiting for one of them to show up in the room, and kept straining her ears for the sound of a vehicle or some bits and pieces of the hummed distant tones coming in from the large window with the shutters open wide. She dozed off to the sounds from the two under the large tree.

She was woken up by the lady tapping her shoulders gently, "Wake up, Tusmo, wake up! The crazies are here. Make haste and get the girls and yourself to the bathroom. You never know when they will stop for you. It's speed and more speed until you get to your destination, which will be in the blink of an eye."

With this, she laughed and helped Tusmo to get the girls up and to the bathroom.

The lady and Tusmo went though the courtyard and passed the almost falling fake door, where the powerful headlights were glaringly blinding their advance to the vehicle. The engine of the Land Cruiser was on, underlying the atmosphere of haste the old lady had told her about. Through the blinding light of the headlights she could see some shadows of movement behind the oppressive glare of two eyes as she got closer and closer to the truck. This mingled with a tape deck playing a familiar Somal tune, and the sound of voices of men.

Tusmo thought to herself if this was meant to be quiet, how much the display of secrecy was actually working. She braved passed the light with the children in tow. When she got past the headlights and was about to pass, the driver called after her and directed her to get in the front seat. She got in with the girls, amidst an inside decorated by a lot of frills red and other rich-colored patterns on the dashboard, dangling with tassels extending from the bound steering, it was just a cacophony of color clash, carpet red, the material resembling corduroy.

There was a display of great affection for the truck, similar to that showered upon the Somal horse decorated and more suitable to this revered animal by the Somal. But in the times of the iron horse, the horse had to take a back seat to this new, even faster carrier of man. This esthetic was passed on to the land cruiser, it had taken if not the mystic and honor of the horse in the lore of the nomad, it was slowly making its mark on the body of new work coming out in this day.

The minute Tusmo was in the cabin, the vehicle raced off, into the brilliant night sky of Somal, the driver was a short man with the requisite paunch, close cropped hair, and an open shirt with a colorful low tank top. One side of his mouth was packed with chat creating a protrusion expanding one side of his face into a tense stretch that seemed to push the skin of his face on one side beyond its natural limits.

After a polite few words with Tusmo and a smile for the girls that created further havoc of his face, from then on he spoke to the men through the partition between the cabin and the canvas enclosing the flatbed of the truck. The men in the back sometimes had their faces right there at the partition.

The vehicle as promised was driven at a maddening speed. It jumped, flew, and pounced off and on the unpaved road a little more than a path. Tusmo thought she was prepared by the very descriptive rendering the old lady had given her, but she had never imagined such a sustained fear of eminent death. It was the girls' bedtime and the hot temperature of the cabin and the movement made the sleep very near the start of the dash to Nairobi.

She on the other hand could not do anything other than pray consistently for deliverance from almost certain death. She almost wondered what in the world had got her here to begin with, and for that matter what was she accomplishing by starring eminent death in the eye. She was aghast at how deftly the driver chewed the chat, smoked amongst other things, while he stirred this projectile fearlessly on, as if to egg it on, like he was stretching his face to the limits. The vehicle's fast and unsteady buoyancy was as if it was a ship caught in the powerful currents of the sea.

It seemed then the Lord had answered her prayers, giving her relief in the dozing off away from this dare devil driver.

She was woken up by her trembling body from the very cold air that now came from both the open partition and the driver's window.

She quickly checked on the girls and saw that they were moving their bodies seeking warmth from each other. She asked the driver to close the partition and his window slightly.

He said, "Sorry sister, the air keeps me alert. But underneath you are some blankets. Cover the young ones with it, and get one for your self."

The girls remained asleep, she, however, lingered for a while, and then went back to sleep. The next time she woke up she was in a maze of endless lights. She had never imagined such an expanse of lighting. The vehicle had now reached the city limits of this large city. They were now on at a reasonable speed, slowly plying through the well-lit city.

The driver was now showing signs of fatigue as he softly announced to her their arrival in Nairobi. She could tell she was in a very different setting. The landscape was greener than anything she had witnessed in a modern setting of skyscrapers and neon lights. The vehicle wound its way through the city, through the driver's deft hands, and finally came to a stop in a well-populated neighborhood that was awake with people moving along the streets.

She saw the large banana leaves used to wrap the chat with, dangling from all manner of stores. She knew she had arrived at the sprawling neighborhood of Eastleigh, a place known to Somals throughout the world, because it was comprised in the main of Somals as residents. The Land Cruiser came to a halt at a two-story building. It was now very early in the morning. Everyone Tusmo saw was wearing some form of protection from the cold, a sweater or a jacket.

He parked in front of the building away from the road, and commenced to sound the horn which sounded like a large orchestra rather than a regular honker. The doors of the building opened from the inside, and Tusmo could see a man fumbling with a great set of keys to open the steel bar doors after the regular wooden door he had already opened, exposing the passageway of the building. When he managed this, he came out with someone else in tow.

The driver told the man who had opened the door in his ma'wiss to make accommodations for Tusmo and her girls right away, stating,

"I will be back later after I finish my business. Find them something to eat. They've been traveling non-stop from the border. They are not used to this. Please take very good care of this lady and her young girls. I will see you later on."

The man, and the one in tow came around her side of the cabin, and helped her rouse the sleeping girls. Tusmo said there was no luggage, so they helped walk the half-asleep girls inside. As soon as they got through the door and into the narrow passage way of the building, the same man with the keys closed the doors behind them, first the iron, then the wooden one.

Tusmo tried to stop to wait for the man engaged with securing the building, when the other man motioned her from behind him to come along as he passed the end of the narrow enclosed passage way and disappeared. Momentarily, Tusmo cleared the narrow passage way, and entered a deceptively large courtyard in the shape of a rectangle. The man from behind passed into the courtyard and advanced ahead them. They followed him to another open frame of a door and proceeded to open a door from the many doors in this enclosed section of the large two-story building. He promptly touched with familiarity the wall, and the room was lit by a naked light bulb exposing two beds that were made with white sheets, each with a dark coarse woolen blanket.

The other man promptly removed the sheet halfway and helped the sleepy girls onto it. The earlier man said he would be right back with something to eat for the girls and her. Tusmo told him not to mind about the girls they were going to sleep anyway, just to bring her something with water. He told her he would send the food right over, and showed her the bathrooms located in the separate enclosure just outside the room, and the keys on the room's key-chain.

He also said there would be hot water early from daybreak onwards. With that, he took off after the other man who had already left. Tusmo was relieved she had finally made it so far without much incident other than a lot of heart wrenching worry and a continuous palpitating heart throughout the journey. She looked at the girls while they slept, glad she had embarked and braved the unknown, while at the same time solemn in her hindsight appraisal of what had transpired so far in their very young lives.

She did not know what would commence but she would strive to shield them as much and as far as possible away from such grim uncertainties. A knock at the door brought her out of thinking about her babies as they slept unaware of the stark gravity of the situation the entire family had been catapulted into.

She thanked Allah for her good fortune nonetheless, she opened the door, and took the tray of tea and sliced bread with jam and butter. She ate the food and looked forward to sleeping in a bed in a place where there was no movement, especially after that quick dash in what seemed to be rocket from the border.

TWENTY SIX

Marital Bliss

. . . .

HOAGSADAY, WITH QUITE A LOT OF DETERMINATION, LOOKED forward to the daybreaks, even though the others were not so enthused by the sheer amount of rugged work he had quite forgotten after leaving nomadic life in search of fortune. Now Hoagsaday had neither the fortune nor the youth of his previous nomadic wanderings. His fighting group consisted of five men who traveled on foot without the requisite livestock in tow. This made them quite conspicuous to the normal band of men in the mist of the herds they were driving.

Light and swift movement was the reason for such a small unit. They traveled quietly most of the time in the light of the moonlight. Always there was a young man who knew the land blindfolded, having spent many grazing years in the wilderness alone or with a small group. Usually, the man would had lived this life in these same local parts or in ones that were slightly removed.

The group carried only water and ammunition for their AK-47s, the pastoralist's weapon of choice. It did not jam up as much as others did from too much firing of the sand from this earth. They scavenged for food through nightly re-consonance missions, canvassing who was around in the dead of night. The land was not particularly built for stealth, but there were ways to hide in the ups and downs of the unevenness of the landscape, the lows and highs, along with the recurring similarity of the trees and the mix of their colors. The trips for food would also give them the formations of any groups of soldiers or larger formations nearby.

At first, most of the lone family settlements were only obligated by close clan ties, and generally it was shameful to not feed the travelers and strangers in your midst. The men survived on barely nothing but water and a little milk from this encampment of the other, always moving, for in movement there was safety in this open expanse. They stirred clear from the military strongholds that had a lot of personnel. They also tried to keep as injury-free as possible under the circumstances. They had each other for company and protection from this world of hostilities.

During the day, they would look for a place away from visibility, make a hasty fire for a meal, on good days of meat, and also, on most days, of tea. They were always on the alert for surprise encounters of any kind. Encounters which could result in death, for most of the camel herders who were also armed with Ak-47s. They never hesitated to protect themselves and theirs because they simply could not afford an alternative existence.

The government and its brutal actions caught the news wire like wild fire as nomads met each other along the way or through the paths of drinking. They were naturally born newshounds. They were aware to even the most minute details of disparate incidents far flung and near. There were still some areas that were slightly unaffected, but by in large the situation was getting wider and wider as the days continued. The soldiers were encouraged in their undisciplined behavior. The people settled anywhere, everyone in small towns to those in larger settled areas were slowly getting pulled into the skirmishes. All in all, the death and hardship of their clansmen was getting more and more acute in the Hinterland.

The situation was also getting worse in the State's administrative dealings with the public in this region. Land was confiscated, children went missing, elders were gunned down, sometimes only after inquiring after a prisoner's status in the State's custody, and by an arrogant soul consumed and overwhelmed by the power of his office, espousing the ruling clan's callousness.

Initially, Hoagsaday started out not venturing very far, staying away from the Somal side for a long time. Gradually, this changed. As he acquired more and more experience he ventured further and further into Somal, staying for long periods, engaging the soldiers of the land. He was always under the command of a veteran who, not unlike himself, was displaced from some life or other with very short notice. In this way, the Government lost more and more of those it would have otherwise duped into believing its clan-blind commitment to the progress of the nation.

Hoagsaday was developing into a fearless and patient soldier. After everything he had previously worked for or believed in was terminated, he went with these veteran commanders who were stern in their commands for survival reasons, but, at the same time, very patient, and took everything in stride from the lack of reasonable or rationale. They would, at the end of exhausting treks at a brisk pace, lie down without a meal.

Water was essential and most nomads were quite resistant to the thirst involved in this constant moving.

They would rest quietly in a corner without too much of a fuss when that day's cook was out of tea leaves. These were men who were forlorn like Hoagsaday from a great blow that was as devastating to their world as it was. Some of them had lived a much more opulent life then Hoagsaday's, but they were few and far between. The majority were the sons and brothers of those who had lost their kin, sometimes witnessing it themselves. The others might have escaped with their lives simply because they were not there.

They were, in the majority, nomads They were the ones that formed the small groups that continually went after the clan state. They were the young men there to avenge the murder of their brothers, sisters, mothers, etc, and who sometimes were irrationally blinded by this hate. But where is reason in this case, when the anointed protector becomes the violent aggressor?

A strong impregnable exterior. He took his commands with a

seriousness bordering passion. He, like the rest in this small group of four, was intense with the business of guerilla warfare. The man leading his unit of four was a little past forty, a former military man not hired for ranking, but who had seen a lot of action during the Ethiopian War. He knew the smell of death and the loss of a tight night. He had fostered a dependence during his time living alone against the elements, where an "us versus them" attitude made for survival of the entire group.

Hoagsaday was in the process of erasing any possible sign of their day encampment at this naturally lowered enclave where they had spent the just expired day of seclusion in. He poured sand over the fire and removed the surrounding human traces. They were told again and again how this could easily steer the enemy in the right direction after them, and so he took great care to conceal their stay there during the day before they broke camp completely.

Very soon after, the sun was completely sunk. The group leader wrapped himself with a bed sheet over his cotton shirt and leather gun-strap. His bullets and water container were all strapped on his waist, over his ma'wiss, inconspicuous from his camel herder brethren. They were all dressed similarly, heading deep into the Hinterland to confront a small detachment of soldiers who were reeking havoc as they pursued their type of band.

A group from their militia attacked a small military scouting mission of about fifteen and had left the others severely wounded or at the brink of death. The more these tit-for- tat skirmishes ensued, the more encompassing the violence was to all who lived around or were caught in the vicinity of the recent strife. They beat up, shot, or maimed the nomads. Hoagsaday's group was short of food and water. They were going to walk through the night to find a nomad's encampment, and, thereafter, for a place to refill their containers full of water.

The young man who led the journey forward pushed on with an unrelenting pace that was second nature to him. He did not feel he had to wait for anyone, whether they were or were not used to this harsh pace. At first, this was quite horrid for the city dwellers like Hoagsaday, but by and by Hoagsaday and the others became more and more acclimated to the fast pace that came naturally to the nomad, and Hoagsaday also learned the resolute endurance of the long tracks with the very little sustenance of water and food, broken by large meals occasionally when they were honored by the slaughter of a goat or lamb upon their secretive thought frequent encounters with friendly nomadic encampments.

Hoagsaday, through his determination, kept vigil not to be perceived as one who could not endure the hardships – at any price – to free himself and others of this tyranny. He had lost everything over nonsense. He did not think of the loss of his wealth much but of the disaster he had faced of one day having no choice but to abandon his wife and young daughters. No one should ever have to go through such a disastrous predicament, ever. The other commander kept his own counsel, as did Hoagsaday. No one knew the details of how he left his position, but they vaguely knew the circumstances.

The main mission for the moment was to gather intelligence and also to pinpoint the movements of some of the settlements that they had encountered. This would be all in the distant periphery, unless that is, the number either favored them or the element of surprise. This would give the very small unit a leg up over a slightly larger number.

TWENTY SEVEN

Stealth

· ·

ALI WAS KICKED OFF HIS DREAM WHEN THE MEN STOPPED for lunch on one of the side-road cafes. They ate quietly, while Ali continued to hide himself behind the dark Persols. He believed in the distant mysterious approach of a superior over a subordinate for obvious reasons. This kept them at bay and always on the back of their heels in a defensive posture. He thought clearly of the mission he was to assume. His number one goal was to get the nomad to hate their assumed liberators.

The several cities surrounding Beheyeah's region were slowly feeling the might of the Government in the way the Government did business, first in appointed regional military-turned-civilian governors who were sent to regions they did not hail from originally. This was not considered an issue when the State was popular. Rather it became unpopular when selected regions were repressed at one time or another and when, as in the case of Beheyeah and others, hostilities broke open to unseat the State. The governors and the people who represented the State in other capacities were slowly gaining a reputation as occupier clan henchmen.

This did not translate to the general public in the far-off, heavily-populated city. In the city, they did not see the Government as a clan or even their wrongful targeting of civilian, but rather saw the Government's actions as isolated responses to power-hungry clan members who wanted to take everyone back to the corrupt days of the previous clan's nepotistic regime of the immediate post-independence time. The Government assailed the clan system. Through its curricula now instituted in the Latin script, lead campaigns to even burn an effigy representing clan-based nepotism. So they did one thing while at the same time empowering the clan and larger clan of the Head of State.

So everyone conventionally continued the previous view of the Government. This they guarded assiduously in the control press, and gave token positions to the very same clan they were secretly at war with.

Ali came to this region. It was his too. His clan bordered Beheyeah's and they were practically the same in almost everything other then a different genealogical birth, which by the way, was most likely not even the case as Ali's clan was probably spawned by the clan of Beheyeah, or visa versa, due to, in particular, the original proximity of their clans.

The people settled in the larger settlements and in particular those in the city were, at first, not privy to the scale of military intervention in the Hinterland. But, as time progressed, they acknowledged more and more the military as the arm of the Head of State's clan and of his lackeys from the spectrum of clans in Somal. These were a group respected by their clan for their achievements within the hierarchy of the State, but they came to be regarded later as devious opportunist's collaborators, who in all reality forsook their brethren for personal gains. They were in part why the rest of Somal had a much slower and delayed understanding of the magnitude of the Head of State's belligerence, pitting one clan against the other. The presence of this group just confused the issue, which would have probably come to a head or maybe stopped at their heels had there been such a stark and open contrast of those who held power with those that did not.

This region as in other regions were feeling the pinch of the State's concentration of power in the capital. Anything you wanted had to be gotten from Mogadishu: passports, university degrees, all types of documentations from really petty ones, to the more important ones. People from these regions had to travel to the city, and if you were from a region that was particularly into playing ball, then even when you got there, you would spend a lifetime going through red tape, spending great amounts of money where others considered it their actual birth rite.

These were the conditions that Ali was getting into, he would work with the governor to counter the burgeoning resistance, he was here to assume this work, and help the governor with intelligence, directly to headquarters. In reality, he was the governor of the regions when it came to actual strategy that was then relayed back to the governor as instructions to him. The locals were already feeling the pinch of marginalization. Their goods were heavily taxed, and then those taxed were used in the capital where the powerful of the President's clan did as they pleased with it, in the name of this or that progressive idea.

The vehicle came closer to the destination of one of the major cities in the North, and Burao, was going to be Ali's base for operations in the Hinterland, with the support of the local Government and military contingents.

The man he was relieving had already been summoned to Headquarters, but this was the least of his concerns. He had done a bad job of keeping the public's opinion on the side of the State, against the collectives outside. He also did very poorly in terms of counter-intelligence to support the military operations in this area.

As a result, they were losing the battle from confrontations from being ill-equipped. Ali kept his briefings and information to himself, and he knew that he had to make some adjustments from the life of the city. He was here on a mission and as soon as he was able to get things going, he would be detailed back to the city. He would try in the meantime to continue his operations as a business broker between the State and those who would rob it, by providing cover.

So he was assured by his new position in this region to quickly get to know the goings on of the town, through the usual greedy in-betweens that would definitely show up in the scheme of things. But his first priority was to establish himself in this new region.

The vehicle came to a stop at a military barracks in the town, and they were led to their new quarters, until something else was arranged for Ali.

The next morning he was briefed by the second in command as to what the operations and the general intelligence reports had so far gathered from the Hinterland. This report detailed the groups and people who had been active in the so-called support of those opposed to the State. Ali had no particular mandate, so he could do as he saw fit. It seems now Ali saw things the way the State wanted him to see things.

Ali called in his two immediate underlings – a major and a captain – and summoned them into his office the very next day. They were both clan friendly, and eager to rise further in the management structure of things.

Ali cleared his throat, and started with his greeting, sitting behind the large sleek metal desk and the many telephones on top of it, arranged just beyond the blotter. The Administration staff had already brought the officers their sweetened tea. The two officers sat in large comfortable chairs facing their new commander, Ali Deray, and, from their vantage point, all they could see was Ali's standard dark shades, setting him off at a distance from a more intimate gaze.

Ali started the conversation with a greeting, "Good morning, gentlemen. I am the new head of regional security. As I am sure you have received circulars to this effect from Headquarters, I would like a briefing now on what is going on at this station, in particular the connections between the Hinterland, the city, and the rebel bases here. This is where we need to focus our intelligence."

"Please go ahead, Major."

"Thank you, Commander. Well, we have established a lot based on the military operations that have proceeded in the Hinterland. In this city, we have imbedded some noteworthy individuals, some who have been compromised in some way or other and others who are not particularly interested in anything other than their stomachs. We also have young officers in this region who believe in the State, and of course we have the common criminal intelligence – listening to conversations in public places of discussion. The really important strategy meetings happen inside clan deliberations, which we have not had too much access to. The captain will relate his side of events."

"Yes, Commander. I'm in charge of extracting information from captured individuals. I am also engaged in monitoring the day to day propaganda of the city. Planting things here and there to make sure there is always an alternative to the Hinterland news that gives the State an upper hand."

"Well, this region has become a hot spot for the Liberation Movement, from finance information to counter-intelligence information for Government troop movement to strategies."

"But who do we have working on their sympathizers inside our institutions?" Ali asked. "This I think will be a first step towards cutting some of the vital flow of information between the inside and the outside. We will be headed tomorrow towards the Hinterland villages and towns so I can see and hear for myself what is going on. Thank you, Major."

"Thank you, Captain. We set off tomorrow at dawn."

"Get some rest." With that, Ali stood up as the did the two who were now saluting him while they shook hands leaving their new Commander's office.

At dawn, a small retinue of vehicles left the sleeping town of Burao on their way to the Hinterland. Ali was alone in his car with the two young officers. There were frequent stops and quick assessments in little encounters, though the people were not particularly giving of themselves in many of the small villages.

Ali spoke to some, but kept aloof and, in the main, listened to the officials on the ground. The trip to him had one significance and that was to show the power and the powerful reach of the State everywhere in the Hinterland. This message was not lost on the local nomads, particularly those who had been caught in the State's brutal repression.

The trip covered quite a distance, and took several days. Ali never let up that he had known these areas as a young herdsman himself. They made stops according to the hour of their chat in the afternoon, only sometimes continuing on and chewing in the vehicle. Ali was silent, unlike his usual habit of talking a lot when he was at his spot in Mogadishu. Here, he had to maintain the distance between him and his subordinates, though it was not just him who cultivated this part. It seemed something the nomads cultivated, but was really not known in this egalitarian society.

They were usually welcomed with the slaughtering of a goat or a lamb with plenty of rice. This the elders or the prominent members of the clan did as a response to the expected hospitality accorded a stranger, borrowed from the culture of feeding the wayward stranger who might, by chance, happen upon a nomadic encampment. This was also the excuse for those in the encampment to eat meat, rarely slaughtered on a regular basis by the host. A stranger was a welcome interlude to the routine of having to be satiated by the drinking of camel milk. So in the villages, as in the big cities, this tradition was carried on.

Ali and his entourage returned after a week of visiting these Hinterland settlements. He then began the business of looking for a place to stay inside the city population so as to ascertain some of its daily moods and mood swings.

He made very little of his position and kept it under close wraps. He wanted to mingle as far as possible without getting the usual fear his work and organization commanded from the public, which was based on fear of this nefarious agency's reputation of being above the law.

He started his evenings after work with a solo chat session at his new residence.

Then, he would go to one of the restaurants, dressed inconspicuously as an ordinary elder would dress. He liked to sit in the more popular haunts the local elders gathered at, to sip the ritual sweetened tea while talking politics – local, clan and international – after the evening's BBC bulletin.

Ali's Somal was the same as everyone else's. Although he was a member of the ruling clan, he was part of the sub clan that the targeted pariah clan was in actuality a clan that could just as well be his. They grazed the same areas, culturally they had more affinity to their immediate neighbor clan, also a sub clan of the pariah clan, than his own clan who were of sometimes geographically distant both culturally based on associations and proximity of geography, and the subsequent genealogical linkages of maternal side blood on both sides of the sub clan. However, in this time as in the old time some of the most vehement violent behavior occurred between these two related groups.

Ali would sit at these nondescript tea shops and listen in on conversations, sometimes engaging and provoking new conversations. He knew eventually everyone would know him and his new position. As things were in Somal, people knew from others what was happening around them. But even then he would still have to function, and in the arrogance of State power he felt, as did many, that they could walk around with impunity, based on the fear of the Government's reprisals on behalf of their officials or another interpretation of avenging their own, a clan member.

At night, this is what occupied him — mixing with the public, developing some sort relations with the locals, and, during the day, listening to the reports from the Hinterland skirmishes — between this regions' clan militia and the military under clan command acting as a neutral force.

The Government was losing in the Hinterland through the many stealthy raids by these militias all the way from the bases across the border. He knew, as would anyone who had had grown up in the Hinterland, that this was the case, first, because the State's lack of knowledge of the areas they were engaged in, and, second, because the State had in reality no support whatsoever from the local populations. This is what Ali saw as lying at the core of the State's failure in their attempt to quell the puny gains by these disgruntled movements in the war of these regions.

He must, he thought, come up with a way to stop this form of growing support. He thought, then, the best way to stop the spread of this clan's behaviors towards the Government was to spread Government power to other regions which might not otherwise make any attempt to question the Government's integrity and which, if so, might not launch an insurrection like Beheyeah's or those of the other clan groups in Addis.

This is what occupied Ali Deray on a daily basis: how to draw a wedge between the clan-based militias and the members of their clan in the Hinterland. This was what he looked for. If there was something he could use to make them unpopular in the own back-yard, then he would have succeeded in isolating them. Ali knew that without the support of the of clan members as recruits or suppliers of food, or scouts, and information of the terrain and reconnaissance reports from the extensive network of information imparted by the ever roaming nomads to their brethren for future targets, the opposition would not last.

This is what had to go, and go quickly. In the city, his juniors kept tabs on the more prominent personalities, keeping a very close eye on local activities for any possible leads. He put the heat on this group first. He instinctively knew of their importance at the head of these clan-type agendas. He continued this ad hoc research and concluded other things from his research, as he had not spoken to anyone.

One evening, while sitting after the news bulletin had blared from the speakers of one of tea houses, Ali was befriended by a man not unlike himself, a small city sophisticate.

In another corner of Burao, a man named Jamal arouse early as was the custom of the small but old centers of settlements close to the Hinterland which were originally a stopping well for camel herds. Because of its permanent wells, the residents were the in- between. Most lived in the town but still had deep roots in the Hinterland, through second families or as part of the family still actively living the life of pastoralism.

The settlement was further developed by the colonials who cre-ated a paying position and chief for every clan in an effort to find some method to administrate to these egalitarian people who did not have natural reverence for a one-man leader but who tended toward the consensus of inclusion. This schema of leadership gained currency through colonial State violence, whenever these paid clan/colonial officials needed the backing of power to elicit absolute dominance over their clan members. This people who increasingly became dependent on colonial favors and monthly salaries, moved to Burao initially to both guard their positions from possible rivals, and also to get closer to the seat of Government in the town.

Some clans already had such a position but it was not config-ured in such a manner. In essence, the advent of positions such as village headman and clan brain were really given meat by the British colonial governments. The local akils, having lost the positions under the new system, were out and about in the city in search of Government inclusion hand-outs from officials.

Ali had received one of these types of solicitations and had entered a class created then abandoned by the new system's way of things. Some after all did manage to continue in some capacity or the other because, unlike the others of their Hinterland group, they had tasted and knew the privileges of governmental power versus those of a clan or an individual.

They knew the Government stood for an enormous wealth that, at any moment, could rain an immense wealth on you, if and only if, you knew how to work with the official whose signature on one such check could make you a completely different man, could make things shake and happen, the official whose wisdom could quickly surpass that of a revered local sage as much more illuminating and profound. This group collectively ran many of the things in the area Ali was in. They were, in outward appearance, impeccable paragons of men in their society.

Jama had a routine in the evening. He would sit with his cohorts, other entrepreneurs of the clan commodity, which met almost daily at these venues, and then broke off the next day only to meet again the following evening. Those in the group were of a shared outlook – 'What is there in it for me?' 'And if there is something, I will do practically anything for it' Frowning very hard on the morality or even the business ethics to a large extent, the end justified the means. Their concept of fellow humans, in particular their clan relatives, was heavily influenced by greed and greed alone.

They were pretty atheistic about what the religion of clan culture dictated in human relations and moral relations. Even though they somehow did believe in a religion and acted as pious, there was a total disregard to, in particular, the moral dictates stipulated. They stole and coveted everything from everyone for themselves. This included the recently orphaned or the destitute old.

Jama lived a little out of the main center of the town, and walked the distance in the morning with the throng of early birds on their way to town. There seemed to be a purposefulness to the brisk pace of their walk toward the center of shops and tea house restaurants. This is where people congregated in the very early morning.

This village of a town was dead by nine o'clock in the evening. Anyone who aspired towards a good reputation would not be caught dead in the act of roaming the city or chewing chat. The maxim was, as in many even larger towns, you did not dwell outside too much after night prayer, but, ideally, would be at home right after. After a long night, most of the residents were up very early, but ironically half of them did not have any particular business that started at this time, it seems they were all up fishing for something to come their way.

Jama went to his relatives' shop and sat outside under a the shade of a tree, listening half-heartedly to the on-going conversions in progress. Most of the men gathered outside this shop were his classmates. He knew some from childhood during the many roams they had together looking after their herds, though now they had all but abandoned that livelihood and were fishing for opportunity to know, for an encounter that would make the rest of their day plentiful.

In the form of money for a meal and the customary bundle of chat, this would manifest through some transaction related to something regarding the clan – either positive in the form of wedding bells, which entitled all males present to receive a small part of the advance of reserved money and closing the door to other would be suitors. Usually there was a dispute between two sub clans or members of the same clan and here there was always adjudication, each salivating the prospect of endless monies for an endless case, always extended beyond the memories of what the original dispute was. These adapted town nomads, like Jama, knew how to make things drag on, from many such experiences.

Jama looked into the door of the large warehouse to see what his clan chief, who was sporting his usual large khaki shirt with many large pockets and a small checkered scarf hanging on his shoulders, had forgotten there this morning. He was a well built man of medium height, large ears, all on a very small dome of a head. He had light-colored brown eyes and very closely cropped hair, left uncovered when he was in the heat of this enclosed warehouse, office, and shop. He was considered very good looking even at his very late years of past seventy.

He was still agile, busy, and full of zest for all matters involving the clan, the government, and commercial business. He was looking down at his desk at some numbers from the sale of imported pasta, an he had stacked them, almost filling an entire section reaching the rafters of the warehouse. He wore his rather large, thick reading glasses and was starring down while he occupied himself tremendously in very deliberate calculation both as a show to add to his mystique as a man who knew the magical workings of the pen, and to keep those who knew he was the chief at bay and always second guessing their entry into his shop to rouse this man who was clearly engaged in something very important.

This rouse did not work for long on the unusually brass nomads. He just peaked their curiosity. After all, he was still a man like themselves, and furthermore was their kin. He played this game with them day in and day out. He learned through the years they were not going anywhere, so they continued these theatrics on a daily bases, him in disdain of their camping out each morning in front of his store, them indifferent with a sense of entitlement to what belonged abstractly to the clan in his person and possessions.

Jama stood at the door for a minute to clear his throat and call out to chief using his title, "Akil, how did you sleep?"

He looked up because he knew Jama's voice. Had he been one of the other idlers he would have feigned hard of hearing.

"Every man and his circumstance," he replied to the greetings. "Jama, you are a bit late, but we must go to the Governor's office today. Remember we have been summoned to go there. You can accompany me there and we can talk on our way there."

He rose from his desk putting his glasses in his pocket, exposing his expensive ma'wiss that was fastened at the waste by a large, dark green ancient money belt. On one side there was a Somal dagger in a leather sheath attached to the belt that went under the folds to wrap the ma'wiss in place so as not to fall off.

He carried his large walking stick that also doubled as a weapon. The nomads were very good at using it in combat.

Jama was similarly attired although he was much younger. The Akil liked Jama because he never crossed him, and always knew certain things about town. In other words he was someone not unlike himself when he was younger.

He was a great talker and socialized well beyond his clan. He was more diverse in his relations, which extended to clan's residence in this town, and he made it his business to know everyone that mattered. This is one quality the chief liked because solution many of the inter-clan problems lay in the home of individuals, who could exacerbate them or tame them. The Akil treated this young man of promise as an understudy of sorts.

They ventured passed the clan congregants sitting outside in a flash before anyone one of them could waylay them. They both knew the routine. They would act as if very busy in conversation so as to ignore anyone who called them from the crowd. They simply did not look back as they moved passed them.

Anyone who had the gumption to follow would be told sternly to wait for the chief who 'would be back.' Even though the title did not confer any real power as it did in the past, the nomads now saw it as an inheritance of leadership that had come a long way, had been in the same family for several generations now. The new State, with its anti- clan posture, could not eradicate this position however hard they tried. They did, however, dilute it greatly. In some cases, a blind eye was turned.

They ventured towards the Government offices located on the other side of town, and made sure to walk on isolated paths so as to have a secret conversation as they walked. Jama and the Akil had many such conversations, more strategy sessions before they hit the officials in earnest.

They knew the Government was engaged in harsh reprisals in the Hinterland against their particular clan, and that was the reason for the venture today – to see the Governor. The Akil asked Jama, "What do you think they will present this morning to us?"

"Well, we both know there were skirmishes in the Hinterland

where as in the previous encounter the lazy, fat Government soldiers were caught with their pants down."

"This is not going to be a very pretty meeting for us and the other clan representatives. As usual, they are going to cast a very suspicious eye in their conviction that we are somehow the leaders of these militias, while we spend all our time here right under their noses. They are aware of who we meet and what we talk about. They ask me all the time what is going on in supposedly the private clan meetings that are illegal in their eyes. But when do we have such meetings? Anyway, the mood will be of great conviction from the Governor and his military and intelligence gathering personnel. They will lay the blame squarely on us for their recent embarrassment in the Hinterland."

"Yes, this I understand. But we must remain as deceptive as they will be of their intentions towards us and other clans. We are one and the same. We are caught between a rock and a hard place. The militias suspect us for our proximity to this bully power. This also renders us suspicious to them because we are members of their clans too. So, Jama, remember that what we still have that is unquestionable is the support of the clan. They do not question my sincerity period. They are very much behind me, but it will be quite difficult to maintain this position when the militia continues to antagonize the Government violently. This will always create a problem from both sides as they engage each other."

"And the losses are felt quite dearly by all of us."

"This State is going to create enormous problems for me, and others like me. I eventually will be the target of both these groups at war. I am a sitting duck in this village, and so are the rest of us whether we are prominent or not."

"Yes, very clear and precise. I have thought of the sheer desperado tactics of the militia which I cannot blame, but they really are determined to get us all embroiled in this war they are waging. The nomads are also sitting targets. It will be very easy for them to be accosted in a cowardly manner by this clan State. Today, as usual, they will be fishing for something we are supposed to know, and they will never believe otherwise."

"They know we are from the clan and likewise we know they are from the clan, but they have the power to pretend they are strictly people who are doing things in the name of progress. We used to call it nepotism. Now they want us to call it something else. Have you met the new regional the purveyor of serenity? No, but I hear he has been brought because he is not soft when it comes to our clan. The other one was considered too soft on the nomads. We know that was not the case. It is just as we are. The man and his camels in the Hinterland are also caught between these two places – the militia and the State. I in particular intend to survive both."

"And there will be the usual suspicions, so we are damned in both cases." "True, very true. We shall have to do our best under the circumstance."

The conversation progressed this way, with frequent looks aside in case anyone was within earshot of them as they walked the street towards the Governor's office. There was always the air of being watched by someone or listened too by the most unlikely of people – a shoe shiner, a common beggar, even a dusty old nomad who looked like his camels were very nearby. How much this was an exaggeration? And how much of this was true? Based on the munitions of now State and former party affiliates in this or that revolutionary group.

Most of them were from the groups who previously held no such political power. They were now members of the police, armed forces, and numerous other forces. It seems that overnight everyone was trained and held a job in a military or a paramilitary organization. This led to great suspicions based on the State's sheer number of workers in this capacity. Anyone could be anything in this new scheme of things. The idea was great, but unfortunately it was all laid to waste and often used to persecute or intimidate innocent civilians, most egregiously felt by those who happened not to be members of the ruling clan, and who had something some greedy official wanted by any means.

The Akil, having maintained his businesses and stature, was always afraid of when his turn would come, especially now that his clan had made it onto the hit list. He was a man not quite unworthy of intrigue, and this is probably why he was intact, while so many others had perished on the wayside of the new administration.

He worked with whomever had continuity for him. His rationale was based on a very poor outlook of being besieged by the prospect of losing everything and becoming very poor, as his father had become shortly before his death, squandering everything he had on his flock, the clan. His father was a communal personal, and took very seriously the righteous path of alms and self-sacrifice, but this led to the Akil's children having only stature rather than wealth, like their contemporaries, some of whom were led and helped on this path by the very own Akil who left his brood wanting very much in the material world.

The children of his friends did not want much nor did their fathers even come close to the wealth of his father, but, at the end, what mattered was how one increased in wealth rather than how much that wealth went to the benefit of humanity. Humanity itself was after partaking, disgusted by such indulgences. Having grown up in this manner, he was a keen observer of how people mostly ignored you if you were not prosperous, even though their prosperity had it roots in your father's initial great assistance. He was determined never to be at the mercy of the blanket insignificance of poverty, and wanted, even more starkly, a great title of standing wealth.

This was indeed a very difficult posture to undertake when the society was communal in almost all of its aspects, especially with his titled position at the head of a small clan sub group. He was responsible for keeping things this way. He collected when there was diya to be paid. He received when it was to be paid, and likewise he distributed it to his charge. Not all of it, of course, most of the time, keeping a lot for himself. They now approached the gates to the large office of the government, agreeing to listen a lot, and be as deceptive as possible, not committing to anything.

They greeted the other clan figures who had also been summoned to hear for themselves what new measures the Government was going to take against their brethren, requiring the utmost allegiance in whatever new plan had been hatched up as a response to the recent attack.

The doors to the large office were open. Several Government functionaries, including Ali Deray, were already seated where the group of clan elders came in and sat at the table alongside these officials. The Governor sat at the head of a massive, elongated wooden table with an almost glass-like varnish coating.

"Welcome, welcome," said the Governor. " I hope all is well today. Lets us get to the matter at hand. As all of you know, there was an attack on Government soldiers in the Hinterland by militias aided by the local nomads, their clan members sympathetic to these self-styled traitors. We have warned you in the past, as I will warn you today, support of these outfits will cost your areas and people dearly. We will go into these areas to quell such foolhardy attempts to mess around with this great Government.

The people must learn that whatever their sympathies, they can not win against such a powerful foe. It is better for all of you to go to your areas and convince your people to stay clear of assisting such silly insurgency. The militias will always take flight after their cowardly ambushes, leaving the nomads to pay for their ill-conceived transgressions.

As you can see, the Government is taking this matter seriously and has sent another security chief to head all operation henceforth. Colonel Ali Deray comes highly versed in these matters. He is devising a plan as we speak to finally stop two things: one he is engaged in the cutting off of internal support for these traitors, and second he is determined to fight these militias to the brink of extinction. Today, you are here sent to make these plans clear to yourself and the people whom you represent. We will provide all with a rugged vehicle you can use to go and speak to your kin. There will be, as per usual, expenses for the trip, for entertaining the clan elders in your respective areas. For that, the usual will be supplied to you this morning in cash currency of the State. The vehicles will depart with you in them tomorrow very early. So, go and get yourselves ready for tomorrow."

With that, he adjourned the meeting and hurried out to another part of the building. The elders were used to this futile approach of unveiled threats, and they were not lost on this prominent group who knew it was a matter of recourse. That is, the Government's open threats to the Hinterland were so far falling on deaf ears. Whatever you said about him, he was good at what he did, which was to convince people that what existed and, quite commonly, what did not exist.

Everyone in Somal, according to him, was completely in support of the State. The common, egregious, wrongful death at the hands of this same very man, however, led many people to great tragedy. People were completely at a loss for how the Clan State might force others to believe what they knew to be entirely false. Such was how the State was loved by those it was targeting. Furthermore, the issue of insurrections was fueled by a few disgruntled former officials who were dismissed simply because they were not capable of performing their duties as put forth based on clan nepotism.

The elders were ordered, each one to his clan or sub clan, to plead the case of the State. They knew this was an uphill battle, but it did not alter their resolve to at least attempt to build some form of rapport, even if involved only a few minutes with the nomads, shouting them down, as they presented a much hated agenda. Most of these encounters were intoned with the veiled threat of State power reprisals.

This is what emboldened these encounters. They were really pointless to either group. They went back to where they had come from, where their actual business was with the clan, but in an abstract non-physical way. What they said was the clan, and clan heard what the clan said through these powerful intermediaries. They, in other words, represented, shaped, and produced both the clan's perception of itself and that of those from the outside.

Instinctively, the two gentleman were very close of heart to the Ali Deray in that their thoughts, deed, and actions were all heavily decided by personal advancement, and only personal advancement. Both groups had to deal with creating perceptions that masked their individual aspirations. For Ali, his charade was creating this benign image of a very real and often belligerent Government that was increasingly becoming a hard sell to anyone. As for the chief and the lackey Jama, their personal survival as men of affairs in the clan set and beyond dictated that their work be within the framework of the State's dictates, which were increasing becoming contra to the interests of the clan.

The chief was a man who saw things in paradoxically long time-spans. He knew the State would move to other hands possibly sooner rather than later, and indeed there was going to be life after this situation. Ironically, however, he did not see other than the changing of personnel. Things like, for example, liberation from injustice through armed struggle were in his eyes just not reasonable at all.

Perhaps he only viewed personal sacrifice as a means to a very personal end. He would work with anyone at all times, but what he would not do is be left out of the loop. For him, being out of the loop was being out of a livelihood. He was put on this earth to accumulate material things. His enemy's poverty had become something larger than life for him. You would think that that if he hated poverty then he would idealize opulence, but in reality he lived a very poor life, non-commensurate with what he had already accumulated.

They left the meeting silent for most of the walk back to the warehouse. Jama and the chief were both weighed down by the treacherous position their ambitions had placed them in. Jama and his mentor walked silently for most of the way. They were very sensitive to what they had been ordered to do, and it was clear that in this case they would have to come up with a miracle to keep any one of the two sides satisfied. If they presented themselves to their clansmen openly in assignment of the State, particularly after the stepped-up aggression of the State in their clan's area, they were certain to become, in the eyes of their brethren, men of no blood, for to forsake one's own clan under any circumstance would be judged a mortal sin for any clan member, but would be judged doubly catastrophic for one who was at the head of the clan.

The chief spoke to Jama briefly before they stepped into the warehouse, "I will see you at my house for lunch today."

Lunch was a matter of a couple of hours away. Jama went to get the chat for what would be a very lengthy session after lunch, given what they were faced with tomorrow. He knew they would have come up with nothing less then a life-saving plan, or this would be the end of both their individual pursuits. For they would, after this, neither be welcome by the State nor by the clan.

Jama walked quite a distance in the blazing sun to the outskirts of the city where the chief lived. The old men rarely ventured the distance to his home before the end of the early evening. Jama could count on his fingers the amount of times he had been to the chief's home, whether day or evening. He collected the bundled chat – enough for himself and the chief – and arrived at the home, tired not by long walk there, but by what they were tasked by the state to do.

He approached the enclosure of the chief's vast barren compound going through the opening of the thorn enclosure, walking inside towards the lone concrete structure, a two- room structure made of concrete brick tiles with a corrugated iron roof. He greeted the elderly wife of the chief and proceeded to settle down in the pre-pared room. The old lady had told him that the chief had yet to arrive and asked him if he wanted to proceed with lunch or wait for the chief. He said he would wait, that the chief was probably not far off from the house anyway.

Jama stretched himself on the cushions hoping to rest a little from his weary thoughts. Before the old man showed up, surely he thought to himself this was not going to be easy for either of them to resolve and save their positions. He closed his eyes, trying to lose himself with a little shut eye before the tasking work of thinking this one out without altering their positions on both sides of the fence.

The old man arrived at his home. He took this long walk every morning and repeated this again in the evening. Although he was a man of means and could have easily afforded a vehicle, the chief preferred to walk, or as the people of Burao would have you believe, he could not bring himself to buy anything, spending money for anything was always a problem with him. On the other hand, he was known to always accept a free ride to his distant home with quite some vigor. He would say that his frugal habits, which included a very sparse diet – near starvation to others – kept him, at such an advanced age, in great shape.

"Wareya, Jama. Wake up."

He woke Jama up by prodding him with his walking stick. Jama woke up surprised that he had dozed at all, given what had been on his mind. He sat up seeing the food of meat and soup enter almost simultaneously with the chief's arrival. They washed their hands and had their meal in the same type of silence they had gone through coming from the house of the Governor.

After a hearty meal of meat and soup, which was rare because the old man never came home for lunch, the chief told Jama to wake him in a little while. He had over indulged himself, and needed to settle his bloated stomach. Jama was also thankful to take a further rest before they both taxed themselves discussing the upcoming events of tomorrow.

Jama woke the chief up after a short nap clearing his mind for the heady battle to find an amiable solution to the near impossible conditions they had been thrust into by, he thought, the idiot Governor.

The old man sat down at the prepared comfortable cushioned and layered table, beautifully decorated and perfumed covers.

They started opening and chewing the chat bundles, silently, as if trying to find the right entry point to spark this much needed conversation. The old man started speaking as if randomly, as if to no one in particular, in a very low tone, absentmindedly repeating what the Governor had said to them earlier that day, "We will send you a vehicle. We will send you a vehicle." He said this over and over again, starring outside toward the open space in front him, with a blank face. Jama was surprised at what the chief was doing. He was not usually given to such behavior, and this only added tension to what Jama was already worried about.

The old man started after sometime, "So, Jama, we knew this was coming, but not in this way. We had not anticipated the vehicles and the open messenger for the State scenario. Our people always see us, and expect us to work with the Government, but only for the interest of the clan. In this case, how do you justify going to the Hinterland in Government vehicles and with Government officials lurking in the background, right after the Government has killed members of your clan?"

"Well, we have gone there with the same message in a more subtle form, but this time there seems not to be an escape route or some way we can camouflage the whole affair as something the Government is correct in doing. We need to come up with some method of alleviating our culpability. We need the usual exit. The issue is what or who. This is where the solution lies, hard as it might be. Otherwise, we might as well start digging our own graves."

"We are expected to leave early tomorrow. This, you and I know, is written in stone. How we will find a way out of this double-edged sword, will just have to manifest itself at some point during the journey. You know, Jama, we will not have a chance to do anything tomorrow. The Government will have their usual eyes and ears accompanying us in the vehicle, and throughout the trip. So whatever we must do to save face must be thought of now or never."

"I have been thinking hard ever since the Governor gave us the assignment. So far I have nothing. I think we will have to wait and see what they are thinking and saying at the village. From there, we will just have to maneuver accordingly."

A few hours later, they wrapped up their chat session. The chief remained home without going back to the warehouse in town, and Jama made his way to his home a little ways from the chief. Neither man slept much that night, in anticipation of their treacherous assignment tomorrow. They were quite astute when it came to intrigue, but the Governor was clearly not thinking of them when it came to their future position of authority or even personal safety.

The chief knew he had to save himself from this pitfall, a pitfall that could have easily been avoided had they been consulted and not commanded to go the their brethren who were seething from the brutality of the Government's recent actions. The chief slept and hoped a clean way out of this mess would come to him from somewhere in his mind, even through a dream during his sleep. He could almost taste the extreme reaction that would ensue if his brethren even thought he was playing both sides. Likewise, he would be done with favors from the State. He would have to wait and play it by ear when he got there.

The Government truck came early for him. There was a gentlemen already seated there. The chief had, more than likely, a guess that this human was the Government's eyes and ears. He slid into the seat next to him, and the vehicle commenced towards the house of Jama. The truck stopped to pick Jama up. He was already standing outside his small thorn enclosure. He had a small cloth bundle in one hand, and was dressed in a dark green patterned ma'wiss, with a shawl draped on his shoulder.

He was a young man in his late twenties, not for a long shot an elder. He got into the vehicle beside the others and it ventured on in the stillness of the very early morning, right after the dawn prayers, which were marked with the early orange tinged rumblings of the sun before it rose to fully light the earth from another long night. The vehicle cruised toward the Hinterland on the lone paved road then went on for another thousand miles to the coastal capital of Mogadishu.

The vehicle rode along this road. The occupants were tense, quiet, and lost each one in their own thoughts. The vehicle moved off the paved road to the open land following the open tracks beaten before it by herds of camel, large trucks, and men winding around avoiding trees, bushes and uneven gorges of rocks, in no particular consistency, trudging along in some places, and speeding in the open flat and secure stretches in others, all bypassing the many nomads families with their herds on the move in this dry season.

The thirst of the land and the people was apparent in the dryness of the faces of the vehicles' passengers, encountered as they journeyed past these moving families. This season was not lost on the chief and the others who knew this life well, having lived it to adulthood. Both the Chief and Jama had livestock and a Hinterland family who continued a life of pastoralism as did their ancestors in this part of the world. The vehicle came to only one small stop after their journey for all the passengers to answer Nature's call. The time was very close to dusk when they arrived at the very remote village, which the Chief represented in town.

They were immediately surrounded by what seemed to be the entire settlement. A large circle had formed around the vehicle. An elder cleared a path towards the passengers. The people recognized the Chief and Jama. They also knew the vehicle was a Government one from its tags. The Chief led the passengers away from the curious onlookers along the path towards an enclosure that served as a tea shop. They sat down and were joined by some of the elders who knew the Chief as a prominent member of their own.

They boisterously ordered tea for the guests, while the shop owner pumped his hand to light the filament of his powerful paraffin lamp. They sat in the half-darkness and exchanged the normal niceties. The Chief asked about the water situation in the season and how far off his second family was from the settlement, as most of the clan was in search of grazing and permanent wells. He was told they were about more than a half- day's journey on foot. He then arranged accommodations for the officer and had Jama escort him to where he was going to spend the night. The drivers would sleep outside beside his vehicle.

Jama came back and they headed with some of the elders to a small Somal module now permanently surrounded by the common thorn bushes forming an enclosed yard around it. There was a tree in the compound and the lone round movable module which the Somal nomads broke down and carried on camels to the next destination. It was covered by leather drapes and canvas over the frame of removed wood pieces to form a small dwelling. They entered the dwelling, the layered bedding had been already arranged for the Chief on one side and Jama on the other. The men and their two important visitors sat in a small semi-circle. Tea was brought to them by one of the women as they settled down to learn of the Chief's appearance in their midst with other strangers from the Government.

The elders and the men spoke briefly with the Chief and Jama inquiring as to what they were here for with the Government. They spoke briefly with the Chief and Jama rather then spending the evening talking as they would have liked to. They noticed that both the men were tired from the convulsive journey to the Hinterland settlement. They bid them a momentary adieu and let them get some sleep.

The elders at the same time sent out messages to some of the others miles away grazing and watering their stock in this very sparse of seasons. Everything was difficult due to the harshness. As so, the efforts from the nomads were increased to sustain the life spans of their stock, by seeking water across long stretches of land. They were usually in the same predicament as their animals. They also had to make due without water or much provisions. The milk from the camel during these times was only a trickle.

In this season, the air was always tense. The nomad was sizzling with tensions from this seasonal situation of barrenness. Tempers flared at the wells over water rights for the animals. The well was not the place to be for the passive or mild during this heightened period of scarcity. It was hardly the place for a herder's congenial niceties otherwise none of his stock would drink. He had to remain forceful at the well to avoid being moved out of the well by another aggressive herder, whose camels, he thought, were more deserving than yours. With all this trouble, there was also the matter the chief was here for. The nomads had a lot of grievances. They were catching fire from Mother Nature and did not need any help in the area of misery.

Their Government was acting like an alien Government at war with them. They had no capacity to withstand this brute force. They were used to resolving inter clan or within clan disputes. They felt a grievance of immeasurable magnitude. The military was openly responsible of some heinous acts, above and beyond the decorum of inter-clan blood feuds. The elders were glad that the Chief was at the settlement, and saw his arrival as perhaps heralding the return to an uneasy détente with Nature. They sent the call out to all within reaching distance to attend as a much needed reconciliation with the Government. In fact, the Hinterland notables had decided a few days earlier to dispatch a group of elders to Burao, to put a stop to what the soldiers were doing. They thought there must be a better way for the government to solve its problems with the incursions, without victimizing everyone who happened to hail from the same clan that was openly hostile to them.

Those who were discerning knew what was going on. Others were indignant for being embroiled in something they viewed as being far fetched from their routine of grazing. They neither knew nor wanted Government positions. They were aware of the politics of representation in clans, but even here they knew they were represented by a stranger they knew only through genealogical relation to them, hardly in person. Every once in a while, when there was an urgent need, this politician or official would show up to bask in his own glory.

The Government Official had breakfast in the morning with the Chief and Jama. During this time, he took the opportunity to make them aware that he was with them here in an official capacity as the eyes and ears of the Governor. He further mentioned how anxious the Governor was. They did not fail in their mission to their brethren. They were both acutely aware of what the Governor wanted. They could also envision the other side's position. But the gentlemen spoke as if the Governor was bestowing benediction to the inhabitants of the Hinterland. Jama and the Chief wondered what planet this man came from. Could he be that ignorant of the pastoralists?

They kept these thoughts to themselves, and did not speak until a long while after the Governor's man had finished speaking. They ate in silence without a word, except for the customary grunts they made for active participation during a long winded monologue.

The chief broke the silence, turning his face away for the first time from the breakfast and spoke, "We understand what is at stake here, in particular for the two of us. We represent the clan and we also dabble in Government in this fashion. What the Governor has instructed us to do here is difficult – even a blind man can see. We will try to do what we can considering the circumstances that have been laid in our path.

"This morning, my brethren are coming from all corners and we will have a meeting with them. After this, we will see you, and, as you know, being a member of the Government does not make you my clan member. So you will not be able to attend our clan meeting. That is a tradition we will have to abide by, but I will do my best in this arena to make it clear what the Governor's position is towards my clan. The power of the State is not lost to me."

Jama remained silently glued to his breakfast. The officer also remained silent after this. The chief and Jama left the officer and commenced to the large open space by the well to a choice tree that functioned as a large open congress for the clan. Some of the elders were already there, there was a group of youngsters milling around. Soon the place would be teeming with the clan from near and far. The chief and Jama sat on the ground a little elevated directly under the large tree in anticipation of a large and very heady meeting to commence. People started coming in small and large groups, and soon the congress of clan members would begin. The old man had lived through many precarious situations, but he never quite knew how to handle them beforehand, at least not completely.

There was now enough people gathered around, sitting on the ground facing the trees. The clan elders of the Hinterland were now seated alongside the chief and Jama, around a natural elevated semi-circle around the base of the tree facing the seated congregants. A respected member of the clan from the Hinterland known a degcheer stood up to address the group.

"In the name of Allah, the most beneficent, the most merciful, May he bless us with rain soon."

The gathering responded, "Amen."

"May Allah make it possible and easy for us to solve that issue that has brought us here today."

"Amen," said the crowd of clansmen in unison.

"May all of us be blessed with the heath and wealth of camels and sons." Again there was the chorus of "Amen."

"My brothers, we have been blessed today with the chief's presence. He has come here today in spite of the many obligations he has of family and business in far away Burao. We have come to know him well as had the ones before who knew his father. He has lead us in the right way and always has our interests at heart. The past days have cast a shadow of insecurity throughout our area, and this is why this man, our chief, has thought it important to bring the Government to witness for themselves and put an end to such blatant disregard for the life.

"We are already going through one of the worst dry seasons for years. We are certainly not a people interested with confronting the Government. I will not say much for now, but I would like Hage Roble to summarize the most recent events as they have occurred against us at the hands of Government without any provocation from our side. This behavior from the authorities has run amok, and is sanctioned now wherever we look. We can not call it the ways of our fathers either, and thus we do not have a clan to address our problems too, or act traditionally in hostility towards a certain clan. I will tell all who are gathered here honestly that we are not sure how to conduct ourselves in this matter. Perhaps the chief will elaborate upon this matter for us, and show us the way forward as he has done in the past." With that, the elder sat down.

The chief went on his knees first then pushed up with the aid of his palms pressing on the ground. In this manner, he stood up laboriously to a standing position. Being quite vain about his virility, he did not like the exposition in front of all the hungry clan members who coveted his position of big affairs on behalf of the clan. This exposition of such a weakness was like a wayward suckling deer to a pack of hyenas. It just served to embolden them further, clearing the way to easy confrontation for those with or without a chance at his position. As he stood up, he thought of his sons and the sons of his brothers, and how all of them were conspicuously missing from the gathering or around his person. It is at these times that such a visible deterrence was necessary, the hyenas would note their presence and curl their tales between their legs and run he thought.

He knew that such a presence was not likely. He had spent his life destroying any potential in them. He kept them at bay and always lacking. He never helped them, only discouraged them whenever possible. They were scattered everywhere with most of them living precariously within the chief's town. They had no education, no wealth of the small city. Neither did they tend to the affairs of their rich uncle. As far as the normal wealth of the camel, they were also lacking tremendously in this mark of respect. Most of them were eloquent and some were wise beyond their youthful years, but no good could pass upon a man with no livelihood to speak of.

The chief salivated in their demise, and they could not conduct themselves in public without the usual pent up anger that others saw at face value as completely irrational. They could not believe that such young people could be so mad with someone as elderly and as accomplished as their uncle. He would sit quietly during these public displays by his immediate kin, without emotion, and sighing in exasperation at the futility of being without able kin to work in the families affairs. He would always add his benign, tireless intervention to save these basket cases he had been dealt in the apparition of kith and kin.

The chief, a master of propaganda, was way ahead of the young men. He paid certain people with favors to pass on his made-up folklore of how he had done so much for his immediate kin, with nothing in his old age to show for it but the anguish of having to rely on others to do what rightfully should be done by his sons or the sons of his brothers. It took this moment of being exposed by the condition of his age as he stood up in front of his kin for him to realize the folly of his ways. His need now for them functioned as a visible deterrent.

He wished he did not cultivate their vehement hate, but he did not regret the mistreatment as a wrong unto in itself. The chief stood up a little bewildered, and very uneasy from what had just been witnessed by the multitude gathered to hear him make a way for them as a group. Nonetheless, he tried to ignore everything, and he cleared his throat and leaned on his walking stick, grasping the knob at the top of the polished walking cane cum bone breaker with both of his hands for emphasis as he looked earnestly into the crowd. He greeted his gathered flock with the usual salaams, which they returned in unison.

"First of all, I pray to Allah to help us through this very difficult time, and also to help me make the right decisions as far as any mere mortal can. It is only Allah that in the end will determine the fate of all of us, through the dry seasons and with the most recent problem we have with the state."

"Amen," said the collective to this prayer by the chief.

He continued holding the stick not for the assistance of standing, but for emphasis to his rhetoric. "We have traveled here at the direct request of the governor of this regime. Like you, we have heard of the unfortunate instances between the military in this area and my brothers tending their flocks."

The governor has said that he will not leave any stone unturned in the matter, and he has asked me to investigate the instances myself, along with an officer of the Government whom he has assigned to me. The governor has sent all of you this message. He will prosecute and pay the diya of those who were killed in this unfortunate incident. That is the governor's position. My position remains steadfast with the clan elders here. They are the ones who were here and who know exactly what has transpired so far between us and the Government. Until such the time as we can come up with a consensus from the elders and me, I urge calm from all of you young men.

"We cannot follow an injustice with another injustice. That would be going against our religion, and our just ways of adjudication. Again, I urge a calm disposition until this matter is solved properly through the usual ways. No one is allowed to take matters in his own hands, even those who have been most aggrieved in these cases. We will hold court here under this tree like you and I have known in our time and as has been done in the past time of our wise forbearers. Each and everyone who has something to say or relate in relations to these incidents or on the matter of how we should proceed forward, will have an opportunity under this tree to speak. The chief sat down ending his address to his kin, with peace be upon you. The seated returned the blessing, and remained quiet for a minute.

Then a man stood up from the group he was seated with. He was dusty, skinny, with wild, unruly curly hair. He adjusted his white sheet that had turned dusty red from contact with the earth when he covered himself during sleep in the wilderness. He moved the strap of his machine gun around so that it would rest comfortably on his shoulder. His eyes were blazing with a certain unpredictable earnestness. It was clear the man had left his livestock somewhere in the wilderness to attend this meeting. He did not wait for anyone to allow him to speak, he just commenced speaking after a mumbled and abrupt greeting to those facing the crowd and the seated gathering he had risen from.

He was in his mid- to late- thirties, a man with a solemnly serious face, with eyes and a weapon that dared anyone brazenly. He began looking straight ahead at the elders in front of him. "I cannot believe that our chosen ones are engaged in trying to placate the government's involvement by dragging us through a long, drawn-out process that is only meant to buy time on behalf of the government. I have something stuck in my throat at what that old man has said to all of us.

"What does he mean by unfortunate incidents and the governor's position? We were all here and, as a clan, we know exactly what transpired here last week, and the month before. None of us are mad. We have witnesses, and the incidents are known to you. The one before, and the more recent one. How in the name of Allah can you stand in front of us today as our chief and act as if there is some matter or other that needs to be investigated? We are not going to accept this time-wasting, cowardly approach. We have here all the people who know that the government mowed down my son along with ten other such sons, during one day.

"They did not ask nor have a lengthy discussion about who or what was wrong. They just started killing then, and they killed again last week, all from this one clan, in different locations. What as men are we going to do to reclaim our dead? The worst of it all is that the people who survived these killings in cold blood have related on many such occasions what transpired. We have not even gotten into the months of hounding by various armed groups from the clan of the president, haven't even dealt with them doing as they please with us at the water wells. We have seen also the increase of incidents from both our neighboring clans and from the soldiers. When the first killings occurred, I myself came here to this settlement, and related how my son and the others were shot.

"We were told to bury our dead, and report this to the government. We did so right here, close to us, where their commander was stationed. We were first humiliated and then we were told the soldiers were doing their work fighting your clans' militia who your son and the others were known members of. Those who were there at the commander garrison knew that out of that arrogant mouth, there was nothing that come out of it but blatant lies. My son as the others were killed at the wells while watering their camels in broad daylight in front everyone at the well. They were killed in cold blood. We, the parents, and all the others know that these boys were innocent camel herders.

"The commander has made it clear with these most recent deaths that the government is the aggressor. And here is the government.

This governor is either mad or thinks we are to accept this charade brought to us by none other than our chief, someone we hold in great esteem. He is doing the dirty work of this murderous regime. We live here and we are clear who and what the problem is. What we want to know is how much longer are we to allow these killings to continue endlessly without redress or even stoppage of further victims? I will not stand for any more of this time wasting. There will be blood on that side too. We do not count the militias skirmishes as just cause for the military to kill our innocent sons while they tend to their camel herds. I have just spoken for many who are not willing to tolerate the previous killings nor any such cases that will surely happen again sooner than later.

"We, the parents and their relatives, will not abide the mockery of ours sons' death in cold blood by coming here to listen to lies and deceit from the government's side. The chief, if he convenes this and continues the path of falsehood, while he knows the truth, will make plain as the daylight, given the killings of my son and other sons of this clan, that he is not of us, and that he speaks for himself and on the government's behalf."

The man then abruptly left the gathering, amidst a lot of shouting, and pointing fingers at those sitting, facing the crowd on the natural dais elevated from the rest.

The elder showed a brave face even though it was clear they were losing ground. Their eyes betrayed their worry. The crowd followed the man who had just spoken, all swearing that there was not going to be any wasting of time, discussing nonsense under this tree. Ultimately, those who were sitting facing the elders were all gone. The elder had lost ground. His flock had abandoned him. They also parted ways without as much as a word to each other. They were clearly stunned at what had just happened. It meant they were not going to have the lengthy exercise in rhetorical skills. No one was having it. The chief and Jama were the last ones to leave the spot under the tree. The chief was clearly devastated by the forceful and convincing speech.

They walked slowly back, away from the tree grounds, and went toward the Somal module to regroup after this disaster. Neither man said a word nor looked each other in the eye.

They sat down when they got to the Somal module. They were both floundering for ideas to salvage what ever it was they could. They were clearly out of touch with the amount of hostility towards the government's recent actions. It had just dawned on them how mistaken they were to think they could easily run this interference, as it was in the past. They were quite out of touch with the blood that had marked a new zone of hate. However, this was what was there, and the chief and Jama had a living to make, which was very much tied to their good relations with the State.

Things had to be done, or things would go out of reach from their manipulation. So far, the old man was at a loss. In the many years that he had been in this business of intrigue, he had never been so unaware or even been troubled in his position as he was today, sitting there like a log lost in frustration. There was no sign of redemption in any shape or form. He and his disciple in crime were both lost in a vast emptiness of anxious anticipation. The old man and Jama had to come up with something extremely important with the impetus to alter an almost certain turn of events.

In the balance hung whatever reputation the old man had garnered through the years as the head of clan. His children, and his fathers would be visited upon by the memory of how he sold his people for personal gain. This he would not allow at any cost. The reputation part of his ruin was overwhelmed by his blind greed. He could not see the end of his lucrative position which he had worked so diligently to foster and keep. All in all, the government's position must be adhered to, and the clan had to be convinced this was in their best interest. He and Jama would stay as long as it took in the trenches to make this happen. He must, however, make a very quick trip back and forth. He needed to see the governor to get some commitments from him.

He also needed to get a great deal of cash, to make heads accept what the mind had rejected. He was an old hand at changing minds, creating sentiment, and he assured himself in silence that this time would not be any different. They were going to have a big pow-wow tonight, but he told Jama what to do in his absence, and he said that he would be back in a day at the latest. His trip should be kept as 'hush-hush' as possible. He instructed Jama and gave him the names of certain elders telling him to brief them on creating some sentiment with the clan for reconciliation with the government, promising a cessation of hostilities with a firm assurance from the state through the governor's office. Then the chief prepared himself for the night prayer, before going to bed in preparation for the battle ahead.

TWENTY EIGHT

Hinterland

· ·

EARLY THE NEXT DAY, TUSMO WOKE UP IN THIS STRANGE
new environment. She looked at the barely furnished rooms with
two beds. The girls were sound asleep on one of them. She was now
far away from the machinations of Mogadishu. She was glad not to
be constantly worried about what was lurking in her path in order
to apprehend and return her to the misery of injustice. She thought
of this journey for a second, but this was increasingly pushed to the
side of her thoughts. Her mind was now considering the unknown,
as on the journey there, but this time, it was occupied more with
what she was going to do next. Asha had told her she had arranged
for some monies to be given to her and a former partner of her husband. She wondered how she would get in touch with this person,
or with Asha for that matter, because she did not know who he was
and visa versa.

   She was determined to continue her journey towards the reunifi-
cation of her family as was planned between her and Asha. She had to
find out how she was going to find her husband or his whereabouts
in Ethiopia. These thoughts were recurring in her mind, like a vast
circus with no way of resolution. She would ask around today, perhaps the proprietor of the hotel, and this would have to do for the
moment.

   She heard a knock on the door, she opened and a young man
entered with a tray of a flask, a plate with bread on it, and mugs.

He smiled at her, saying something or the other that she could not understand. He looked different from the people she was used to seeing all her life. His features were different from the pastoralist. He reminded her of the people from the Riverine areas of Lower Juba in Somal that she had seen a lot of in the Mogadishu, though she could not understand their language.

He placed the breakfast on the floor and left closing the door. Tusmo opened the top of the flask letting out a steamy fragrance of the spiced sweetened tea she was so familiar with. She poured herself a cup, consuming it with the buttered sliced bread she enjoyed tremendously. She thought the butter, jam, and sliced bread quite a treat. The bread she was used to was not this sliced loaf, nor was it buttered with jam where she came from. Before leaving, the man had also ushered a women wearing a large khaki-type of overcoat over her long dress that reached mid-way past the knees.

She also spoke to her in a language Tusmo did not understand. She gave her fresh towels and tiny bars of soap, and pointed to the towel and motioned her to follow past the door. Tusmo got up and went with the lady who bent down to pick up a steaming bucket of hot water and placed it in the bathroom. She placed an empty bucket under a tap and filled it half-way with cold water. She then went out, motioning her to follow. She opened a door adjacent to the bathroom, and showed her the toilet with an enamel basin embedded in the floor. There were foot grooves on the top of the enamel at the level of the floor, slightly higher than the enamel. Tusmo knew this place for Nature's call was a little different from what she was used too Tusmo returned to the bathroom, mixed the cold with the steaming water and had a long bath using a container to dip into the already mixed water, to pour over her body.

The weather was much colder in Nairobi than she was used to. She dried herself. Shivering, she went back to the room where the girls were still asleep. She poured herself some more hot tea thinking about the previous things she had set out to do. She thought she would, first of all, inquire who was here at this hotel in terms of bloodlines, and she would also ask how she was to make contact or find out if Asha had already made some form of arrangements as she had discussed with Tusmo earlier in Mogadishu, with the business man who had worked with Hoagsaday in the past. She mentioned there was also some monies here for her to go further on to Ethiopia.

She would wait to give the girls breakfast and a bath. Then she would go to see the owner of these lodgings to inquire about certain important things such as what arrangements the driver had made for them, or, if there were none, what she should do.

She entered into the courtyard a little shy in front of the gathering of men drinking tea at tables engaged in conversation, speaking Somal. Most of the men gathered were all visibly Somal. This she found a little strange because her idea of this country had not included common conversations in Somal. This emboldened her to ask one of the men where the owner of the lodgings was. The man directed her towards the front of the courtyard. She went through an opening in the far corner of the courtyard. She saw a physically well-built man, dressed in a suit jacket, wearing a sweater underneath with a koofiyad placed on his graying coarse hair. He was between the ages of sixty and seventy.

There was an air about his presence that belied a rather otherness in the way he wore his clothes. First, most men his age did not wear this type of more Western attire.

But she found his presence somewhat comforting, other than his more Western-type of presence, for his features reminded her of her uncle's.

He smiled at her as she approached him. He seemed to have a knowing look about him, and he greeted her with familiarity. Tusmo greeted him and began to relate who she was. The old man interrupted her, saying that he had heard of her through the driver, who had brought her to the lodgings.

He explained his bloodlines to her, which she immediately recognized as being a major clan affiliation through a cousin of hers. She was intensely affected internally with this news. She was weary from travel and the like, and this bit of information hit her like an avalanche in the sense that it cleared away all the uncertainties in the same way an avalanche would roll over anything in its path. She was emotionally keeping a lot of things inside, as she was taught, and as her mother before her was taught – to be stoic in all kinds of weather. And, therefore, she tried as much as possible to conceal her forlorn relief from this encounter so far away from her original home.

This was not what she expected or even dreamed of.

The elder owner of the restaurant said he had heard of the terrible things that had happened to her, her victimization and her fleeing their home in a great haste, from his fellow clansmen.

He said he was very sorry to have heard this, and he began to assure of her safety while she was there.

He told her that he had a very important errand, but that he would be back to take her to his home where his family was. He asked her not to worry from here on out, that from now on she would not have to worry about much other than raising her children. He had messages from the front. She thanked him and went back to the room to check on the girls and see how they were doing.

She got to the room and to her surprise there was not much of a stir in the girls' log- like sleep.

There was a knock at the door sometime in the afternoon. The old man, the owner, came in and said they should prepare to leave towards the house of pain.

There was not much for Tusmo to pack. She had been introducing the girls, who were busy playing, to their uncle, and she told them it was time for them to go with him.

The old man led them to a car parked close by, which he opened, and then motioned for her to step into. He put the little pillow case that comprised their belongings on the seat next to the girls. They proceed towards the home of their new found uncle. Tusmo watched the roads, the buildings, and forms of the people as they went by.

She was now certain she was in another country. This country seemed to be buzzing with much activity – a lot of selling and moving of produce on two-wheeled, man-driven carts, weighed down by the weight produce, possibly retuning to the farms they came from to begin with.

There was an urgency in their movements. They seemed to be on a quest, or in search of something. Everyone was in this heady motion towards something. There were a lot of cars at this time of late afternoon. People thronged the sides of the road, peering for something in the distance. Some were reading, others talking. They were all occupied with this urgency that transcended their reading and conversations. The old man must have known or realized the intensity with which Tusmo was engaged in her surroundings as they floated by, at times in a rush and at times at a standstill pace of affairs.

He said the people she saw were trying to get home after a long day of toiling employed in some manner or other.

He said this was one of the busiest times in Nairobi. It was called the rush hour. Then he went on to describe the various areas they passed and what the people were doing. He said the ones who were in suits and the women who were immaculately dressed were all working either for the government or private corporations. But all were lower administration staff; all were educated here, working in one form or other in intellectual labor, 'pushing paper' as some would say.

The land was beautiful in its greenness. There were a lot of trees of all kinds, and amidst the greenery there was a dryness still from the sun's intensity over the previous hours. The heat and aridity she recognized and was familiar with. She was really taken aback by the immaculate women standing at the bus stop on their way home from work. This she did not know of in Somal. There was a work force of women in many capacities, but something was a miss compared to this type of gathering. Here, they were truly a force embedded in the landscape of the workforce.

Most of the men were wearing coats in the European fashion, with ties, quite well kept and neat, with groomed hair and polished shoes, all belying their frequent, lively treks to and fro. The production accumulates in many forms, piece by piece.

Tusmo, like anyone else who had her experiences as a reference for processing what she encountered on the way to her uncle's abode of living, compared and contrasted what she saw with what she knew in her past. The girls were also aware of the difference in their surroundings, but they were too engrossed in the scenery to exclaim as loudly as they had on the journey there. Somehow what they saw was so intense that they were really at a loss for words. Not the usual for her children.

They knew from the little reference gathered over their short life spans that this was a different place all together, but with some familiar elements to grasp at in their memories, like the gentle face of their uncle now driving them in his car. They were also not used to such an old man made to drive his own vehicle. In the Somal, this was done mainly by younger relatives on behalf of their elders. In fact, for the most part, the elders there did not know how to drive, having only driven camels in their youth.

They reached a nice walled-in home similar to the one Tusmo had lived in in Mogadishu. The only difference was that was made of carved rock, dark in color, made out to be a well-proportioned rectangular block with a rather picturesque garden, lush and green with all manner of trees. She also noticed a small wooden house in one corner. What soon became evident to her was the loud barking of a dog.

This was indeed probably the strangest thing to her and the girls. The girls were frightened by this unfamiliar sound, and their old uncle thought the response to the dogs rather funny. As the girls refused to come out of the vehicle, he reassured them that it was secure, and that they could come out. Tusmo was astonished because this was hardly ever done in Somal.

The dog was considered a filthy animal in Somal, and since these ideas came from religion it was, thus, widespread. The old man, on the other hand, thought nothing of it. Tusmo followed suit and also reassured the children, and they, together, went out into the large bungalow. Inside, they were met with a small woman, rather old, whom the uncle then promptly introduced as his wife, Sarah. She was short and typically dressed in the Somal derah, her hair drawn under a tight cover.

She welcomed them with a smile, asked the servant to carry her belongings, instructing him in another language, and, at the same time, asked Tusmo to bring the girls to a room in the house that seemed to have been freshly prepared for their arrival.

"I have many children — I guess not children anymore — but there are eight of them," she began. "I have a small girl, the last one who is the age of your oldest one."

She then commenced to show her the bathroom, and the separate toilet in the house. Sarah was very talkative it seemed, and her voice was as deep as a man's, but somehow it still retained a very womanly quality, a sort of bass with delicate edge semitones. Having arrived at the house just around dark, she looked the room over, and was very thankful for the modest, clean bed, with freshly pressed linen. She could not imagine such good fortune in the midst of such circumstances.

The next morning she woke up to the clamor of the many half-adult children Sarah had mentioned in passing rumbling through the household. These children, Tusmo found, were mostly boys in their teens, with two girls slightly younger. They were all hovering in and out of the kitchen, and were all dressed in some odd fashion, their work uniforms like those of the men of urgent affairs, with jackets whose colors had some sort of relation to the colors of what ever else they were wearing.

Sarah was in the midst of this commotion, and it seemed that all of them were asking for more tea, bread, or something, all at the same time. Sarah was struggling to keep up with it all. She looked up from the stool next to the steaming kettle of tea on the charcoal stove standing on minute legs on the floor. But Tusmo just observed this morning commotion, and understood it to be the morning rush to school.

Sometime in the late afternoon the uncle came in, as usual. She could tell it was him from the noise of the car and from the glaring lights of the highlights pushing forth as the guard swung the large gates open. The dog now loose, he grabbed instinctively as soon as the gates swung open on their own momentum.

The old man waited in the darkness of the Nairobi night outside the gate. His car doors had been shut unconsciously from the habit he had developed when he began his journey from where the lodgings were. The gate and the guard were all now part of the nature of this ever-growing city which was both increasing in number of resident as well as in the distance between the haves and the have-nots. Each night, under his breath, the old man frequently turned from side to side looking for any person or shadows from the thick growth of bushes, trees, and hedges that grew around the outside of the walled compounds.

He was always tense, wishing the guard would hurry up with the gates. Every so often, the papers would cover the many victims not unlike himself as a result of this deadly combination of natural foliage and the wait outside one's entry gate, shutting the poverty outside with the help of large treacherous structures with pieces of glass imbedded in the concrete wall, further fortified by razor wire, or, for the more industrious, electric shock wires. For a someone new to this scheme like Tusmo, relations between the inhabitants of the same city were absurd. Even though she had previously lived in a walled-in enclosure, she now knew the use for them. Other than what she thought before, before she realized it was meant for demarcation from other compounds more so than for keeping their fellows residents at bay.

They exchanged the normal greetings once he got inside the household, and his faithful wife had already placed his dinner on the table in the corner of the living room. He was a jovial man given to humor, and was a very good story-teller of recent events.

He had a knack for enlivening even the very mundane. And he had already developed a healthy relationship with the girls, though they were already asleep by now. He had given them pet names, and always brought something home for all the children, especially the girls.

They seemed to live a different life from the contingent of boys that he had of various ages. Both he and his wife seemed to have to make due attitude with this part of the household. They lived in the outer margins of the enclosed house, and came in and out of the enclosure without any interactions with the main house. Only during meals did they sometimes show up around the kitchen area, and always for a look at what was for dinner and when would it arrive at their part of the house.

Tusmo had stayed now for a while with her uncle and was getting very restless as to what was happening to the connections between herself and her husband. Between herself and Asha, no word had come from the last contact she had with the driver who she thought might have some connection to Asha. It was becoming clear to Tusmo now that perhaps there was no such connection. Suspecting as much, she had decided to ask her uncle to find some relatives she could contact in Ethiopia, but, alas, he was still searching for some persons with reliable information.

He continued searching for the whereabouts of Hoagsaday or for his cousin Beheyeah. He was trying to get a phone number from anyone around this group in Ethiopia. So far, there was no such luck.

Tusmo, in the weeks she remained in the household of her uncle, was continually surprised at the wife's behavior towards her. This woman took every opportunity to slight Tusmo and the girls. She increased the antics every week to includes days where the girls would barely eat anything for some reason or the other. She would starve Tusmo regularly, showing her through this action and rude commentary towards Tusmo that she was not welcome there. One day, shortly after these incidents kept recurring, another one of her relatives had come to stay from another town in the interior.

She stayed with them and was quite excited to meet Tusmo and her daughters for he first time even though they were not that close but were related distantly through a more general affiliation to the same clan. The visitor was very sympathetic to Tusmo's treacherous flight as was her uncle and she assumed a motherly disposition towards her. After several days at the house, the visitor noticed what she had seen before, given her long-standing relations with the house: that the lady of the house was quite peculiar in the way she would single out relatives of the old man, and, behind his back, make their stay there unbearable to the point they would voluntarily leave.

Meanwhile, the wife's husband merely pretended not to know this because he knew there was no way he could change this lady. He played along with the deception and tried to ameliorate her transgressions by his sheer presence alone. He also could not find a way out of this relationship which had born him so many children, some of them still very young indeed. He was resigned to playing along, pretending oblivion, but at the same time, he made contingency plans to get his people out of her reach as soon as possible. And he did this in particular for Tusmo, who was not just a visitor who lived somewhere, but who was someone who needed to start almost from scratch – to either move on or reside in the city while she gathered her own contingency plans for her future reunion with her husband.

Her uncle called her in and told her in front of his wife that he had found a place for her and the girls to live in until, at least, Hoagsaday's location in Ethiopia had become clearer. Tusmo was glad and happy to get some control over her life or whatever was left of it; and she was even happier to get away from the clutches of this petty lady. Quite uncommon in the eyes of Tusmo, this wife had really flaunted the mere hospital ethic afforded to a visitor who was also a relation, a visitor who would be regarded as almost sacred to the Somal.

He said that he had had a visitor a year ago from the Somal, a very religious lady from Somal, who was sent there by her family to pursue an education. Her father was an old nomad who had joined the rank of the adventurous youth along the seaport of the Red Sea who had sought prosperity and the risk of adventure through the life of a seaman.

When working in numbers, Somals were often stowed away in ships. Sometimes, they were mortally unlucky when they came out after days of being from where they had been stowed away. And other times, the ships could not turn back when there were no other Somals on board. They were quickly thrown overboard.

The lady's father was now settled in Cardiff where there was a large community of Somals. He had come back to Somal every so often after his initial marriage which had produced his beloved daughter and he sent her money and encouraged her to pursue her education. He was to let her stay with the uncle and his family, but when it came out that this was just not an option for a long term stay, due to the old man's wife's petty and often cruel behavior, he decided to put his daughter up elsewhere. He would send her money for her school and upkeep through the old man. The old man was quite different from his wife in that he was kind and sensitive in the most admirable of human kindness.

"Tusmo, tomorrow I will come back very early from the lodge to pick you and the girls up. Please pack everything you have. We will be headed to the house of our relative, Dheka. She is waiting to meet you and the children of Hoagsaday."

"I will be ready very early. You may come at any time. The girls and I will be waiting for you here."

As she said this, her heart leapt for joy. She had had enough of this petty wife's antics. The girls and her were literally starving. She tried to sneak some supplementary things through the servants when the wife left the house, which was rare and never for more then a few hours.

She did not wish to embarrass her uncle because she knew that she was already way beyond the breaking point. Her uncle did not go further into this conversation nor did his wife inquire about it. It seemed to Tusmo this was a compromise reached a long time ago between the couple, and the wife would not question where her husband was going to take his relatives or even show some feigned attempt at the indignity of moving a guest to another abode. It was clear to both where their boundaries lay.

Tonight, Tusmo could not bear time. She was conscious of every second. She had been feeling so terribly that she had let this happen to her girls, and she had tossed every night thinking of the type of mother she was that she allowed her children to barely eat, while saying nothing, acting only to sneak milk and sliced bread which they all learned to horde and eat mysteriously within the confines of their room. No matter what this lady was doing, it still got to Tusmo that she was showing her girls behavior that was weak and deceptive. They had never had to think about food and the lack of it much less contemplating the hording and hiding of it. Thinking of these things, she dosed off waiting for when daybreak would come.

The next morning, there was the usual commotion in the kitchen made by the boys. Tusmo knew now why they kept coming to the kitchen; they themselves were at the mercy of their own mother's machinations. This confounded them as children because it really jeopardized their sense of security and belonging. Tusmo could never understand such cruelty in a mother, not even in the harshest plains of Somal, where there was ample reason to be so inclined. But even the nomads within those dire conditions were not disposed to see food as more important its purpose, which was in reality to sustain their living.

Morning did not come soon enough for Tusmo. She had woken up half-crazed from the combination of hunger and had stayed up awake and anxious to get her girls away from the clutches of her own inability to stand up for them, her failed duty which had so far became their main fare in their very young life. She wanted to escape her own inability to stop either the State or this petty, incredulous women who took such joy in victimizing her very weak charges.

Tusmo had forced her girls up and moved them to a standing position one by one. She had decided to force the issue. She would not wait for her uncle to return even if it meant that she would break his routine. She was going to seize the day. She got the girls and herself ready, and had packed everything quietly so as not to rouse anyone in the house. She made sure she used the toilet and bathroom before the household had entered into the full commotion of its early morning preparations for school.

She was now ready, sitting dressed up and alert, waiting to hear the sound of her uncle talking in grunts over the cacophonous barrage of conversation made by the screeching pitch of his wife's voice. Tusmo had long since understood from the noncommittal grunts of her uncle in response to his wife's endless ingratiating conversation that he had long been disappointed in her mean behavior. To Tusmo, this was a marriage unlike her own. It lacked the luster and verve of mutual endearment.

Hearing the usual grunts he made every morning during his breakfast, Tusmo was now preparing to go outside regardless of the previous instructions her uncle had given her. She was determined not to wait until he came back for her later on in the day. She waited for her uncle to go for a few minutes and got the girls next to her, stood them up in their room, behind closed doors. She was gathering her courage to step through that door, on to the living room and outside to the car. Thank god, she thought, the guard already chained the dog inside his wooden house.

She paused for a second amidst the barrage of noise emanating from that person, and held her daughters hands tight and close to her while she managed their worldly belongings in the pillow case. She took a deep breath and rushed through the door with the girls in tow, struggling to stay balanced as she thrust them forward through the living room.

Her sudden appearance startled the two people in the room, one of whom looked at her with a slice of bread half stopped in route to the mouth. She ignored them and commenced through the front door, onto the garden and drive way, where she now stood resolutely in front of the backseat car door. The girls stood there in silence with the mother facing one side of back passenger car door. Tusmo heard the screeching voice from behind on the verandah of the house speaking to her back, a voice toward which she would not turn.

The voice kept saying, in an almost beseeching manner, "My sister, my sister, where are you going so early? Don't your uncle and I at least deserve a goodbye? After how much I have done for you while you were here! How ungrateful can your relatives be, Hassan? She has neither spoken to you, nor said anything about this. How shocking this all is!"

With that, Tusmo heard a slow starting and then an almost growling beginning of what turned out to be an extended short wail which quickly fell back to a growl whimper.

"I tell you every time this happens not to bring your ungrateful relatives to our kind home."

Tusmo heard the sound of her rapid fit trailing off back into the house, seemingly grieved by yet another ungrateful relative of her husband's clan.

He came out as she left. She heard him with her ears as she stood still, with her back to the house facing the vehicle. He came next to her and then passed her, stooping a little to open the vehicle without a word. He was quite flustered and apologetic in demeanor. It did not bode well that a man of his stature really had no control over what happened in the house. In part, it was also that he was so ashamed of the pettiness his wife espoused in general, and particularly given the idea that food in his society was considered public. It was shameful to be concerned with the hoarding and denying of food. It was considered, amongst the Somal, reprehensible and surely a mark a very low birth.

Her uncle let the girls and Tusmo in and slid into the driver's seat without a word. They drove for a while before he started talking again. He started to describe Dheka, what a wonderful girl she was, and how she had also come here by herself. Her father had spoken to him via telephone a day before she arrived in Nairobi. She was also at him house for a week. It was now almost a year and a half since then. She was a very pleasant girl, he said, though she kept to herself while attending school.

"She is living with a lot of other women," he continued, "in a house where they share the rooms. The house is owned by someone I know, and some of them have children like yourself. I spoke to her yesterday. I was waiting for a vacancy, and it has finally has come.

"Tusmo, I cannot explain why or how my wife began to behave in this terrible way towards in particular my relatives. You are younger and probably do not see why a man of my stature has not been able to exercise more control over his household and children, a very basic thing for a man. But I have learnt to live with her and the children are many. They have also learnt to deal with her as being their one and only mother.

"They know they can not get another one, and I have realized the same thing. I have made amends on behalf of my children more so then myself. In this way, she becomes tolerable. I try not to take anyone home, but by the same token, I can not leave the women at the lodge, it is not a place for them."

The car pulled into the streets of the busy neighborhood of Eastleigh. Tusmo recognized it from her brief stay at her uncle's lodge.

"Uncle, this house is not too far from my lodge. It is actually very close to where you are going to be staying."

The car pulled into a side-street and stopped around the middle of it. There was what seemed to be a back door to the enclosure, leading to a spread out courtyard style bungalow in a rectangle formation. The rooms and dwellings faced the rectangle of the common space which was the long rectangle courtyard.

"Wait here," he said, and left the car and knocked the door hard. There was a quick answer to the knock. The door opened from the inside and he came back to the car which was quite close to the door and opened the door, motioning to the girls and to Tusmo to come out.

He went, passing the man who opened the door, followed by the girls and Tusmo. They stepped into a world within itself – lines and lines of clothing. The courtyard was full of the clothlines. The floor was wet, and the day was overcast and cloudy. The water was everywhere from the clothes. Tusmo could not see anything beyond these heavily strewn sheets soaking the cluttered courtyard. They followed the lead of their relative almost blindly. Then, they came to a halt as they went through the little gap made between the end of the lines.

They came to a stop at one of the doors facing the courtyard. A door was opened by a key her uncle had, and he quickly switched on the lights exposing the rather small interior. The room was bare with two wooden beds that were made, separated by an equally small wooden chest.

"Tusmo this is going to be your home for now, until I am able to figure out how to contact our relatives in Ethiopia and Somal. You will be able to cook here at your own discretion, that is what most of the families do here. You will soon get well adjusted."

"Is Dheka here?" he asked the guard who Tusmo had not noticed was behind them. The guard answered, "No she's gone somewhere, but will be sure to return."

"Okay, make sure she meets this new family. Tell her this is the family I was telling her about. Also, make sure that you get them everything they need to cook, and the rations. Here is some money, Tusmo. Make sure Dheka takes you to get the things you need."

He spoke to the guard again in the more commanding tone he had cultivated during his lifetime when dealing with instructing workers under his charge. He spoke to the guard in Kiswahili which Tusmo did not understand. He latter explained what he instructed to the guard again in Somal so that she would know what was going on. He made sure to give her what she needed to the best of his ability, even though the whole move occurred sooner than expected.

He suspected that it was too early to rouse Dheka, and this what he detected in the guards hesitation to answer the simple question when it was posed regarding Dheka. Finally, he spoke to Tusmo while smiling at the girls who were as usual running around and jumping on the bed. They had also become attached to their uncle who truly loved children. They grabbed at his pant legs, and leaned on him while he talked. At times, they forgot their mother was around. He spoke to Tusmo in parting saying he was not far at all, and that he had also instructed the guard to bring her to the lodge when ever she needed, till she could get around on her own.

With this, he left, and Tusmo said her thanks to him. She was very happy despite the reality of being nearly abandoned in this new environment, where for the moment she could not even communicate with the only other adult, the guard. Her mind made a quick inventory of the rooms and the surrounding courting strewn with long, wet bed sheets. If there were families around she could only hear their chatter from a far. From where she was, she could not hear the familiar noises of life. Perhaps she thought to herself that it was just too early, cold, and overcast – not the greatest time for a frolic in the deluge of water on the concrete fine polished floor of the courtyard. Even the girls did not want to venture out of the room.

They preoccupied themselves, as children do at play, with just about anything. It was the cabinet drawers this time. They pulled the drawers out and in, out and in. She kept a peripheral mother's surveillance about her, just kept tabs that the drawers would not fall on them. Luckily the dresser was quite short, and she reminded them to be mindful not to jam their fingers in the process. She removed the beddings and remade the beds. She was at last free from that petty food ogre. She was just someone that made her, considerations as bad as they were, stop to take a look at how some people were entirely in a crazy world of their own.

She settled down in her new quarters. The girls were on one of the beds with her, asking her questions in between their play with the chest drawers, then rushing to the small window frame that allowed you to peer outside. The view was of the drab clothes lines and the wetness of the equally cloudy day.

She sat there for a while, when suddenly there was a knock. The guard brought in a hearth of red charcoal which he carried in a limestone vessel at the ears. The vessel had a flat button like a large incense burner, and he placed it on the floor of the cold room. He pointed at the fire and made a sound, and then wagged his fingers at the girls, to warn them playfully not to play with the fire. He left immediately after. The room instantly become very cozy despite the polished to a fine finish cement plaster layer floor. The cement added to not only the drabness of the outside day but impacted the temperature, it remained cold for hours and days after the sun had warmed and scorched the day.

It was seasonably cold in this very high-altitude city, compared to the more temperate climate of the sea level coast of Somal.

The hearth was a thoughtful addition to the sterile, no-frill concrete room. Tusmo and the girls fell asleep a little after the fire was brought in. She had hardly slept during the weeks she was at the ogre's house, and last night only compounded her exhaustion to a heightened-bordering-mental state of affairs.

A few hours later, Tusmo woke up to the playful orchestra of the children's high pitched sounds, with the staccato interruptions of adult conversions here and there.

There was a soft knock on the door. Tusmo opened the door to a most beautiful tall and slender young woman of barely twenty, she was wearing a long flowing skirt and her head was covered with a multicolored headscarf. She was stunningly attractive with large, intelligent, light-brown eyes, dark, full lips, and a lean body shaped and accentuated by voluptuous hips in contrast to a tiny waist hugged tightly by a long sleeve turtle neck.

She looked at Tusmo and smiled through her beautiful white teeth, introducing herself with a very sensuous raspy middle range soft tone, "Hello I am your cousin Dheka," she said as she offered her hand, then she rushed to the children and started hugging them as if she had known them for eternity.

Tusmo sat down right next to Dheka, smiling in spite of herself. She immediately became quite comfortable with her. She was dressed modestly but, within tha,t quite fashionably. She had a lot of taste and flair in the way she adorned her wear and in the choice of what she wore and how she wore it. Instantly, Tusmo thought of things she had forgotten like beautiful clothes, and perfume, the times she spent when making herself ready for a wedding. All these things came back with Dheka.

Her hair was teasingly exposed in bangs loose beyond the wrap of her head scarf, dark shiny and curly. She had a raucous low-tone laughter that had Tusmo and the kids bedazzled. There was something other worldly about this gorgeous young woman, a delicate balance between the more traditional and the new, with an air of independence that oozed self-affirmation. Tusmo thought her quite unlike many woman she had seen. She knew women that were uncompromisingly independent, but they did it within the convention of feminine demure, or at least expected demure.

They sat down and exchanged stories of where they came from and what they were doing. She said that she was waiting for her father to arrange for her to join him in the U.K. and she was here to improve herself through education. She wanted to be a nurse, she said, and was not in a hurry to marry, even though there was an endless line of men from every corner it seemed that had proposed or were in the process of proposing to her, in the hopes that they could spend the rest of their life with her.

Dheka brushed most of them off. Not that she was not attracted to men, but rather she had her own plans, and in these plans there was no opening for a man at this period of her life. This was tempered in part by the many subjugations she had witnessed of husbands' wives which she had seen, including that of her mother in Somal.

She was a pleasant sight. Her conversation was very passion-ate and concerned with Tusmo. She knew some of the things that surrounded Tusmo's appearance in Nairobi, but only in very broad strokes. Tusmo was enlivened by Dheka's positive zest for life. She, for a moment, saw the brighter parts of things, and it also comforted her that she was surrounded by this very different young lady, who saw ways out rather than the more common 'No Way Out.'

She called someone from where they were seated. The guard came in smiling more than Tusmo had seen him prior to this. He also was clearly under Dheka's spell. She said something to him in Kiswahili, and he vanished for a minute and came back with a flask of the Somal staple of sweetened tea. He merrily placed the transparent thick glasses and poured the steaming hot tea in it and left immediately.

They smiled at each other, and he left. "Tusmo, this is a very dif-ferent place from where we are from. There are many things that are going on so fast that one has to take a deep breath before he or she can plunge into the depths of no return."

She giggled at something or the other she was in the process of trying to make clear. She was also concerned about the news at home; she asked about the city, the people and the government. Tusmo talked minimally about these particular things as she was more inclined towards forgetting at least for the moment her ideal situation. She was also quite interested in whatever information she could get about the Somal exiles in Ethiopia, whether some had relatives here and there or some other form of communications that went to and fro. She had the notion that this young lady knew a lot about her surroundings.

They drank the tea, with a promise for exploration of their just-outside environment, laden with similar exiles whom, as it were, des-tiny had placed in close quarters in search of the solace of belonging to the same.

Dheka, Tusmo, and the girls ventured out into the courtyard toward an opening creating by the end of the clothlines close to the end of the enclosed space where there was a communal faucet and space enough for the tenants who lived there to wash their things.

Before the exiles, these had been South Asian dwellings that were built to suit the needs of families and their extensions through the marriages and children, accommodating the increase in demand for space which occurs over the generations. It had always been a sanctuary of sorts from the external outside world of displacement. Though not their original homes, exiles felt comforted in the enclosed idea of it. In the mind, recreated in this confined space, they were away from colonial intrusion, from others that come with the displacement.

Dheka greeted everyone of the ladies who were busy talking, washing, or cooking on a small stove right outside the last doors closer to the end of the enclosure. Tusmo sensed a little reserve in her companion as she made this round with her. She told them collectively who Tusmo was, and they were either interested or preoccupied with what they were doing. She noticed a sneering face amongst one of the ladies, round about the same age of Dheka, who was clearly aggravated by the presence of Dheka.

Dheka continued to speak, and Tusmo answered some of the questions posed to her like who was her husband, this being an alternate way to answer the question of whether she was married or not at the moment, and if she had other children she which she might have left behind in Somal.

Dheka commenced to her room after this brief meet and greet tour. She was definitely not too enthused by it. The girls on the other hand were delighted to see other children around them of various ages, especially those who were close in age to them.

Dheka's room had the same flair she had. It exuded a lived sanctity of both refuge and comfort. There was perfume, colorful drapes on her windows, a wooden chest, covered with portraits of her father, brother, and relatives in some western country. Most of them were of people laden with heavy layered clothing, pictured in the snow. The snow or the uncommon landscape of snow took both the children and Tusmo back. Dheka tried to explain this but could not, for she herself had not seen or felt this strange phenomenon. Indeed, Tusmo and the girls saw the snow in the pictures and knew it existed, but it remained a mystery for them, nonetheless.

. . . .

They stayed in her room as she poured some more tea. Dheka said they would have to go shopping for warmer clothes both for Tusmo and the girls.

"Tusmo, I have been here for a year and a half now and," she continued in that musical voice, "there are many things you have to do. I will slowly try and show you around to the point that you are capable of it yourself. The first thing is we have to enroll the girls in school. This will take a little time, but they should learn whatever they can, even though you have no idea how long you are here for. We will also go shopping and do the rest of things that need doing."

TWENTY NINE

Nairobi and the Exquite Dheka

IN THE VILLAGE THE ELDERS GATHERED FOR A LONG LUNCH session with chat afterwards. The major topic would be how to get the deliberations to the table of what the chief and Jama were pushing. The chief had asked for a select group of people to attend, the ones he had long dealings with, and were similar to him in makeup.

Jama opened the floor after the hearty meal, and the bundles of chat had been distributed to all. All were sitting in traditional-style on the mats.

"Cousins and brothers, today we are here with a hard earned victory from the governor of this region. We have won things with a great fight from our venerable leader, the Chief."

For our brave chief came a chorus from the seated and satiated clan member "One, is that no stone will be left unturned until the right soldiers are court marshaled for their murder of our beloved clan sons. Second, is that all the families of the bereaved will be handsomely compensated to the satisfaction of you the clan elders. This, the great chief, our leader, has managed to fight for in Burco tirelessly. He is always there when he is needed. He is unlike some of the other clan chiefs. He is dedicated to his clan's affairs in the town, far off from where anyone can honestly keep a watchful eye on what he does. Yet, he remains steadfast in his obligation to represent the clan. Now we must consider his proposal to us, listen to him, and let us make a wise decision after he speaks. Remember also how many times he has led us to the most prudent path. Please speak, Chief."

Jama sat down and cleared the spot for the chief to now launch his agenda.

"I will not say much. All of you know the tragedy that has occurred recently and you also know how unreasonable that makes the aggrieved. So much so that one father, during the gathering we had, accused me of being in cahoots with the State." Here, the elders could be heard laughing as did some others of the gathering, loudly.

"We know that it is painful to lose one son, but it is to become delusional, to believe that the state is not interested in killing people because of their clan affiliation. No! No! That is simply not the case. However, we do have very young, hot-headed soldiers who do grave things without thinking. But these are individual acts and not the Government's policy. I am here to tell you that we have a generous portion from the governor to settle the matters at hand. We must get away from certain old ways. We are a nation now, and the State is the one to address murderous crimes between civilians and members of the governments, such as is the case where the soldiers are impli-cated. We cannot go and do it the old way; that is, it would simply not be legal.

"Everything must be done through the proper channels. You must all convince the fathers, and in particular the one who accused me to accept the fate of Allah, and to forgive, even though one is given a god-given right to act towards an eye for an eye or a life for a life. But it is also better in the eyes of Allah to forgive and take the diya instead.

This is the more blessed way of a Muslim."

The elders in essence were a cheer-leading team for the chief. None of those who were vocal about anything or were unbendable to the lootings were branded intransigent. The chief was spinning his masterful yarn. He had crushed their independent wills with so many layers and layers of propaganda, that he could nearly taste the defeat of the father who was so crude to him.

This gathering was crucial in that it was to convene before the big and public meeting of the clan. Under the same tree, everyone from the clan who could attend would. The gathering continued their chat session until the sun set. The meeting under the tree was to convene the day after, and all had been notified to attend. Here, the clan would decide whether to take the traditional compensation of around a hundred camels for each person that was killed by the Government's soldiers."

The old man and Jama went for a prayer and an early night in anticipation of a final confrontation between the camp of his wife and the elders, whom he had fed and to whom he had secretly doled out some of the cash. They were also anticipating their share of the clan portion of the compensation in camels. The chief slept, restored and quite happy, with another battle won in propaganda victory. He snickered when he imagined what would surely await the belligerent nomad when he went home to his weather-beaten wife.

Ali Deray got wind of this rather weak stance of the governor and he went to see him immediately. He burst into his office and began to scold him as if he was a school boy.

"What a weak man you are," he told the governor, "You are a member of the most powerful clan in Somal. Why are you given to such squander with good will when you have such brute force behind you?"

He asked him to come to the window in a rage, "Look out there what do you see?" The governor was clearly awkward, showing visible signs of fear of this junior clansmen.

"What do you see Governor?" he asked again. The governor looked again, and he saw, parading outside in his compound and beyond a sea of brown khaki, berets, armored vehicles, trucks, and a sea of gun-totting soldiers. Instinctively, he could now see what Ali Deray was getting at, but he still demurred and said nothing.

"You coward." Ali continued, "How can you let these nomads tell you what to do? You know they would do the same to us. Why are you trying to speak to them in a language they don't understand? The only thing they must understand is fear. How the hell do you think our clan is able to remain on top of it if you give up to their ideas of what is just? We will lose everything, and must, absolutely, keep everything!"

He was shouting now uncontrollably. "You will not compensate anyone," he said while they were still at the window. He forced the back of the head of the governor and smothered his face on the window. "That power you have outside is what you will use. Kill them like flies, if need be." Ali walked out to the car and was driven to his office.

He dispatched a communication to the nearest Hinterland military installation and spoke to the commander there. He shouted some instructions down his throat, and made him understand what his orders were.

" Commander, you can not fail in this." "Yes, sir," the commander said.

Ali had reasons to become so frustrated with everyone. He had come here on a quick shock-and-awe mission, which turned out to become such a lengthy unending mission that increased by the day rather than showing any signs of ending. He had left his beloved situation where he had run of the city, where he had had all the power, money, and a jet-set life that he had become accustomed to. He had had none of these crude and sorry excuses for humans here in the Hinterland. He was now here and kept here by his mentor the general. Everyday, the situation become worse it seemed. The governments attacked, killed, and reeked havoc. The rebels would respond in kind. It got to a point where the military was overwhelmed by so many ambushes, crazy feats of bravery by the rebels. To cap all of this, Ali was avoided by everyone, everywhere, including members of the clan, state and especially the public in this, what he saw as a hostile town.

He was both much feared and hated by the people in this area, they knew him up close and personal. They had lost many members of the clan to this individual's orders. Absolutely no one talked to him willingly. He had his chat with his bodyguards, and with freaked out women companions, none of whom wanted to be within ten miles of him, much less sitting next to him.

The very brave, ruling clan, was known out in the open in this region. There was no more camouflage. Everything had descended to out and out raw murder between the military and a part of its civilians. If there were any uncertainties, Ali made the decision by Beheyeah to fight the State quite clear. His mentor was still confident of victory and encouraged Ali's maniacal approach. Soon the government was losing so badly in the all these areas, they were replenishing troops, by arresting youngsters from poor families, and shipping them in the dead of the night to the front. They in turn, when confronted with horror, deserted in mass, and the nomads joined the cause in masse.

The government was losing to rebels, and the amount of resistance and capture of military hardware from fleeing conscripted soldiers was a losing game. Ali Deray, Kumanay, and the powerful clan, had become blind in their rage to subjugate the naturally independent nomads. They incurred heavy losses as did the nomads, but they were committed to end this clan tyranny.

Yusuf was himself running amok in the city. He had taken Ali's position, but was much greedier than Ali; he was also very insecure about his Hinterland ways. His self-consiousness become a tragedy for the city dwellers, he could not fit in like Ali fit in, and the fear he generated with those who used to have business dealings with Ali made him lose most of the access to deals Ali was privy to. The problem became that he was increasingly using, and accompanied by all manner of rogues who were not necessarily members of his clan, but were plain petty criminals. This is the company he was comfortable with, and Kumanay was too busy with the hinterland rebel groups to put a lid on him. He was dangerous himself, but Yusuf took this to another level altogether. Regardless of who you were, Yusuf and his street urchins were liable to take whatever you might have, without blinking an eye at murder. The resources were getting more and more depleted by the all out war with the rebels in the Hinterland, despite, of course, the Father of the Nation's reconciliation with his fellow dictator in Ethiopia. They agreed to deport the opposition groups from their territories. This meant both countries witnessed an increase of rebel fighting from all the factions within their borders. Whatever the rationale, it worked against both the regimes. There were skirmishes everywhere, and nowhere was the State allowed full control of the nation.

This atmosphere of dwindled resources and wanton fear for public safety from marauding groups who took orders from no one made the clan government visible to the masses. The unhappy lot of parents of disappeared youth conscripted into the military made the city dwellers follow the path of Tusmo took years ago.

There was no one who could stand Yusuf and his henchmen and the many others like him, all intoxicated with clan power. They resorted to pillaging everything, when their original backers, the clan state, ran out of resources to sustain their greedy ways. People were leaving by the droves to seek safety elsewhere.

Kumanay, with his benefactor gone, found it more and more difficult to get the arms and money he needed to sustain this clantocracy. The Father of the Nation was traveling everywhere, looking for support. He was often confronted by protesting Somals overseas; ironically he was the one who sent them there in the first. Somehow, he and his trusted clan general believed they were capable of sustaining this system indefinitely. Until at least there was a quiet, cowered and subjugated Somal. Unfortunately for the clan state they were taking heavy losses.

The elder convened the gathering under the tree and all were in attendance to see and know what the chief had in mind. Other than those who were privy to the invite, the younger men, or those who might see something amiss were none the wiser. The Father who previously questioned the chief was there, seething with anger. He had had a very big fight with his wife when he got home after the chief's visit. He was confronted by his wife who had, rather bizarrely, gone wild from the very controlled person she was. Even in her mourning she had been very careful not to alarm her mostly grown children, and their children, with the sense of loss she really felt. The minute he arrived she had started a tirade. This really disarmed him.

"What do you want to be the memory of your son and this family? Do you want your grandchildren to be nicknamed the decendents of the intractable one? The one who does not adhere to the wisdom of the court of elders? People lose their sons, but know how to be humble before the will of Allah. Who is grieving more than me? You know how he was my heart. I am not going to let you bring misery to other people. You must learn to forgive and accept the fate of Allah. Our son is gone now, make peace with the world. Take the offer of reconciliation that the government and our respected elder have come here to offer. Stop the blood. The other father has also agreed to this. The governor has sent out protestations to the military and has assured the akil that everyone of them will be court marshalled by the state. Accept! Accept, you stubborn fool! You have always been stubborn. How are you going to kill the military?"

The father of the son was shocked at this confrontation. He did not know what had possessed his wife. Before, she was more adamant than he was that there must be a life for her beloved's life. What changed her so? He was so shocked that he went out of the module and slept outside that night with the camels in wonderment. She had not told him but he knew that old corrupt bastard had been over while he was away. He could not believe how low this person was. This man, the clan revered and thought was beyond morale reproach. Wow, he thought, city people are quite an amazing bunch. They have no boundaries of moral conduct. He did not sleep much that night, and thought what an impossible position to be in when the mother of your son is convinced that the murderers of her beloved son are also the good guys. Amazing, he thought, just amazing. *What treachery that old man abides by! He has no fear of Allah!*

The father slept confused and was not sure what to do the next day at the gathering. He just lay there, looking up at the open sky, beyond anger. The prospect of the private meeting between the fathers of the dead and the chief with his lackey elders along with some of his very close cousins kept floating in and out of his mind: running interference of his thoughts underneath this bright-starred night in the warm open air of the hinterland.

His wife also slept convulsively, not knowing whether he would accept the way that the chief would see it. She thought it was just his stubbornness, and eventually she thought, his indignant anger would subside, as it would have to, with the wages of time, as it was for herself.

 THIRTY

Deya

. . . .

HOAGSADAY HAD BY NOW ADAPTED HIMSELF TO THIS LIFE of forays into battles and skirmishes. They lived in the hinterland from hand to mouth, but were getting more and more in numbers, and victories of the states' soldiers. The forays had hardened him in constitution; he did not flinch much at the sight of death. He become quite accustomed to the wizzing of bullets, grenades and the close proximity of the smell of blood.

Their logistical support had gotten a little better, but day in and day out, the clan became more and more desperate in their violent deeds. They attacked anything moving day or night, in turn they became highly susceptible to any kind of movement. They were always weary of some ambush around the corner, while they slept hidden in the day. Hoagsaday much preferred the danger of attacking a military camp or ambushing and guarding installation then making a run for it. He relished the encounters between the soldiers, who became increasingly very low in morale, more and more reluctant to fight on behalf of a pretentious nation. A lot were not privy to the power base, because they were not part of the ruling elite, but had bought into the national army charade.

The years had made him resilient in his resolve to end this misery for everyone — for his daughter, and those who were coming after them — Let them not be part of such terrible times. And, in Allah's name, they will not. He hoped he might come out alive someday to

return to the normal everyday things he wanted to have: long conversations with his daughters, the caressing and cuddling of his wife,
all in the peaceful land of his birth. However sweet the future was, the
present distracted him from it with a very ugly reality. The people of
this his clan and region were suffering tremendously from a military
intelligence officer who had, for some years now, made everything
smell the bad stench of death. The people were beyond the precipice
of return. He had the power, and he visited his might upon innocent
civilians. The level of death and torture he was sanctioning, as a de
facto governor, was atrocious.

Hoagsaday's group had earned the position of one of the most
elite of the small militia units. They had been involved in many near
impossible missions, literally in the jaws of the lion. The mere mention of Hoagsaday brought shivers to the soldiers who feared him and
others for their notorious suicidal bravery against all odds. Ali Deray
knew he was the man he had ordered arrested years ago, when on a
whim he thought the guy had too much, and the general encouraged
it because he was trying to get at his school mate, Beheyeah, whom
he despised virulently. Hoagsaday did not know the intrigue behind
his arrest, but one thing he did know was he was innocent. He also
knew that it was Ali Deray who had ordered him arrested. Quickly,
he inherited him while he was alive.

He secretly had been lobbying the commanders, whenever he
could, to get an operation going. He wanted one not unlike the dare
devil ones he had been in before. He wanted to hit two birds with one
stone. He wanted to rid the region of this nefarious regional commander. This would completely demoralize the clan state and their
supporters. The absolute prize would be that he would in turn be the
one to capture Ali Deray as he had done to Hoagsaday through his
underlings. This commenced the ruin of many a life from that point
onwards. His family's life became shattered. He was biding his time
for just that day when he would get the opportunity to confront
Ali Deray.

The next day the father got up and left very early towards the
trees. He wanted to get there early, his anger had turned into a quite
determined rage. He left the tending of the camel to his son, and

commenced to the gathering. The walk today to the settlement took him a little time. The hours it took to get there at a brisk walk seemed to subside as he got closer and closer to the gathering trees.

He got there just when the little makeshift tea shops with the ground for seats were serving their first customers. His clan settlement was abuzz with others like him, who would normally be tending to the herds, came into to the settlement just to attend or have their say at the meeting. Everyone who could speak did about the situation in their regions, it had affected everyone drastically in some way. They wanted to hear what the chief had come up with. The hate for the clan state had reached enormous proportions. Their lives for the past several years had known repression only and untoward government soldiers laying siege to their lives and property.

The father ordered tea with camel milk, and sat there on the ground, quiet. He was absentmindedly making a buzz sound from sipping the very hot tea. He leaned against the post and nodded off after he finished his transparent hot glass of tea, tired from last night's lack of sleep.

The settlement was now getting crowded and people were beginning to go towards the trees. Some were making sure they had choice places very close to the proceedings.

The soldiers were around too, looking menacingly at the people. They knew there was going to be more people here than normal. They were also weary of a larger than normal nomad gathering, especially one hostile to the soldiers. They would outnumber them with guns. Most had an AK-47 with them at all times, a very old tradition.

The chief, Jama, and the others started occupying the natural dais. The father had secured a spot for himself right next to where the elders were. This is what he came early for – to be very close to this treacherous soul. He wanted to see if he could spot anything unusually devilish about him.

An elder with a beautifully kept beard had started the meeting. He started with the normal praises to Allah, and did not linger much, speaking after blessing the whole crowd. The crowd responded with the great "Amin," then he sat down.

Jama started with the usual flowery accolades for his boss and partner in crime, the chief. He extolled the virtues of his grandfather, then of his father, and finally of himself. He groveled shamelessly, but now the father saw clearly through this groveling. He then launched into a tirade against the soldiers, who he said acted independently of orders, he added about the governors' tireless efforts to see justice prevail. He then went into the extraordinary work of the chief needed in order to get the governor to compensate the families with such short notice. He mentioned how he single- handedly fought the state to expedite the court marshal of the perpetrators. The chief, he said was a god-fearing man, advocating tirelessly for his clan in a sea of hostility. It was finally the turn of the chief, who this time did not sit down completely, fearing a repeat of that awful getting up on all fours display he did the last time.

He looked into the sea of his flock, feeling very satisfied with his propaganda coup the previous night. He pretended not to see the wild-looking man who had questioned and berated him so severely the last time he was out. He had a much more serene look. Today he was the picture of confidence.

"My brothers, I bring you many heartfelt salams from the governors and his condolences. He sends this to you my brethren. He is personally committed to see that the soldiers who opened fire on our sons will be dealt with severely. He has already made great strides to that effect. He and I both urge you to be patient and not to confuse the government who are fundamentally against such actions with the soldiers who acted on their own. We are living in troubled times. There is a bad drought on top of all these other problems. These are some of the most trying of times, and even though it is difficult, we must stick to the ways of our faith. The dictate of forgiveness, that is better in the eyes of Allah, than the taking of another life instead.

"After all, it is Allah who has ordained what is so, and it is as he wills. Recent times have tested and continue to test this clan, especially the parents of the recent dead in particular. I want you to know that we stand with you in your loss, and understand your pain and circumstances. For several days now, the elders of the clan and myself and some of the aggrieved parents think it is prudent now to consider the more than adequate compensation the governor has offered."

The father who was privy to such agreements grew monstrously livid. He thought about the bitter fight this man speaking had caused between him and the mother of his son. She had never gone to the extremes she had with him the night before, not ever.

A blurry vision of his helpless son came to the fore of his mind. The chief became an animated moving mouth in the background of the vision of his son laying wounded at the well, breathing very hard as he took his last breaths on this earth. The father rose from his sitting position and unlocked the safety guard of his AK as he stood up. He moved the AK from his shoulder strap in a matter of seconds, grasping the machine with both hands. He shouted as he unloaded the weapon blind with rage. He shouted as he mowed down the chief who fell as he was jerked around by the force of the bullets as they connected with his flesh.

"He is not your son. You will not make a mockery of me nor the memory of my dead son. Let this be the last time you lie to all of us." The spray of bullets from the AK wounded Jama severely and the other elders on the naturally elevated dias. The other nomads in the gathering gunned the father down to stop him from killing and wounding more people. He lay there frothing at the mouth with sweat pouring from his forehead, with blood flowing from his bullet wounds, dead.

THIRTY ONE

Last Legs

. . . .

THE NEWS OF THIS BEREAVED FATHER'S SHOOTING OF HIS chief hit the nomad grape vine from corner to corner.

The military's actions were increased as was the militia's. The fighting continued raging on and on.

The rebels were gaining ground and weapons from the conscripts every day now. It was not even a fight at times when a whole group of soldiers would lay down the weapons for the safe passage of the rebels at the consternation of their commanders usually members of the ruling clan.

The security around Ali became tighter, everyone in the region wanted a piece of him. A hated man, yet he was still quite oblivious to the state of affairs. The clan was losing the battle to the rebel groups. They had all moved into the borders of Somal and were forced to fight the military for footing in the country. They simply had no other choice after they were thrown out of Ethiopia.

The rebels had decided they were going to launch a massive attack – no more hit- and-runs. They would take over the major cities in the Northern region, and the other Liberation Front would go on from the mid-South all the way to the capital. Kumanay, in a last attempt to stymie the operation, paid recruited white mercenaries from South Africa, still under apartheid, to bomb civilians in Beheyeah's region of the North of Somal, a region which had undergone many forays by the Somal, the Somal Air Force doing the same on many occasions in the town of Hargeisa in the same region.

Hoagsaday got his chance to go to Ali Deray's Headquarters. He was going to be one of the men who would simultaneously attack the fortified barrack which also served as Ali Deray's home. Others contingents were assigned to attack other military installations to wrench them finally from the regime's soldiers. Hoagsaday volunteered to go to the fortified barracks of the intelligence head quarters, he new his prize would be there. Hoagsaday's group was the most experienced in surprise attacks. They were the ones who were to lead the operation at an hour before dawn for the element of surprise, and to keep the soldiers from mounting any form of coherent resistance by knocking out the place where both intelligence and reinforcements would come from. Hoagsaday's group, at the minimum, was to keep them as preoccupied as possible so as to give sufficient time to the others to overwhelm the military which would be isolated from headquarters by then. It was three A.M. and the small attack groups spread out and walked quickly with light arms, grenades, and bazookas. The stealth would be their only advantage. They kept moving closer and closer to the large walled military barracks.

They took out the forward look out sentries very quickly. They moved in the dark without a sound, all in all there were about five groups of six, all fanned out along the wall, inching closer and closer to where there was going to be a very big show done.

They climbed the walls coming around and killing the other sentries, letting all them through the main door. There they fanned out again, attaching themselves to the walls of the buildings. Any movement from inside the camp by the soldiers was quickly marked and silenced by hand, as the others continued to surround the soldiers' sleeping quarters. The big guns sitting high on the wall were the first ones to get commandeered by the rebels. In the dark, they now sat high overlooking the town. Some turned their guns towards the city anticipating some reinforcements or if some soldiers were coming back. All the other guns in the towers were now trained on the inside of the camp.

When they were all in place Beheyeah waved his hand and they broke the silent night to the horror of the soldiers. Their movements were so quick and well coordinated, they were stunned by how lax they were. The rebels did not fire a shot, at first. Hoagsaday went around to where he assumed the commanding officer was, asking the posted sentry who was there. His soldier had answered no one.

He shouted a command, "Bring the commanding officer here" to his men. The frog marched the officers to Hoagsaday. The identity of Ali Deray was known by the rebels. They turned the camp upside down, but could find no Ali Deray. Hoagsaday was extremely disappointed. He had been waiting for this moment for a long time, in fact he never thought it was ever going to present itself. He would wait here for the day to break, and he told the men to identify and separate the officers from the regulars. He told them also to separate them in relation to crimes they had committed in any way while they were in command. His men knew who had done what in this region. Hoagsaday sat there in the largest camp, dreaming of how this was the beginning of something very different and new. He could not wait for the day to break and to gather intelligence on the other raids – their successes and failures.

He had heard a lot of heavy fighting just very shortly after the allotted time he had given Hoagsaday to have completed his mission. He wondered, did some one get Ali Deray before him? He sat in what was obviously Ali Deray's chair and office. There was a huge picture of General Kumanay and the venerable Father of the Nation.

That night, Ali Deray slept as he sometimes did at the house of one of the many mistresses he had in the town. This time, he was unaware of how this saved him. He heard a lot of heavy fighting which woke him up enough to pace the floor, and he thought about what to do, whether to go back to the camp or to let his second-in-command handle whatever it was. He in no way expected anything as drastic as what was really happening to be going on. He did not know the half of it, deluded as he was by his arrogance. He couldn't have known that a man he had probably forgotten had just missed him.

But instinct had kicked in at some point because a lot of things were not right through the night and through the very early morning.

The operations radio was unusually silent. The fighting was very close to the airport and other important places, he could tell by where the sounds were emanating from. He stepped outside the bungalow and onto the compound. His driver was sleeping outside the vehicle on a mat. He went to the armed guards that had followed him, searching for them around the compound in their usual places. He still could not figure out what was nagging him, but it was quickly turning into a scare. The darkness of this early morning was now very quiet after a lot of gunfire, for what seemed like hours. He tried his radio and got no answer. He tried again.

"Commander Cheetah to Base Cheetah." No answer: dead quiet. His suspicion was piqued further. He went inside, armed himself, and decided to get to the base quickly. He shouted at the guards to be on alert and to ride straddling the doors of his vehicle along with the small army that followed him everywhere in jeeps. They moved fast and at great speeds through public places. Ali was never seen by the public. His windows were always covered with the bodies of his guards who stood upright on the car running boards, holding onto special hooks on the car. They faced the passengers on both sides. There were four of them carrying machine guns with loose hands facing the opposite side.

There was hardly any movement this morning. This also added a lot of worry to Ali Deray. He got in the vehicle and began the speedy journey to the barracks. They wizzed through a sleepy town in the wee hours of the morning, and the quiet gave Ali some repose. He thought that perhaps he had just gotten carried away with all he had imagined. It had probably just been some nomads getting wasted by the soldiers this morning.

The car moved faster and closer towards the barracks. The gates were closed and everything seemed quite normal. As they got closer, the rebels who were now manning the tower guns signaled an approaching vehicle. They remained silent and saluted Ali as the gates were open. All Ali could see were his uniforms opening the gate.

He was let in and surrounded by Hoagsaday's men. They were all captured with the firing of a bullet.

When the rebels took Ali to their commander, he was shocked and showing signs of faint. He just trembled to bits when he understood he was the prisoner of the people he never imagined would ever get the upper hand.

"What is your name and rank soldier?" he was asked by a man standing next to Hoagsaday.

He replied, "Colonel Ali Deray."

In a flash, Hoagsaday got up, eyes blazing. He thought to himself, Could this be? Is this the man? Clearly, Ali did not know Hoagsaday. He just stood there, his posture, shoulders slumped and disheveled of spirit, a far cry from the rod-like arrogant stiffness Ali was known for. Hoagsaday looked and sat down with the weight of this encounter.

He was trying to clear his mind, not believing that this was actually happening. He just sat there dumbfounded with the name Ali Deray. Replaying in his head was the voice, "I am Colonel Ali Deray; I am colonel Ali Deray."

All of a sudden there was a lot of noise outside. Hoagsaday's soldiers were trying to force their way into the office, each blocking the other's way in a hurry to get to Ali. They were each shouting their own threats, the gist of which was "Let me take care of him." Another would say, "No! Let me skin him alive!"

Yet another was issuing threats to the others, "Listen guys, none of you will touch him. He is mine. Do you know what he has done to me?"

Hoagsaday was of a mind to give him to the crowd. Let them tear him to pieces as long as he got the biggest one. Ali could hear the men outside, and knew that, sooner or later, the door was going to give way.

He let out a shriek, begging for Hoagsaday not to let the crowd get to him. He was trembling with streams of tears rolling down his cheeks. He was truly a man who was staring death in the face. Hoagsaday knew he could not get his men to back down. Ali's name was synonymous with the clan-state victimization of other clans. No one there from the group was asking for calm. Ali's capture had unanimously whipped everyone into a bloodthirsty frenzy. Hoagsaday, despite his own wishes, went out and told the other man inside not to let anyone in. It took him a while to get everyone away; and that was nothing, he thought when the town heard of Ali's whereabouts, they were definitely going to storm the place. Hoagsaday's instinctive crazy reaction to this horrendous figure subsided.

When he considered the maddening hate he had brought out in people it could be heard harrowingly clear, just outside the door. As it were, the winds of fate had placed Hoagsaday and Ali Deray, his tormentor, in one room. The banging on the door was getting louder the more desperate the crowd got. Ali let out a shriek every time the audible danger became louder. Hoagsaday saw the frailty of this coward. His eyes were darting around like a nervous rat. Afraid to sit or stand, he could see his violent death before him. Hoagsaday went from feeling violent rage, to a pettiness, now to disgust with this pathetic thing here in front of him. He waited for the crowd to simmer down outside, then he would send him to the leaders of the movement to decide this heinous creature's fate.

At five p.m. the city dwellers all crammed the cafés and tea shops, a ritual everyone agreed upon. With the likes of Yusuf on wild rampages now, they kept these gatherings, at least, intact. Today as they did everyday, they all listened to the ritual B.B.C. at 5 p.m. in the Somal language.

The announcer came on:

"This is the BBC London, read to you by Ahmad Sulieman Hashi. In the news today, we have confirmed reports that rebels have captured a number of the major towns of Northern Somal, and here is a cominque from the Somali National Movement, 'After heavy fighting early this morning and movements after the coordinated battle with the forces of the dictator Mohamed Said Barre in the towns of Hargiesa, Burao and other Areas in the North, the Military incurred heavy losses and all these towns are now in our possession. They are no longer in the hands of the fascist dictator, the so called Father of the Nation. We have also captured the brutal colonel head of this region's nefarious National Security Service, and other senior lack-eys of the brutal clan dictator.'

"'Another report from Somal today also confirms that the USP has been moving towards the middle of Somal, and is also now capturing the middle South, as follows.

The stated goals of both of these Movements: to liberate Somal from a one clan despotic rule. The leaders both claimed that it is only a matter of time before the dictator and his henchmen are forcibly removed and tried for crimes against the Somali people. The nation need no longer live in fear of these thugs.'

"This has been the BBC in London bringing the world news in Somali." Everyone in the city was astounded by the news and were secretly happy to be rid of this crazy state. However, there was always the fear of brutes like Yusuf who would stop at nothing to get any-thing, stop anyone for nothing. On a whim, people were killed in these encounters. The city dwellers, those who had for years now been seeking refuge elsewhere – they could not leave like this in a climate of anything goes at any time. The news was also received by the top brass of the State. It shocked them that they had under esti-mated these groups' resolve from the inception.

The writing this time was on the wall for them, the brutal ones. Most of them had pillaged the country to the bone. What everyone knew was coming hit them as a big surprise, and still they thought only in terms victory. They truly saw what others saw to boot – the power and wealth would never move or concede without a fight.

People in Mogadishu were scared but yet so desperately wanted the way things were to end. Those who could, continued to stream out of the country; those who could not, stayed and continued the business of living.

THIRTY TWO

The Beginnings

. . . .

THE BROADCAST REACHED ALL THE CORNERS OF THE WORLD. It summoned different spirits in different people.

Kumanay was in his expansive office: the Father of the Nation at his Presidential Palace; Yusuf in one of the many houses he had taken possession of. The news reached Beheyeah at the religious commune of his forefathers, as it did Tusmo's uncle at the Hotel in Nairobi.

As promised earlier, the rebel movement was just outside Mogadishu. Late at night, the father and Kumanay mustered their clan loyalists. Kumanay and the other elite members of the clan prepared for this eventual confrontation with the zest of victorious generals. The Father in his arrogance became even boisterous at times. It was lost to all of them, including Kumanay, that defeat was sure and certain. Their ignorance held forth to the last minutes.

The forces came in as the city dwellers took to the streets. A crowd gathered everywhere – looting, shooting, filling the streets with a storm of weapon fire. The rebels moved in like a hurricane, easily fending of the Regime's last dying kicks. Apart from a specialized unit composed of his very next of kin, no one from his vast coterie of lackeys was anywhere to be seen. The young, and the old were all getting out of the mayhem. The entire population was now in open insurrection, a total state of anarchy slowly bubbled to the surface, a euphoria of freedom in anarchy. There was a movement of the masses spilling onto the major routes out. The highway was thronged with a sea of people. The young and the old, women with their children strapped on their backs stretched for miles on end. The multitudes of humanity carried their possessions on their backs. Fear ruled their lives for the years of the Father, and now fear was moving in one direction away from the madness they were trying so desperately to leave behind.

Kumanay went to his safe. He had a lot of money in foreign currency in a safe at his mansion. He loaded an automatic pistol and stuffed the currency into his pockets. He dressed in casual clothes, sandals, and got into one of his luxury 4x4's. He knew if he was stupid enough to linger in this mayhem, he would either be burned by the marauding crowds, or caught by the in-coming forces. He started the vehicle and headed out of the gate. He was headed across the border to Kenya. He started on the roads that were just now becoming impossible to pass with the amount of debris from burning government vehicles and the litter of all manner of stuff strewn on the streets. Some were engaged in skirmishes all around him as he tried to pass with this expensive vehicle as unobtrusively as possible. He got further and further away. Most of the thugs hesitated to open fire on him, probably because they thought he was better armed than they were. He slowly got further and further from the close quarters of the city. He was headed for the highway and was quite relieved that he was just about there.

As he made the turn to get on the main road, he was shocked at the amount of people thronging the highway. It was too late to turn back. He had gone in where it was a little sparse, but he quickly got jammed in the sea of people all fleeing with their lives, like he was doing, but on foot and with all that they owned on their back. The vehicle became stuck on all sides, and Kumanay could neither move forward nor could he move backwards. People were, it seemed, in a trance. They were all far away, burned with their souls. They knew not where they were headed. Kumanay sat behind the wheel, crushed with anxiety. A thud shook the back windows, and he turned around slowly to see, and saw only shuddering stares. Greedy and intent on him, they sent shivers down through his every inch of soul.

THIRTY THREE

The Expert

. . . .

HAROLD BRATHWAITE WAS NOW A RETIRED AMBASSADOR.
He lingered in bed reading with the television on the news chan-
nel. He kept it there as background to his reading. Looking over the
book covers to watch something that had piqued his interest, the
anchor blared out, "The capital city of Somal is in total anarchy. After
the blank, the entire population is engaged in creating a mayhem.
The dictator Siad Barre has just fled to the Hinterland under heavy
pursuit from the rebel guerillas who had entered Mogadishu in the
midst of this anarchy.

Harold was in disbelief at what was happening at his former post.
The T.V. streamed to the mass exodus of humanity wide and thick
on a road he barely recognized, the one he used to go down to visit
the beautiful green areas beyond the city. He looked at the sheer suffering of the babies on their mothers' backs. The children and the
elderly were all walking with their heads and shoulders loaded with
personal belongings. The women were devoid of the colorful earth
tone pastels. No smiles or boisterous conversations. What he saw was
not what he had ever thought possible or imagined he would ever
see of Somals. A melancholic gathering, a giant snake of humanity
pushing on the road away from the familiar.

He saw at the top a brand new land cruiser and he immediately
thought of his close associate in the Somal government, Kumanay.
He was encouraged to deal with him through the notes of the dead

American Ambassador, the efficient local Somal, and the other foreign diplomats.

They all described him as amenable, western-educated, and open to swaying the government his way. Harold remembered the first time he met Kumanay at the height of the Soviet-type Revolution, when the country was teeming with Soviets. It was at the German Ambassador's residence in Mogadishu, where it was the beginning of many such clandestine meetings between him and the then Junior Officer Kumanay, though even then he was quickly rising through the ranks. He remembered their frequent conversations. He was much more sophisticated than Brathwaite even though the former was actually western.

He had a very good command of the English and Italian languages. He read widely in both, and through the years, Harold would bring him books back as gifts. He remembered one particular conversation amongst the many he had had with Kumanay at some embassy or the other. It was years ago when Harold was acting and not quite yet Ambassador. He remembered the missive from stateside urging him to find ways to influence a change from the Soviet to the American backer. This gave him a carte blanche so to speak. After the many strategy meetings, particularly with the Somal embassy staff, they agreed he would pass on a secret message to Kumanay.

They met for the first time, and Harold remembered it vividly, as if it were just the other day.

The Major was ushered into a well-decorated room inside the German Embassy's private residence. He was looking very dapper, young, and energetic. He was wearing a suit, well-cut, and it draped his slender body exquisitely. He entered the room where Harold was to meet him with an air of self assured confidence.

"Welcome, Major Kumanay. Please sit down," Harold had said as he rose to pour him a drink, "What will it be Major?"

"A rum please – ice and coke."

They sat down and got comfortable on the sofas in the well-furnished office.

"I will be very straight forward with you. Since you are a man of intelligence, I will not try to pretend we, my government that is, are happy with your Government's very close association with the Soviets. We want to know what it will take for you to help us change things around here in Somal."

Kumanay was a little pensive but Harold could see his eyes were lit up, and that he was quite interested in what Harold was saying.

"I think we need support, aid both militarily and in other areas such as business, as well as with monies for influence over my colleagues who will ultimately make the difference. You see we would also like to get rid of our own Soviets. It will be a long drawn-out process, but our powerful party stalwarts are very popular now. It will not be easy, but it will happen if we will get rid of them. You must guarantee an open check to do this. There are going to be many repressive measures, but rest assured it will only affect the Soviet's areas. Most of us are not interested in the Soviet System. We want a western-type of government. This I think is the only solution for Africa. We must follow the well-tested steps of, for example, your country. There is no clan nepotism there. We need a system that can do that for us too. We need to become a nation. I am ready to be your development and progress partner, Ambassador, but we need your help to get from the chokehold of certain members of the politburo."

"Consider it done. I am authorized to fully support you and your country towards this great path."

Harold was back again, looking at the sea of humanity trudging along the road with the trucks and cars stuck inside, moving at a snail's pace, surrounded by the ever- looming large crowd.

Kumanay sat looking back at the figures who keep taunting him with their harrowing stares. He became restless, locked all the doors. He sat in the vehicle, scared, his palms pouring sweat like a faucet all over the steering wheel. He became increasingly nervous. Death emanated from every corner of the crowd , he thought. He started to go delirious with the fear of anticipation. He saw for himself a tragic fate, if he stayed marooned in this crowd. He started honking the vehicle as if shouting from the seat that he needed to go carry the sick and wounded much further down. The crowd on his side gave him space to get on the off road. He honked, shouted, and finally a gap occurred, and he stepped hard on the gas pedal, almost landing the 4x4 on its belly on the off road. He did not look back at the crowd. He could not get far enough from them in his mind. He drove for a while until the overwhelming feeling of fear returned to him.

He got out of his brand new vehicle, afraid it would bring him undue attention, and he abandoned the vehicle altogether, taking off on foot, not knowing where he was heading. He walked and walked until he passed out in a delirium of fear, hunger, thirst, and exertion.

Harold continued to watch the news as it captured the city in destruction from the population at large. He saw there was a lot of cross fire, and it really baffled him how all this had happened. The extent of the mayhem and violence made Harold remorseful and quite ill at ease in his Potomac home. He could not imagine the virulent hate the civilians en masse were manifesting against the government. He knew the Head of State that he was watching on the news, fighting the rebels. He saw how hated this government he had propped with cash was, and how weapons were being precipitated into the abyss of the base instincts of the city. He could not tear himself from the responsibility in front of him. The book dropped on his lap as he became overwhelmed with the flashing images of Somal in violent upheaval. He realized it was the first time he had really seen the people of Somal.

CPSIA information can be obtained at www.ICGtesting.com
Printed in the USA
LVOW071750220812

295488LV00003B/72/P